The Rhythm of their Souls

L.D. PACK

CONTENTS

CONTENT WARNING

This book is a healing romance and may be triggering or unsettling for some readers.

Please note that the content is intended for adult audiences.

Please do not continue reading if you are sensitive to the following:
Addiction, abandonment, bullying, body shaming, childhood trauma, emotional abuse, explicit death scenes, explicit sex themes, grief, mental health awareness, mental illness, neglect, night terrors, substance abuse, and mature language.

ADDICTION AND MENTAL HEALTH SUPPORT

(Substance Abuse and Mental Health Services Administration)

SAMHSA National Helpline: 1-800-622-HELP (4357)

The above helpline is available 24 hours a day. It provides informational services for family members and individuals battling mental health and/or substance abuse disorders. This administration provides referrals to community-based organizations, local treatment facilities, and support groups. This novel explores the themes of mental illness stemming from trauma and generational health issues, as well as addiction and substance abuse. I want to emphasize that I approach all these subjects seriously. My portrayal of the above topics is drawn from personal experiences and my perspective, and I recognize everyone perceives them differently.

We all face mental health struggles and unwanted challenges in life, and having someone to talk to is vital. If you ever feel alone, please reach out to me—I will always be a listening ear.

This book represents a part of my healing journey, and I hope it helps heal at least a heart or two along the way.

PLAYLIST (SPOTIFY)

Noah Henderson- Tired of Healing
Outer Banks: Midsummers (guitar theme)
Billie Elish- Ocean Eyes
Goo Goo Dolls- Iris
Amber Run- I Found
Myles Smith- Stargazing
Cigarettes After Sex- Nothing's Gonna Hurt You Baby
Samuel Burger- Cinema
Lana - Heaven
Benson Boone- In The Stars
Anna Clendening- Help
Novo Amor- Anchor
Novo Amor- Keep Me
Vincent Lima- The Only Thing Left
Wilfred- Everything We Need
Tom Rosenthal - It's Ok
Fleetwood Mac- Dreams
You me at six- Take on the World

To my beautiful departed big sisters, Megan and Stacy, thank you for protecting me as best you could. Although you are not here today, know that you both inspired me to address the uncomfortable subjects often silenced. Your battles did not define you. May you both be at peace from your sufferings. I love you always.

To my last living sister, Tracy, I hope you know how proud I am of your strength and how far you've come. I know our sisters are proud of you, too.

Lastly, to those fighting battles in silence: Please know I hear you. You are not alone. Keep fighting. You, my beautiful, deserving friend, are beyond worthy.

Olive

CHAPTER 1

At the tender age of eight years old, I casually discovered that the dangerous cocktail of drugs and alcohol, when intertwined with the fragility of a wounded soul, swiftly plunges one into an unyielding vortex of destructive turmoil.

How did I learn this at such an adolescent age, you ask? Well, my mother didn't hesitate to rub it in my face every time she cracked open a chilled beer or set flame to a pipe at all hours of the night.

The sad thing is that even in those harrowing moments, I was just grateful to have her home. You see, her absence became a constant in my life. Another unwanted lesson was when I realized that her random "store trips" meant she would vanish out of thin air for two to three days.

It became normal to the point where I stopped wondering why and accepted the shitty life that was rudely handed to me on a broken wilted platter.

But she wasn't always this way, you know. She once radiated from the inside out. Maybe I was young and naïve, but there was a luminous light about her. She was beautiful like a blossomed flower, with her long brown curly locks and doe-like eyes.

She held a huge piece of my heart. After all, she was my mother, the one who birthed me and held me for the first seconds of my death sentence. The fucked-up part is that I only got a glimpse of her unconditional love. Somewhere in my short existence, she lost her motherly instincts. And it was then that I had no choice but to befriend loneliness. It cradled me on the nights my mom didn't come home, and adapting became a permanent part of my vocabulary.

Did I mention that I have a big sister? Her name is Nora Ray, and she's five years older than me. She was the only normalcy in our house as a child; together, we endured the finest of trauma and disappointments early in life.

Nora was my protector, my first best friend, and by far my favorite person. I've always admired her confidence, humor, and welcoming aura. There were disastrous times I wouldn't have survived without her protection. She illuminated my darkest days, keeping the monsters from under my bed at bay. I was fortunate to have her.

Where is our father in all this, you ask? Well, our deadbeat dad, who goes by the name Joseph, abandoned the three of us when I was around five years old. Aside from his constant drunken episodes directed towards Mom and Nora, I remember little of him because he wasn't around much. When he *was* home, he spent it outside in his shed.

Once, he surprised my sister and me by building our own treehouse. We loved that damn treehouse. I guess it's the most fatherly thing he ever did for us. And the day he vanished, my mom never searched for him or spoke of him again.

I think she was relieved, in a sense. If the word "fickle" were a person, it would accurately describe our sperm donor. His mood swings were the absolute worst. He never lashed out at me; maybe it was because I was so young, but there are some recollections buried deep inside me, memories that do not want to reveal themselves. They say when you encounter generous amounts of trauma, your brain goes into defense mode. It tries to suppress certain traumatic events to protect you from the aftermath. Maybe that's why I have vague memories of him. The few that I have are not pleasant and certainly ones I wish my brain could forget.

And the day he left, it was almost as if it lifted a small burden from our home, really our lives all around. Our mom seemed beyond relieved considering he was hardly ever kind to her and smelled like fermented beer most days.

I think it's safe to say that his absence has become a blessing for our little dysfunctional family. It was just Mom, Nora Ray, and I, completely content in our little tan trailer on Circle St. We could finally live a normal life; we didn't need him, did we?

One thing is for certain: Blessings do not last forever. Mom made it about a year before she met her new boyfriend, Timothy, and things changed when he came into the picture.

Mom had her attention mostly on him. They would stay out late at night drinking at bars.

I never got much sleep on school nights. It didn't matter what time of night it was. They'd bust through the front door like a herd of elephants. Mom seemed happy, so we just dealt with it. She deserved every bit of happiness thrown her way.

The thing about happiness is that it can be a short-lived fairy tale. When the round-the-clock fighting began, the drinking habits became more consistent, and I'm not talking about a yelling contest with curse words thrown back and forth. This was some Jerry Springer-Steve Wilko-type shit, and my sister and I had front-row seats to their scuffling escapades.

We had no clue that Mom could throw hands like a man. I don't know if it was from built-up anger caused by our dad's previous behavior. Or maybe this woman was an MMA fighter in a past life.

At first, we felt terrible for him because I don't think he knew what Jewels, aka our Mom, was capable of. One night, we heard him yelling from her room. I frantically ran to Nora's bed, and we checked it out together. When we opened Mom's door, we saw Timothy lying on the floor, yelling for help. Mom was kicking him profusely in the ribs.

Horrified by what we were witnessing, we didn't dare get involved. We slammed the door and hurried back to Nora's room. I slept with her that night. *Nora Ray, my sweet protector.*

We figured he would be long gone after his brutal ass-whooping because surely his pride was somewhere on Mom's bedroom floor after she stomped it out of him. Nope, we can all laugh together. This fool continued to stick around and get his ass handed to him, and that's when I decided I would no longer feel remorse for that loser.

We wondered if he enjoyed getting manhandled by a woman. Little did we know that all it would take for Timothy to run for good was a car accident that left Mom with permanent damage.

I was seven when he and Mom got in their bad car wreck. They were driving home late from a bar, drunk. Mom was passed out in the passenger seat, and Timothy took a little nap while driving. His car went around a curve and viciously rolled down an embankment.

He left the scene in handcuffs with nothing but a few scratches on his face. Mom was left on a stretcher in an ambulance with a fractured spine.

Timothy spent a couple of days in jail until our mom quickly paid his bond from her hospital bed. Just for him to go to our house to retrieve his few belongings, and we never saw him again after that. He didn't even check on Mom after the accident or thank her for bailing him out. She was once again abandoned without explanation while now recovering from a back injury caused by both of their careless actions.

This was a huge hit on her for sure. We saw a daunting shift we hadn't quite seen before. A person can only bear so much. This was when our lives spiraled into something tragic. This was when addiction busted down the front door and claimed our broken mother.

I was ten when my heart broke for the second time. The morning I watched Nora walk out the front door was a hurt that made my bones ache. She was running from our family curse. But can I blame her?

I was relieved for her in a sense, but a part of me envied her escape plan. I'll never forget her haunted expression, eyes brimmed with tears. She quietly opened the front door and slowly looked back at me with so much guilt in her eyes. "Stay strong for me, Olive; I'll come back for you."

In that painful moment, I slowly nodded. I felt a sliver of hope, but in the back of my little damaged mind, I knew there was no saving me. I was the little sister being left behind to deal with our mother's chaotic shitshow.

Nora went to live with her high school sweetheart, Jake, and his easygoing parents. He was just a couple of years older than her, and they were "in love." Shortly after moving in, Nora got a serving job at a little place called Bebops. Jake's parents didn't charge them rent to live there or anything. She just didn't want me to go without. Mom was reckless and struggled to keep the power on at home.

She never cared to explain when inconveniences happened. I would just always assume she blew through her disability money. It seemed like her booze and drug habits were more important than the essentials we needed for survival.

One afternoon, I walked home from the bus stop, but there was no power at our house. When Mom finally came home, she said no word. *Nothing new there.* We went almost a whole week without power. We ate from cold aluminum cans and managed to stay warm during the brisk nights. We would snuggle up together under massive blankets.

And in a way, I loved those cold nights; it was the closest I'd been to Mom in a long time. And I'd desperately take anything I could get from her to subdue my aching needs as a child.

I appreciated school days more during this time. Sometimes, I would sneak off to the bathroom to embrace the free, cozy heat. It took six days for Nora to find out about our living conditions. She was livid that I didn't tell her, and I don't blame her for it. It's not that I didn't want her to know. I just didn't want her to scold Mom, even though I knew how wrong the situation was. Plus, we would have only had to suffer one more week. Then, Mom's disability check would have been deposited, and just like that, we'd be back to civilization.

Nora paid the bill, restoring power to our small trailer. She restocked the cabinets with food and gave me enough money for a week of school lunches. She always tried her best to make sure I didn't go without. I always felt bad asking her for anything; I wasn't meant to be her responsibility, and I felt like a burden most days.

Unfortunately, we had to mature at an early age, which is a harsh reality. Survival is a word that still clings to me. I am still to this day just thankful to have someone like Nora in my life. Because without her, what would be the point of my survival? She is the best big sister.

It's appropriate to say that we received the last shit pickings in the parent department. Maybe that sounds cruel, but does it seem wrong?

Life can be so damn ruthless. It will take something that was once pure and set it ablaze, and then it will take a seat and observe the destruction it caused. And I truly believe some of us are born broken. Why? That's a question I don't have the answer to.

All I know is that our parents are both examples of it. And somewhere along the road to misery, Nora and I became very much broken, too.

And as I grew older, the monsters crept out from under my bed and infiltrated my mind insidiously. They manipulated my emotions and evoked feelings I struggled to put into words. The relentless monsters inflicted unhealable wounds deep inside me. They had discovered their perfect home and resolved to make it their permanent abode. I was to be internally feasted upon for the rest of my existence. I quickly realized that there was nothing to shield me from them now, not even Nora Ray.

This was when I discovered trauma and mental illness, two very real things. And I don't think people understand the dynamic of the two, working together to destroy anything in their path. Leaving behind debris that sticks to everything like thick honey.

Olive
CHAPTER 2

Today is my birthday, and it's just another day—there's no need to make a big deal out of nothing. I lost interest in celebrating it at age nine when my mom didn't have the decency to at least come home for my birthday. She missed two of them after that and showed up days later like nothing was wrong. There was no birthday phone call and no trace of where she was. Thankfully, I had Nora there for two of my birthdays before she moved out.

As a young teen, she tried her best to make it special for me. She would make strawberry cheesecake muffins and use a lit match as a candle. Those few birthdays, I made the same wish every year. All I wanted was for my mom to choose me over the drugs and the temporary men in her life. My wish never came true, and that's when I decided my life was futile.

And well, fuck my birthday.

My best friend Danielle seems to think otherwise. She made that clear by rudely waking me up at 7 a.m. with the song "Birthday Bitch" by Trap Beckham blaring in my ear.

This was her new *tradition* when we moved into our apartment three years ago. I was sixteen and beyond, ready to get out on my own. Danielle was two years older than me, so things worked out the best they could. We've known each other since we were in elementary school. We grew up inseparable in the same lovely trailer park and promised each other that we'd one day live together. So here we are, *"roomie besties"* in our little boring town.

Danielle plops down on my bed beside me. "Get up, Olive."

I roll my eyes and blow out a loud huff. "Don't you have anything better to do other than torturing me?" I say through gritty eyes.

She smacks me with a pillow and annoyingly chirps, "Uh, hello? It's your nineteenth birthday! Get your grumpy ass out of bed." She can be a sharp thorn in my ass sometimes.

I glare at her but force myself up and go to the bathroom. Looking in the mirror, I see nothing new; I look the same. The age of nineteen sounds so bland. I don't see the hype in celebrating it.

I walk to the kitchen and contemplate feeding my growling tummy. Danielle is already standing by our kitchen island with her arms crossed, giving me a sly look. I pinch my lips together in annoyance. "What is it?"

She gives me a massive grin. "Don't forget our plans for tonight, birthday girl." *Damn it.* Somehow, I let her talk me into going to a random house party. It just landed on the same day as my birthday. Taylor, an acquaintance from high school, bought her first home a few months ago in a town called Marshville. The only thing I know about this place is that country singer Randy Travis grew up there. I've seen on the internet that they have a mural of him on a building.

We heard through the grapevine that Taylor started dating a guy near there. They're not living together, but they're only fifteen minutes from each other—about an hour's distance from us.

Danielle says a lot of faces from school will be there, so it's sounding more like a high school reunion to me. I have instant anxiety just thinking about it. Danielle is really the only person I have a relationship with from school. I have a few girls from work that I keep in touch with and see occasionally outside of my work. Aside from that, I keep to myself, which means less drama.

I discovered close friends can backstab you just like anyone else. My old snake friend Chloe made that clear when she fucked my ex-boyfriend, whom I dated for a year. Long story short, I don't trust many people.

It's Friday, and Danielle begged me to take off a month ago. She doesn't believe anyone should work on their birthday. I started working at a Call Center three years ago. It didn't take any experience aside from a school diploma. The money is decent; I talk to strangers all day on the phone. And for some odd reason, I get constant compliments on my country-drawn accent.

Hey, if it makes the customers happy, I'm all for it. And the good thing about working over the phone is that even when I speak to the occasional asshole, I'm able to flip them off or even mute the conversation to say how I feel.

For example, grumpy Brenda from Arizona does not know that I called her a snooty fuck twat. It's quite therapeutic in a sense.

I'm sure Danielle has a whole weekend planned for my birthday. I'm already dreading this party tonight. Some days, I love conversation and interaction with other people. Most days, I want to be left the fuck alone. I guess it's a happy medium somewhere in between.

So now I need to prepare mentally for human interaction. I decide to message my big sister Nora to see if she'd like to grab lunch at our favorite eating joint, What-A-Burger. Retrieving my phone, I didn't realize I had multiple unread messages. Oh, right, it's my birthday.

Nora: Morning, love muffin. HAPPY MOTHER FRIGGING BIRTHDAY.

Me: Why, thank you, sis! Care to join me for a Witch Doctor?

Nora: Sure, what time are you thinking?

Me: Let's do 11:30. I love you, big sister.

Nora: I love you most, Olive.

Things have been off with Nora lately; she's been through the wringer. Five months ago, her boyfriend Jake had a tragic accident that left him unconscious at a friend's house. There were at least eight people there at the time of the accident.

The ambulance and paramedics arrived quickly, but there was no saving him; he passed on the way to the hospital. During his in-depth autopsy, they discovered he had overdosed on Fentanyl laced marijuana. It was under investigation for months, but law enforcement could not prove someone guilty. It was a bad batch, and he was the one to test the waters first. Fentanyl is becoming a common cause of death in this generation. I'm recognizing the names on many gravestones.

Jake's passing took a huge hit on my sister. He was her first everything; they had lived with his parents until he turned twenty. After that, they found a small two-bedroom ranch home for rent just miles from his parents. Two months after his funeral service, Nora broke the lease and moved back in with his parents.

I offered for her to stay with Danielle and me, but she refused multiple times. She didn't have it in her to leave his parents alone with broken hearts. Jake was an only child, and they adored him. I don't blame her; his parents were more involved in her life than our mother.

I'm just worried about Nora and her mental state. I know she still feels guilty for what happened. She had worked that afternoon, and Jake wanted her to take off so she could tag along. She believes the outcome would have been different if she had been there. It's been hard to convince her that there was nothing she could have done to change how it happened.

All I can do is continue to be there for her. We've been through the wringer throughout life. Our mom made sure we got a good taste of chaos early on.

And I can't imagine the hurt she is feeling internally. A human can only survive so much.

Nora arrives fashionably late, but it's okay. I'm happy she's here; we don't see each other as much as I'd like. She looks exhausted and worn but still stunning as ever. Her beautiful long brown curls form perfectly around her frame. Her big smile is contagious and could snatch any guy's attention.

Damn, I miss seeing that smile. The light she once desperately held onto is dulling in her eyes. I can almost see it flickering, painfully struggling to stay lit. Something about her is different; this isn't my beautifully broken, strong Nora Ray. I quickly mask my concern before she catches me having a deep conversation in my head.

We spend around an hour talking about my job and a little about our mom. And how neither of us has visited her in quite some time. We talk briefly about Jake's parents and how they're doing. I tell her about the stupid party Danielle is forcing me to attend. I invite her to tag along, but she swears she has things to do back home.

I'm sure it's just an excuse not to go. It's fine, and I will not push her on it. She needs time to heal, and God, do I want that for her so badly. I hope she knows that I'm here for her, just like she has always been for me.

Once I return home, I am greeted at the door by my sweet Lottie girl. She is a miniature Pomeranian. My mom purchased her when she was around eight weeks old. She was a gift for my fourteenth birthday. Maybe it was her way of apologizing for her absence during prior years. Lottie is by far the sweetest, cutest ball of hair with four legs. We've grown up together, and I don't think I've ever loved a pooch so much. She is a blessing that I surely needed.

I didn't feel *as* alone when Lottie came into my life. When I was younger, there were nights that I'd shut myself in my room and cry. And it's almost like she understood my pain. Her sweet, tiny self would nestle up to my neck and stay there as long as I'd let her. *My little Lottie Love.* She approaches me and wags her tail to say hello; I scoop her up for quick kisses and snuggles before going to my closet.

Danielle isn't here, so I assume she's out shopping for a new outfit for tonight's dreadful party. That girl will buy new clothes just to wear to the mailbox. I spend a good thirty minutes trying on different options. I peer at my figure in our full-body mirror. All I can say is thank the lord for growth and puberty. I was that awkward, skinny kid, and I caught a lot of shit for it at school.

I never enjoyed getting called anorexic by my classmate Bennett Weaver. He had many nicknames for me growing up, like Trailer Trash and Crackhead Girl. The not-so-funny thing about that is my mom was keen on a little rock in her pipe occasionally.

Bennett's bullying caused a lot of self-doubt that was difficult for me to shake. I never understood what his problem was with me. I guess he had insecurities and needed to project them on someone else. I was the easiest target to aim for.

Somewhere along the way, life decided I deserved a little grace in some areas of my life. Or either it's one good thing my mom passed down to me. I was a late bloomer, and my appearance changed drastically by the age of sixteen. And damn, was I relieved to break free from that long awkward stage of my life. I was always so hard on myself. I'm now a little on the taller side of five foot seven.

Some would say I was gifted with a long torso and legs and a small waist with a donk like the ones T-Pain talks about in his songs. My ashy silk brown hair flows down to the middle of my back. I didn't get my mom's full curly locks like Nora Ray did, but depending on the weather, my hair is wavy in different styles. The only tight curls I inherited are around the frame of my face; they come out to play only on humid days.

I finally go with a short-sleeved, form-fitting sweater dress. Its sage tone meshes beautifully with my olive complexion. I pair it with my favorite white sneakers. I'm going with a subtle makeup look: a touch of mascara on my long lashes and a shimmery highlighter on my lower lids to bring out the warm honey flecks in my light brown eyes. I dust my high cheekbones with a pinkish blush and gently color my ample lips with a mauve-shaded gloss.

This small primp says a lot for me, considering I usually only doll up for work. I dress comfortably on most workdays, considering I sit in a cubicle all day. My go-to attire is baggy shirts or sweats. If I knew Danielle wouldn't scold me, I'd show up to this party in what I slept in last night. Hopefully, she's impressed with my quickly thrown-together outfit. She can kiss my ass otherwise.

Olive

CHAPTER 3

5th grade

On the school bus, I squish the side of my face into the window as hard as I can— anything to distract myself from Bennett's harsh words. Every day is different with him. Some days, I am nothing more than a ghost in his presence. Other days I know as soon as he spots me, venom will shoot from his sinful lips.

"Oh, here comes the trailer dump princess!" Bennett spews out.

This kid has had it out for me since we were in third grade. It gradually got worse once Danielle left me for middle school. Now, I'm just stuck dealing with this alone. I try so hard to be cordial and kind, but the nicer I am, the meaner his words spill.

It doesn't help that I live in a trailer park and ride the same bus as him. You see, Bennett grew up with happily married parents. And no exaggeration, they live in a mansion on their own private road. So through his eyes, I'm just as useless as a pile of dog crap on his well-manicured lawn.

Early on, I discovered that you're judged in school by where you live and the brands you wear. I remember when I wore my brand-new Payless sneakers to gym class years ago. I was happy for once and excited to wear them. Bennett destroyed any joy from my mind.

We were sitting on the bleachers, waiting for our gym teacher. I watched Bennett as he scanned the class, almost like he was looking for me. When our eyes met, he immediately brought his beady eyes to my shoes.

He lifted his finger, dramatically pointing at me. Then his wide mouth flew open. "Haha! Look, Olive got a new pair of shoes from Salvation Army." It's a memory I'll never be able to shake.

It didn't help the situation when his little conniving group of friends joined in with his laughter. So much anger and embarrassment built inside me, and all I could do was sit and let their pestering simmer out. I never wore those shoes again after that day because God forbid I wore a pair of shoes that didn't have a printed logo on the side of them. How dare I be so careless.

If I wasn't called out for my clothes or where I lived, he spat in my face about how skinny and poor I looked. This is just what I need, another reason to hate myself.

If he knew how disturbing my life was back at home, would he continue to be so cruel? Honestly, it would probably fuel his fire. I'll never forget the time my mom let the power shut off, and I had to wear the same clothes two days in a row. You would have thought I was unaware of the very clothes on my back. He reminded me at least ten times. *You are worthless, so useless that no one pities you.* Good, that's the last thing I want, pity.

There have been many times when I'd get home exhausted from playing the tough role against his bullying, that I'd walk in the door, head straight for my room, and plop on my bed screaming into my pillow as loud as I could. This couldn't be normal. I'm only a child, so how can I bear so much stress and worry at this early age?

Bennett Weaver was a mean, snarky kid who got everything generously handed to him in life. And then there was me, the weird, defeated kid with an absent mother and father.

I was damaged, but I had a good heart. Our situation was a prime example of what's wrong and right. I know I can stick up for myself, but what was the point? I did it for my best friend several times; no one would mess with her, and I wouldn't allow it.

Maybe It's because I don't love myself enough to think I deserve the same treatment. All I've ever received is heartbreak. And if I was given this difficult life, then I was to endure all its suffering. *Olive Sage Landers is a burden to society.*

Olive

CHAPTER 4

Danielle turns up the radio and puts the sunroof down. The air is warm and smells of early summer. May is right around the corner. We're heading to Taylor's new house and should arrive around 7:30 p.m. I love our car rides together; we have our own free concert every time.

"I Got a Feeling" by The Black-Eyed Peas comes on the radio. Maybe this is a sign of a good night? I sure as hell could use some more positivity in my life right now.

Danielle and I sing every single word flawlessly. We do this with at least five more songs during our ride. She knows how to bring me out of my funky "moods." I can't help but smile at her presence; I'm so lucky to have her in my life. I've had many letdowns, but she has always been there for me.

My phone dings twice, and I glance down to see a new message.

Mom: Happy birthday, baby.

Mom: Have any plans for this evening?

Me: Thanks, Mom. Danielle and I are going to a small get-together.

Mom: Please be careful and don't stay out too late.

Me: Sure thing. Love you.

Mom: Love you, Olive girl.

I haven't visited Mom much, but she appears to be better. I've noticed a pattern with her. She goes a month or two without using drugs or alcohol but then relapses. I decided a while back to love her from a distance; being around her too much brings out a side of me I try to keep locked away.

It's not necessarily her; it's that house, too. Some memories painfully seep into my pores every time I step foot into that house. Nora's treehouse and mine are the only things that haven't been tainted.

I check in on her occasionally. I don't have it in me to leave her without. Nora and I take turns keeping the power on at the trailer and food in the cabinets. Lately, it's just been me here. With everything Nora has endured in recent years, I expect little from her.

Sometime later, Danielle pulls off into a gas station parking lot. "We are officially in Marshville. I'm going to get us some basic bitch White-Claws," she says, full of excitement.

I nod my head at her. While she runs inside, I take a gander at my surroundings. I see nothing out of the ordinary; it seems to be a regular town with small shopping centers like it is back home. Not sure how Taylor came across this place or a boyfriend from here.

But it feels nice being in a different city where no one knows me. I can be anyone I want to be. I wish I could say the same for this house party, but I'm sure I'll be running into many familiar faces. *Yay me!*

After leaving the gas station, we pull up to a two-story white vinyl house with brown shutters. It has a massive front porch, and it looks like her few neighbors are far away. Large trimmed bushes and dainty flowers are wrapped around the foundation. She must have a lawn care service; everything is shaped to perfection. I spot one tree over to the right side, which looks to be an apple tree with fruit dangling from thin limbs.

Overall, it is a nice house. We park along the side of the street. It already looks like a slew of people have scattered their cars throughout her yard.

"How many are supposed to be coming?" I anxiously ask Danielle.

She quickly responds, "Girl, I don't know. Quit worrying; it's a damn party, so let's have some fun!"

As we head for the front door, empty booze cans are already on the lawn. Loud early 2000s music is playing from what sounds like the backyard. We make our way to the front porch and knock on the door. Within seconds, the door flies open, and Taylor stands by it.

"Oh, my gosh! You guys came!" she shouts dramatically.

We exchange hugs and forced smiles and congratulate her on her newly purchased home. Taylor doesn't acknowledge that it's my birthday, which she probably doesn't even know it's today. *Thank fucking God.*

She introduces us to her new boyfriend, Ryan, sharing how they met at a random coffee shop months ago. Ryan was visiting family in the Concord area. And now, here they are in their cupcake phase of a relationship. Taylor gives us a quick tour and tells us to make ourselves at home before clasping hands with Ryan and heading for the backdoor.

I am already uneasy with the amount of faces I see. I notice multiple people from school and many new faces. Taylor must have made friends since moving to this town.

Danielle notices my grimace and hands over a White Claw with a nudge of her shoulder. "Get out of your head, Olive, and just enjoy yourself for once." She then gives me a wink before heading to the kitchen area.

I let out a slow sigh and give a nod. Anxiety will be the death of me.

I try to replace my worrisome thoughts with positive ones. Okay, it's my stupid birthday, and I didn't have to work today. I guess things aren't so bad. I pop open my White Claw and scan my surroundings.

Once I go to take a sip of my drink, I lock eyes with someone standing directly across from me. *No fucking way. What are the odds of this?* I am currently being eye fucked by *the* Bennett Weaver. We have not seen each other since the end of eighth grade. His parents put him into a private Christian school. I never thought in a million years I'd see the guy who ruined my self-confidence as a kid.

I look so different now, and damn, so does he. He's sporting a classic Busch-Lite-inspired gut and looks to be balding at age twenty. I guess money can't fix everything after all. Or karma finally slapped his mean ass one good time.

He slowly trudges towards me. I can't help but scan his unimpressive features. "Uh, Olive Landers?" he nervously asks. If there weren't so many people in my way, I'd make a mad dash for the front door. I glance over his shoulder, finding the front door easily accessible. Escape scenarios run through my anxious mind.

I let out a defeated sigh and finally respond, "Yep, it's me, ole crackhead girl." Wow, *Olive.* He stares at me with concerned, beady eyes.

I could punch myself for saying that dumb shit. I take a generous chug of my bitch beer, waiting for him to degrade me and tell me what a waste of life I am. But instead, I see disappointment in his expression. "You have changed, Olive. I hoped that I'd run into you here." He picks at the invisible lint on his shirt.

I can't say the same, bud.

He takes a deep breath. "I wanted to apologize for being a dick all those years when we were kids." I watch him lightly kick his shoe at imaginary dirt on the floor.

Distasteful words stain my tongue, but I refrain. "No problem, Bennett, it's in the past," I say with a forced smile. His shoulders relax a little. We then give each other a weak grin and clank our beers before guzzling the cold liquid. He gives a quick nod and makes his way into another room.

I take another gulp of my drink, almost emptying the can. Thank God that's over. I would have been just peachy never seeing his face again. He's lucky I didn't crush his hopes and dreams with vicious words. The younger me would have handled that conversation differently, period.

I stroll into the kitchen and spot liquor options on the

counter. I might as well start on something a little more stout. I have a full weekend off from work. And after that encounter, I need something stronger.

Why not live it up for once? I have a DD tonight; Danielle ensured I knew she would drink responsibly.

So I make myself cranberry vodka and immediately take three big gulps. I can feel the alcohol pleasantly creeping into my bloodstream. I decide to check out the backyard commotion. After walking through multiple groups and nodding at familiar faces, I locate the back door.

Danielle intercepts me, and we make our way out the door together.

To the left, there are people laughing while playing beer pong on two long tables. To my right, there is a stone patio with a small lit fire pit. Chatty Kathys sit around the fire, probably talking about their exes or the Kardashians. And no one seems to notice or care about the not-shy girl straddling who I presume is her boyfriend. It wouldn't be a party without that one careless couple creating soft porn in someone's backyard.

Good for them; at least someone's getting laid tonight. Danielle gives me a pouty lip. "I hope to straddle someone like that by the night's end."

I scowl at her and roll my eyes. Honestly, she wouldn't have trouble finding her a good-looking guy to straddle.

Danielle and I walk towards the back of the yard, where there is a decently sized bonfire. People are standing close by, talking while drinking their beverages. I've always enjoyed the scent of burning logs and the bright, sizzling embers.

As I inch closer to the fire, the weakened breeze changes

course. Standing maybe seven feet in front of me is a mysterious man. The fire's smoke must have concealed him prior. My eyes start at his feet and scan every inch of him until they reach his demanding eyes. The fire's natural gleam beats against his sculpted jaw, and even though it is dark, I can see his eyes' vivid coloring.

They are as blue as the purest oceans, and around his pupils, they're gently caressed by an emerald green with a hue of sunshine. I've never seen eyes so full of life. I don't even realize that I'm standing as still as a statue, mesmerized by a stranger. His plush lips curl up into a wicked grin. He hasn't taken his eyes from mine, and I damn sure can't pull mine from his.

My heart feels like it's about to pound its way out of my chest at any moment. I can no longer hear the loud music or the chattering of all the people surrounding us. We're frozen in time; and right now, it's just me and this attractive man.

I just stare in awe as he strides towards me slowly; his movements are smooth like rich velvet. Within seconds, he is standing inches from me. Up close, he is even more breathtakingly attractive. A lingering oak scent invades my senses. It reminds me of a forbidden forest with hints of earthy undertones and wood. His thick, dirty blond hair lays neatly upon his blessed head.

I clasp my drink with both hands to avoid reaching up and running my hands through this guy's gorgeous wavy locks. His strong stature is a good six inches taller than me. If Chris Hemsworth and Paul Walker had a younger brother, he's the one. This man is exceptionally gifted from head to toe.

I completely forget that my best friend is right beside me;

at this point we look like conjoined twins with how close we're standing together. I pull my eyes away for a split second to examine Danielle; she is big-time gawking, just as I am. *Looks like she's getting laid after all.*

"I haven't seen you around here before," mystery man says curiously. God, his deep voice sends warm shivers down my fragile spine.

I don't even realize that he's speaking directly to me until Danielle aggressively elbows me in my side. She then mumbles through closed teeth, "Earth to Olive."

I gather my thoughts and go to speak. "Um, well, that's because I don't live around here."

His perfectly symmetrical eyebrows pull together. "Olive, such a delicate name for a pretty face like yours."

I nervously clear my throat and rattle out, "Why thank you, sir." Wow, if I could teleport myself anywhere but here, damn it, I would. I can't even look at Danielle. I know she's burning a hole in the side of my head.

He chuckles softly before running his large hand through his hair.

"What's your name, anyway?" I blurt out. I'll say anything at this point to hear this man speak.

He gazes at me. "Theodore Ace Rivers, but you can call me Theo." He just gave me his full government name. I'll be doing my detective work when I get home.

This man is too sexy, even down to his name. I'm going to assume he's probably a criminal or some shit. No way he looks this good and has a clean record.

"What are you thinking about in that cute little head of yours?" he croons with a grin.

I have got to do better about zoning out around people. I could drool at this point and wouldn't have the slightest clue. I chew on my bottom lip before locking eyes with him again. "I was just thinking about how it's getting late, and we have a long drive home. It was nice meeting you, Mr. Rivers."

Yep, I'm buzzed out of my ass. I immediately turn around and rush for the back door. Once I get inside, I try to focus on where Taylor's downstairs bathroom is. After bumping into multiple people, I spot it across from the living room. Right before I reach to grab the door handle, two girls jump in front of me and slam the door in my face.

Stupid bitches. It takes everything in me not to knock that damn door off the hinges and hope it lands on those snobs. Instead, I take a few deep breaths and grab my phone from my clutch purse.

Me: Danielle, let's head home, please…

Bestie: Girl, I was just texting you. Why the hell did you run off like that? This beautiful man has the hots for you. WTF Olive?

Me: Yeah, well, imagine I give him the time of day, and then he sees the shitshow that I am. He will be the one running next.

Bestie: Okay, Ms. Dramatic. You are freaking gorgeous and deserve a good time with a hot guy. It's literally 9 p.m. But it's your birthday, so if you're ready to head back, then I guess let's go.

Me: This is why I love you. I'm heading to your car right now. If you run into Taylor on your way out, tell her I said thanks for the invite and nice crib.

I left Ryan's girlfriend's party around ten. I would have gone sooner, but I didn't want to look like a complete jackass for leaving so early. After meeting *her*, I couldn't focus on anything else. I tried to play a round of beer pong with Ryan and a couple of other guys from school, but my curiosity got the best of me.

This girl sparked my interest, and I can't seem to remove her from my thoughts. And now she's the girl who got away. What a fucking moron I am. I didn't even attempt to stop her. Honestly, though, how crazy would I have looked chasing her down, a stranger at that? She probably would have knocked the shit out of me.

But there is a small piece of me that thinks maybe she

wanted me to follow her. I know what I saw. And when our eyes locked for the first time, the feelings were mutual in some weird way. I was drawn to her instantly, needing to know more about her.

At the age of twenty-three, having a relationship has been the least of my worries. It's not that I don't believe in it. It's just that the girls I've tried to connect with just don't click. It has nothing to do with looks. I've had multiple gorgeous women attempt to be what I need. The problem is that looks fade, and many women place their appearance on a pedestal, forgetting that their soul needs nourishment. You can perceive yourself as a model on the outside, but you can carry an ugly soul on the inside.

And I've yet to come across anything different with the females I've encountered until now. Meeting her tonight gave me hope for something. The beauty of her radiated from the inside out. I couldn't pull my eyes from it. I've seen nothing quite like her, but there's more to her I desperately need to explore.

There's a brokenness filled with pain and tragedy that hides within the shadows of her expression. It's almost like her soul has been in a war most of its existence.

It's captivating in a way. How can someone so beautiful bear so much devastation? She carried herself so well, accepting her fate. I've tried to picture if my life would have turned out differently. Would I be as strong as her?

I know nothing about this girl, but I know she has experienced something daunting in her life. My biggest question is: How is she alone? I would have swooped her off her feet if she had let me. I'm assuming that since she came with her friend instead of a man, she is like me, single. Considering her friend willingly stuck behind and gave me her name and number, if there was someone involved, it's not serious.

What if we were meant to cross each other's paths? Maybe our souls were acquaintances in another life, and they've spent an eternity searching for one another to finally be together again.

Something shifted inside me when her presence was in clear view. From this point on, I can't shake what I'm feeling. And even if I fail and she wants nothing to do with me, I won't stop trying to know her until she tells me otherwise. Olive Sage Landers, this is just our beginning.

Olive
CHAPTER 6

We arrive at our apartment around 11 p.m. Danielle insisted we stop and grab a bite to eat. I didn't disagree with her on that. I inhaled a juicy cheeseburger within minutes. She bought me a birthday brownie sundae afterward. And thank the good lord above, grease and sugar replaced my alcohol levels.

My belly is full, and now I can't help but replay this evening in my head. I made a fool out of myself at Taylor's party. I was in arm's reach of the hottest guy I think I've seen in physical form. Leave it up to me to sabotage a conversation.

I don't know why I get so much in my head. It's a habit I clung to during chaotic moments with my mom as a child. And it's been stuck with me ever since and is another burden I bear daily.

After preparing myself for a good night's rest, I plop down on my bed from exhaustion. My birthday has been interesting. I faced my childhood bully, put toxic liquid in my body, and scared away a hot male who, for whatever reason, wanted to talk to me. *Classic Olive.*

Now it's time for me to put my detective cap on and search for a dude I'll never see again. Just as I go to open Google, an unknown number pops up on my phone. Who the hell is texting me at midnight?

Unknown: It was nice meeting you tonight, even though you jolted off before I could even get your last name. Oh, and Happy Birthday, Olive Sage Landers. -Theo

My phone flies out of my hand and onto the floor. My heart is running a marathon in my heaving chest right now. Holy shit, how did he get my number? Oh, my fucking gosh. *Danielle.* That's why she was in such a hurry to get to her room and "go to bed" when we got home.

I'm going to strangle the life out of her in her sleep tonight. I anxiously scoop my phone from the floor and ponder on my response.

Me: You are quite determined, sir. Texting strangers at this time of night. Don't you have better things to do? Or other females to bug at sleeping hours?

Theo: Do you call every male "sir"? Or do I just look old and formal to you? I was unaware that there was a time limit on texting. And I'm sure there's someone out there who would love a response from me, but I'd much rather talk with you. I'm intrigued.

Me: No, only mysterious males I've known for less than five minutes. How do I know how old you are? And what shall I call you since "sir" is bothersome? Also, I don't know if I should be flattered or concerned.

Theo: You're a sassy little thing, aren't you? I like it. I'm 23 and far from retirement, so I guess you could call me by my name. May I call you Olive? Or shall I call you madam?

Me: It seems you're a little spicy yourself. So, how can I help you tonight, Theo? And yes, Olive is fine.

Theo: I've never been called spicy. But coming from you, I'll take it as a compliment :) I would like to know more about you. You had me at… sir.

Me: Now you have jokes. Well, Theo Ace Rivers, there isn't much to know about me.

You get what you see, and my life behind the curtain is a disaster. Save your time.

Theo: You remembered my full name, so you must be a little interested in getting to know me better. And if anything, your disasters make you a storyteller. I'd say it's a blessing in disguise.

Me: It's hard to forget someone who stared a hole through my face. I'm not used to people looking at me that way. And you don't know anything about my life; it's not something I'm proud of.

Theo: It's hard for me to believe that men don't crawl to you daily. I would have stared a hole through your gorgeous face all night if it didn't consider me a freak. You're right. I don't know your personal life. But I do know you've had two previous underage drinking tickets. You little criminal.

Me: You ass! Did you do a background check on me? And no, I don't normally give boys the time of day. Most are pricks who like to break hearts.

Theo: I sure did. Are you going to lie and say you didn't do one on me, or at least think about it? You won't find much. And I'm far from a boy, Olive. Maybe if you get to know me, you'll learn the difference between a man and a boy.

Me: I appreciate your confidence and for taking the time to reach out and attempt to turn this into something other than a late-night conversation. Unfortunately, we live in different cities, and I doubt we'll be seeing each other again.

Theo: Talk to your best friend. I think we'll be seeing each other very soon :)

Me: What are you talking about??

Theo: Sweet dreams, Olive

Me: Hello?

Me: Theo??

Me: SIR???

What a prick! What the hell is he talking about? Glancing at the clock, I realize it's now 1 a.m. I can't believe we texted for that long. How am I supposed to sleep now?

He left me hanging on purpose. My mind is turning flips, and so is my stomach. I am seconds away from barging into Danielle's room and beating answers out of her with a pillow. She is so sneaky sometimes. I don't know what she's trying to accomplish behind my back.

We know nothing about this Theo dude aside from how freakishly hot he is. And he seems quick with his words and the meaning behind them, which I find rather sexy. Okay, I need to take my delusional ass to bed. I decide to sit on it for the night.

Danielle and I will have a lovely, in-depth conversation over breakfast today. After what feels like hours of running different scenarios through my mind, I finally close my restless eyes and drift off to sleep.

Olive
CHAPTER 7

I quickly woke up from my childhood bed.

— drip, drip, drip.

What is that noise? I rise from my bed and listen again.

— drip, drip, drip.

Why is it so quiet in here? Where is my mom? Where is Nora Ray? I slowly walk from my bedroom. The bathroom light is on across our small hall. The noise is coming from in there.

I hesitate for a moment but head towards the bathroom door. The mirror is foggy, and this room is muggy and eerie— drip, drip, drip. The bathtub curtain is shut. I pull back the damp curtain. My heart sends a jolt through my chest. I can feel the hairs on my arms stand on end.

Before my eyes, I see my mother, clothed underwater. Her

eyes and mouth are closed. She looks to be in a peaceful dream. Her gorgeous curls float above her, forming an enclosed maze around her face. There is a syringe with a liquid substance circling the tub's wall. I go to grab her and pull her to the surface. As soon as I reach for her shoulders, her eyes fly open, and so does her mouth.

She is screaming underwater. I use all my strength to pull her above.

It's as if someone invisibly hovers over top of her, keeping her from coming up for air. I'm not strong enough to fight the force that keeps her held under. I can see life leaving her eyes. Burning tears pour from my eyes. Now I can't breathe. My lungs are closing. I can feel her pain deep inside me. No, Mom, no!

My eyes fly open, and I gasp for air. My body, clothes, and mattress are drenched with sweat. I can feel every inch of my worn body trembling. I quickly look down and can almost physically see my heart pounding from my chest.

Fresh, salty tears slowly caress my cheeks. I frantically look around, still feeling confused. I'm at my apartment, in my room. Lottie is lying across my right arm, facing me. She tilts her head and gazes at me.

She's seen me waking up in a frenzy so many times. I can see the concern in her little, beady brown eyes. It wasn't real. This was another bad fucking dream. They haunt me more than I'd like to admit. I sigh out of frustration and reach for my phone to check the time. It is 6:30 in the morning. Still no response from that jackass.

I feel so gross, covered in sticky sweat. I take a deep breath and drag myself from my bed to the bathroom to wash off.

Hopefully, scalding my body will motivate me to confront Danielle. Once I'm out of the shower, I peek at myself in the bathroom mirror.

I feel rested even after having night terrors last night. But there's something about my eyes, a sadness trapped behind them. I try to imagine myself as someone else looking at me. Can others see my internal screams? Do they see the demons lingering, bearing weight on my shoulders? Or do I look pleasantly happy and content?

When I stare back at myself, I can see all my inner flaws manifesting in my deteriorating body. Past and present wounds mark every part of me. I try so hard to run from my fractured soul, but the faster I try to run, the more it consumes me entirely.

Most days, I desperately reach for distractions, like an addict chases a high. Studies show that if you have a relative or parent in addiction, it's most likely imprinted in your blood. So I've concluded that I'm an addict, but not in the way you think. Drugs have never really been my thing. Probably because I resent what they did to my mother. I was jealous of drugs in a way. How could something equivalent to a stranger pop up out of nowhere and steal our mom from us?

So yes, I resent them wholeheartedly. But I won't lie and say I've never dabbled. Believe me, I have multiple occasions. In my head, I wanted to know what was so special about them. I needed to know how something could be more important than flesh and blood.

I may or may not have gotten around a bad crowd during my teenage years. Danielle had graduated two years before me. I had to talk myself out of not dropping out and being done. My mental health took a turn around tenth grade. And with Danielle gone, I felt so alone and miserable. I didn't understand the emotions running through my head.

The last thing I was going to do was talk to someone about it and expose my weaknesses because that's all I've felt most of my life: weak with no control. So, I bottled it all up and looked for distractions instead. No, I'm not proud of some of my choices in life. But who was to tell me right from wrong? I had no guidance aside from Nora Ray trying her damndest to fill shoes that weren't hers to fill.

So I said fuck it, most kids turn out like their parents anyway, good or bad. Why not prove the world right? Statistics are always right.

I've fiddled around with a few different drugs. If I was going to try something, why not go all the way in? Cocaine is how I discovered I had raging anxiety. At first, the rush it gave me was exhilarating. It was the perfect combo with alcohol. And damn, did it make me want to party. I could drink like a fish and felt indestructible.

The music, the dancing, I for once felt so alive and vibrant. It didn't take me long, after a few weekends of abusing it, to discover the wearing-off effect. This is where my heart and my head both teamed up against me. The pressure in my stomach, the racing heartbeats clawing at my brittle chest. The rambling thoughts crowded my vision.

The short ride was an adventure, but once my Uber ride was up, I was left abandoned, shivering on a dark street with nothing but my gloomy thoughts. Why would anyone want to feel that way?

Heroine is where I feel I stopped at my lowest. I knew who I could communicate with to get my hands on it. It was obvious who did what in school. So, I wiggled my way into a small group of troubled girls from geometry class. I was troubled, too, so why not hang out with people I could relate with? I was tired of being alone, exhausted from faking a smile every day. I contemplated my decision for a while.

My heart was telling me no, but my brain was telling me to do it. I had already tried an upper, and that didn't mix well with my overthinking mind. Maybe a downer would be different for me. This could be my opportunity to finally understand why people are destroying their lives and families over a stupid, meaningless drug.

The girls brought me to some sketchy condo with guys who looked to be at least ten years older. That place was screaming with red flags, but I would not be a pussy and back out. I've seen some pretty horrid shit, so I could handle it.

I remember the dude's sitting around a weathered coffee table. The place reeked of cigarette and weed smoke. There was this dark, tar-like substance on a tray. Old stained bottle caps lay on and around the table. It looked like they were mixing it with water and transferring it into syringes. I watched all three girls individually take a syringe with the substance and remove the needle. They then proceeded to shoot the substance into their nose. It wouldn't be too hard for me, right?

It was my turn next, shit. Every human sous was watching me in that place. You would have thought I was preparing to perform for them. This made my anxiety skyrocket. One thing about me. I dislike all eyes on me; I don't give a shit where I am.

A dude with acne scars all over his face hands me a syringe. He explained to me what to do like I didn't just watch the girls simply shoot liquid into their noses. I take the syringe in my shaky hands. On the inside, I am an earthquake ready to destroy all in my path.

But on the outside, my face gives away nothing. I stick the syringe to my nostril, and before talking myself out of it, I inhale the substance through my nose quickly.

Instantly, I feel a heavy rush surge through every vein in my body. With each second that passed, the voices in my head were muted one by one. All at the same time, I feel nothing but so much. The pain that consumed me daily, the racing thoughts, the rage, the sadness, is all gone. I feel so numb, yet so alive. It is as if the liquid comes in with no remorse. It knocks my mental door down and kicks out every negative thought from my brain.

Now I sort of understand why depressed people turn to this. I haven't felt this calm in a long time. Nothing matters. I don't give a single fuck about anything except for this overwhelming numbness.

It wasn't until my head spun that my vision went completely black. I realized the mistake I had made. This is where my memory fights to recollect exactly what happens from this point on. There are tiny kernels I hold onto. Flashes of people surround me, examining me under a microscope like I am some new lab-discovered species. I remember feeling like I was floating on a cloud headed into a dark abyss. Whatever this is, it's happening at rapid fire.

There is a burning sensation in the pit of my stomach. It

feels as if lava is traveling through my insides. The last thing I remember is hovering over a toilet, puking my entire insides out. I had never in my life puked so much. By the time I make it back home, my insides feel like they had been in combat war for years. Danielle is the only one that I tell, and I make it clear it's never to be discussed. Fuck that, never again.

As a child, I think my "addiction" began. I constantly chased love and acceptance. I wanted to feel love and be the cool kid at school. Which was hard to receive since Bennett made sure everyone knew where I lived. So, as I grew older, the constant letdowns outweighed the high I could never fully suffice. So, I said fuck love and fuck fitting in. I found a new craving: distractions. It's the only thing that temporarily blocks out my racing thoughts.

Reading is my companion. I'm not much for sitting still, but if I have a book in my hand, I can escape this dreadful reality. Books are so kind to me. They allow me into their worlds with arms wide open. They evaporate all my mental pain and replace it with adventure and wonder. Books are the only thing that truly understands my fight against myself.

The problem is that I can only visit their fictional reality briefly. Once I put the book down, all my thoughts and worries grab their pitchforks and force their way back into my mind. The impact of their absence feels as heavy as a solid block of stone every single time. So when I am able, I take what I can get—my small fixings.

Once I am dressed, I prepare myself for this conversation with Danielle. I still can't believe I stayed up late bantering with a stranger from another town. And more so, I can't grasp why my best friend is scheming. She knows I loathe that shit. Maybe Theo was messing with me. I hardly know him, but he's the type to play around like that and leave me wondering all night. Either way, I am going to figure this out because I am driving myself crazy just thinking about it.

When I walk into the living room, Danielle is sitting on the couch concentrating on her hot cup of coffee, like she's Moses preparing to part it like the Red Sea. "Good morning, love," she says softly.

I throw myself onto our loveseat directly across from her. Lottie greets her before jumping onto my lap. I stare at Danielle so hard you'd expect lasers to shoot from my eyes. I blow out a lazy sigh. "Anything you'd like to talk about, roomie?"

She squints her eyes at me. "Well, Olive, since you seem to have trouble speaking to hot guys, I took matters into my own hands."

I'm seconds from chucking a decorative pillow at her head. "And what matters do you speak of, Danielle?"

She wrinkles her nose at me. "Oh, come on. Don't act like you didn't hear from a certain someone last night. Don't be sour, but one of Theo's *single* friends has grandparents who own a beach house in Cherry Grove. They're going down Thursday and staying until Monday. Theo invited us, and I may have told him we'd ride down Friday evening after you get off work. And I'm off all weekend, so it just worked out." She shrugs.

It takes all of me not to dive across the living room and throat-punch her. "So you didn't think you should ask me first? What the fuck?" I snap, gritting my teeth.

Danielle sips her coffee and rolls her eyes. "Nope, because

I know you too well. You would've said no before even hearing the plan. Just shut up and accept that someone has the hots for you. You can't run from guys forever, Olive. You'll be miserable if you do. Stop comparing every male to Noah."

Damn, she is right, though. I'm always sabotaging things. Noah fucked my head up. I look for the bad in everything because I've often been let down. And damn, I'm tired of disappointments.

I'd rather be alone than deal with another dude like my ex. He reeled me in, just to turn around and leave me on the ground, gasping for air like a dying fish. It was by far the most toxic relationship. And I lived in it restfully, maybe because it reminded me of my already haywire life. It took a so-called friend fucking him in the back seat of his Mustang for me to realize the fool I was for sticking around. It was an endgame for me then. I let Chloe know she could have my cold leftovers.

I'm mentally exhausted from my unpleasant night terrors. So, I choose not to fight Danielle on this one. She wouldn't let me hear the end of it if I backed out. I'll let her have her way this once. Plus, maybe a small piece of me wants to figure Theo out. Something about him draws me in. And I can't help but want to know more.

My silent thoughts are enough for Danielle to know she's won this argument. I see a small, annoying grin form on her lips. She's lucky that Lottie's perched on my lap. Or I'd knock her smug ass off the couch.

Danielle smiles at me. "Girl, I have a feeling next weekend will be one we never forget."

I stay quiet and drift into my thoughts. Something inside me tells me that she is right. I can feel it down to my aching bones. Theo is going to be hard to shake. It scares me but sends a pleasant rush through my body, easing my heavy chest. *A new high to chase.*

Today, I'm going to take it easy and get some things done around the apartment. I might even kick back and start on a new book. It feels nice not having to work and taking advantage of being able to do whatever the hell I want after last night's ventures and waking up from a mini heartache. I'd say this is an opportunity worth using.

I decide to ride down to the local coffee shop with Lottie. She adores car rides with me. She doesn't mind getting a "pup cup" now and again, either. I'm feeling fancy, so I get myself a large iced coconut caramel latte. I'm feeling good now, with no bad thoughts or racing heart. The air smells of early summer, with a hint of honeysuckle. I picture myself on the beach, listening to the crashing waves. I need more days like these.

Once we return to the apartment, Lottie licks her tiny pup cup clean. She looks up at me with a white foam mustache. She's so damn cute. It's now getting close to lunchtime. My tummy is protesting. I could devour an entire meal right now.

Just as I start rummaging through the fridge, my phone receives a text.

Theo: Good morning, Ms. Landers. Did you sleep well?

Me: Morning Mr. Rivers. I guess I slept okay. Btw it is 11:56.

Theo: Indeed, it is, which means it's still technically

morning time :) Did you dream about me by chance?

Me: You're already on your shit today, I see… and no, Theo, not a single dream about you. Will you be able to survive the day knowing you're not "all that"?

Theo: Ouch, I'll be sure to stay clear of harsh Olive. But even if you didn't dream about me. I know you've thought about me at least a little. Don't lie.

Me: Maybe a tad.

Theo: I knew it. I'm irresistible.

Me: You didn't let me finish. I thought about how you left me hanging last night, which is a rude way to start a friendship.

Theo: Well, considering you've continued to throw it in my face, I'm nothing more than a stranger. I figured it was only appropriate to allow you to have that convo with your best friend. So, we are friends now? That's a start.

Me: Slow down, sir… that's not what I said. We'll see how next weekend goes.

Theo: So you are coming? I like it.

Me: Danielle insisted we go, and I think she's curious about your friend at the beach house. Who is he, and what's his name?

Theo: Well, I like Danielle already. His name is Chase, and he is single. You would have met him at Taylor's party, but he has cousins visiting for the weekend. We grew up together. Our moms have worked at the same bank since we were around nine years old.

Me: That's sweet. It sounds similar to Danielle and me. We grew up together in the same neighborhood. By the way, she is not looking for a bf—just a good time.

Theo: He's a good guy. We wouldn't be as close as we are otherwise. And the same for him, but hey, you never know. Sometimes, you don't search for it, and then a good opportunity falls in your lap. Wbu, Olive, what are you looking for?

Me: Nothing particular, but definitely not a bf. I haven't had the best of luck in that department. So, I choose to be alone.

Theo: Someone hurt you? That's a sad way to live your life. There is someone out there willing to tear down the world for you.

Me: I don't want to talk about it, especially not with a stranger.

Theo: Damn, harsh Olive shows her face again. Noted.

Me: I'm joking, sort of.

Theo: So you are a comedian as well. I like you more and more, Olive Sage Landers.

Me: You seem okay yourself, Theo Ace Rivers. I think it's time I go. I just realized I still haven't eaten today—my poor tummy. Have a good day.

Theo: This is a start. I look forward to officially meeting you. Let's pretend we didn't meet at the party and start fresh in person. And in the meantime, let's get to know each other better. Let's give each other one fact a day about ourselves. What do you say?

Me: Deal :) We'll start the fact-sharing tomorrow.

Theo: I look forward to it. Talk soon, Olive.

Me: Bye, Theo.

I set my phone down on the kitchen island. I can't help but feel a wicked smile form across my face. What am I getting myself into?

When I talk with Theo, I feel relaxed and comfortable. Which is strange to say, considering I barely know him. But I'm great at reading people, and normally my anxiety flares when I catch weird vibes.

Something is soothing about him, and I just can't pinpoint what it is, not yet at least. In a way, I am looking forward to this beach trip. For some odd reason, I want to see him again. I can still smell his addicting oak scent lingering around me.

I can feel his damning ocean eyes burn through me, scanning every inch of my body like a starving lion. I can sense myself wanting more of him. This could go wrong, for so many reasons.

All I know is that I can't pull away from this overwhelming sensation, not just yet.

Olive
CHAPTER 8

I still vividly remember the days when I lay sprawled out on the bed, blankly staring at the popcorn ceiling while my boyfriend Noah rushed to the shower to wash off. It's something he's always done right after we had sex.

I know how crazy it sounds, believe me. But I had stopped asking him why. It used to make me feel gross. It's like he was trying to wash any evidence of me off of him. I grew accustomed to it. Honestly, I wouldn't know much of what was normal in a relationship. My parents failed me in that section, too. Aside from making out with a few guys here and there, Noah was my only relationship and pretty much my first everything.

Okay, I take that back. I met up and had a one-time fling with a guy at the drag strip. I ended up giving him head in the bed of his truck. I know how sloppy that sounds. It was my first time doing anything like that, and for once, I wanted to do something spontaneous.

Danielle may or may not have given me the confidence boost I needed. She was hooking up with his older brother in the car beside us. We agreed that if we ever did anything raunchy, we'd do it together because that's what best friends do, right? It's a memory I'd only want to have with her. And it's our little secret.

Noah seemed different from what I expected out of a guy. He wasn't much of a touchy-feely type. Only during our sexual escapades would he caress me in a way. Don't get me wrong, our sex life was far from tedious. Not speaking on the size of his dick. But I had learned so much since being with him. And foreplay seems to come naturally to me.

But it never felt so much like love, more like a good fuck. I eventually assumed that all boys were different, and maybe this was all I deserved since my life was full of inconveniences. I should have been thankful that he chose me and was in a relationship with me.

Why would anyone want to deal with my mental struggles and a dysfunctional mother? He chose me and was a part of my crazy life. So, I accepted that maybe that was the best I'd get.

Noah and I met at a football game during our senior year of high school. I was seventeen, him eighteen. Our teams were playing the field, the last of the season. I'll be honest. I know absolutely nothing about football. I know they chase each other with a ball, but it's never grabbed my interest.

Danielle and I had made a last-minute decision to go.

We had nothing better to do that evening. Long story short, Noah was standing with a group of guys. I caught him staring at me while I was shoving a funnel cake down my throat. I wouldn't call it romantic by any means. I had powdered sugar all around my mouth. I attempted to smile with a full mouth, and a piece of soggy funnel cake smacked onto the pavement. It horrified me, but he busted out laughing. So, I smiled back at him, red-faced and all. And that's pretty much where our rocky ass journey began.

Danielle immediately had her suspicions, and so did I. However, he easily fooled me in the beginning. He was kind to me, bought me flowers, took me out for dinner, and held my hand everywhere. I was definitely "love-struck" by his commitment.

I thought, for once in my life, I was finally receiving something good for my damaged soul. The thing is, he knew I was still sacred, untouched. And I think that fueled his fire. He pampered me for months, waiting for the perfect opportunity to shoot his shot. He made me believe I was the only girl in the world for him. And my dumbass believed his fake agenda.

Things changed drastically after he took my virginity. No more touching aside from intercourse. I could never touch him until he gave me specific commands. I was his own personal sex toy. This quickly spiraled into another problem in my life that I couldn't control. Control is something I've never had. I couldn't control my mother's actions. I couldn't control the absence and loneliness I felt since I was a young child. I can't control the thoughts and suffering that taunt me daily.

Now, the one thing that was once my sanctuary and security has been cruelly taken away from me. And it wasn't out of love. I was probably just another young, innocent girl on his list for bragging rights. He knew I was vulnerable and desperate for attention. And I allowed it. I fell for his stupid, greedy trap.

Everything about us was toxic. If we weren't fucking; we were fighting. There was a lot of yelling and throwing things. There were close times when I could see it in his eyes. Moments where I knew he wanted to physically hurt me. And I was prepared for it. One thing I can say about my mom is that she did not back down from a fight. And as many as I've witnessed with her, best believe I was ready to box any mother-fucker that tried to put their hands on me in a violent way. And to be quite frank, I think Noah knew that too.

He learned quickly the night I caught him fucking my friend Chloe in the driver's seat of his precious Mustang. I snatched her conniving naked ass right off his mediocre dick and dragged her through the parking lot.

And that was the last time I saw Noah. He is the reason I have little to no faith in boys. *Good fucking riddance.*

Olive

CHAPTER 9

And just like that, it's my last day off. Then it's back to reality tomorrow. I slept heavenly last night. I don't recall having any nightmares, which is a plus. I'm pretty sure I fell asleep with a grin, which is so unlike me. Last night I had laid in bed, replaying my and Theo's chats. I met him out of nowhere and barely even conversed with him. Now, Danielle and I are going to the beach with him and his friend we've never met. This is so different from my usual decisions.

For some strange reason, I feel all giddy inside. This scares me to my core. I hardly know anything about Theo. Yes, he seems genuine and mature. But what if it's all for show? Danielle is right, I can't compare him to Noah; it's not fair to him. But what if it's a similar scenario?

I can't handle another letdown. And oddly enough, I am already feeling something unexplainable. It's as if I can feel my existence gravitating towards him. It sounds absurd, but that's the best way I can describe it. And even though I only heard his voice for a moment at the party, I still feel his rich, comforting tone curl around me.

I love his sarcasm and how he plays around. It meshes well with my personality, and that's saying a lot. I can only imagine the fun we could have together in person. The problem is I know myself, and sometimes I push people away. If things seem too good to be true, it scares the ever-living shit out of me. And I'd rather run before potentially getting hurt.

I know how toxic and unhealthy it sounds. I am quite aware of that. But do you blame me? Life hasn't been easy on me. I've forgiven others many times throughout my life. And what have I gained from it? Disappointments.

I refuse to stress myself over something that hasn't even happened. What harm will it do just to test the waters a little? I will stick it out and see how this beach trip goes. If there are any red flags, I'll call it quits. Plus, it's too early to assume the worst when Theo hasn't given me one reason to think otherwise. Noah is in the past, and I want to keep it that way.

It's been a year, and I can't continue to let him linger in my thoughts. He ruined me before, and I'm only letting him win by allowing the damage to spread like wildfire. With that being said, here's to letting go and moving on.

Nora hasn't reached out since Friday. I hope she is doing okay. I like to keep in touch as much as possible but also try to give her space. We both like our alone time. There's just something off about her. I want to be there for her as much as I can. Since I'm returning to work tomorrow, I must run by the grocery store. We are low on food at the apartment, and I want to get a few items for the beach trip. Jake's parents' house isn't too far out of the way. I make the rash decision to drive by and check in on her.

Once I arrive at their house, I see my sister's car parked in the driveway. It's covered in pollen and doesn't look like it's been driven in days. I knock on the front door a few times.

Jake's mom opens the door shortly after. She's aged since the last time I saw her, which was just a few months ago. She is heartbroken, and it makes my heart hurt for her. She gives me a weak smile. "Oh, Olive, it's so nice to see you, honey."

I return the smile. "It's good to see you, too, Michelle. How have you and Derek been?"

She looks down at the ground for a moment before answering, "We're doing the best we can, considering everything. We are just so thankful to have Nora here."

I gently grab her hand and give it a small squeeze. "Please let me know if I can help with anything. And I know Nora appreciates the two of you. Thank you for caring for her the way you do."

I can see tears forming in the corners of her grey eyes. "She is family to us, and Jake loved her with all his heart. And I hope you know that we're here for you too, Olive." I give a quick nod in thanks. We walk inside.

Their house hasn't changed one bit. I always get a nostalgic feeling when I come here. Their home is a two stories. There is only a bonus room upstairs, which is Jake and Nora's room. Even when they moved out, his parents never touched it. I think they always hoped they'd one day move back in.

Michelle informs me that Nora has barely left her room since meeting me for lunch on Friday. She doesn't seem concerned; she, too, is grieving Jake's death. I replay Nora telling me she had so many things to do over the weekend, which I had a feeling was just her way of getting out of going anywhere. I approach her bedroom door; I look down and see there's no light on. I softly knock and wait for her. I hear no movement in her room.

I slowly creak open the door. Aside from light peeking from behind the navy window curtain, the room is dark. This room looks to be in shambles. Clothes are thrown all over or in piles in different places. I walk over to the dresser and see photos scattered all over it. Some photos I've seen before of her and Jake.

I pull out my phone to use the flashlight. She and Jake took so many pictures together. Some are from when they first started dating, others more recent. They fell in love so young; I believe they would have made it last.

The thought of him being gone sends an ache through my chest. He was everything to Nora. He saved her from our childhood in the best way he could. And now there is nothing left of him but pictures and memories. I fight back tears that try their best to escape my eyes. I turn and see Nora curled up in bed. She looks relaxed and content.

It's three in the afternoon, but maybe she was up late looking through pictures. I notice her purse lying beside her bed; it has fallen over, and items are exposed on the floor.

I see a small baggie sitting on the lip of her purse; it looks like a rolled-up cellophane. I crouch down and shine my phone light on it. There is something nestled inside of the baggie. Just as I go to explore the strange item, Nora shuffles in the bed. I quickly turn my phone light off and tiptoe out of her room. I stand by the door for a moment to see if she wakes.

She slowly rolls over, and I hear a long sigh leave her body. I refuse to disturb her sleep. I'm sure she has many restless nights. I quietly shut her door and head back down the stairs.

I let Jake's parents know she is sleeping and that I'll give Nora a call later. On the way to the store, I can't help but question what's going on with my sister. I can't make hasty assumptions, and while I'm not an expert, I know what is typically in cellophane. This concerns me. Surely Nora would tell me if she's doing something wrong. Why wouldn't she? Knowing what the outcome could be. We watched what drugs did to our mother. They destroyed her, snatched her motherly instincts, and threw them out the door.

Do I have any room to talk? Nora would beat me if she knew what I dabbled in before. But are her intentions the same? Is she just trying something out, curious like I was? Or has this become her normal?

I knew something had been off with her. I saw the change gradually grow after Jake's death. Yes, I know grief changes people. But this differed from that. I don't want to pry and upset her. And I damn sure don't want to accuse her and be wrong. I'm going to figure this out. I can't let my sister fall into our mother's habits.

Once I return home from the store, I put everything up in their rightful places. I realize I haven't heard from Theo today. I'm sure he's at work and most likely waiting for me to reach out first.

Danielle should be home around six. We plan to have pizza delivered this evening for dinner. Maybe a glass or two of wine and a movie. I love we get to have our little girl evenings. It makes me think back to when we were kids. Even though my childhood was gift-wrapped in shit, there are also memories I will cherish forever. And some of those memories are with my best friend.

It'll be another hour before Danielle makes it home from work. I suppose I've waited long enough to text Theo. I'm sure he's dying to hear from me. *Yeah, right.*

Me: Good afternoon, Theo.

Theo: There's my spicy Olive.

Me: Wow, that's one I've never heard. How are you today?

Theo: Good. I'm not much for sharing, even down to nicknames. I'm doing well, and I'm almost done with a job. Wbu?

Me: That's good to know, lol. Unfortunately, I'm going back to work tomorrow. Today has been interesting. Where do you work, if you don't mind me asking?

Theo: Anything worth sharing? And yeah, I mind.

Me: Nope. Not something you'd understand. And damn, sorry for asking. What are you, a stripper or something?

Theo: I'm joking, Olive. I work with my dad. We run a family-owned landscaping company. Stripping is my weekend night job.

Me: Oh, I love y'all work together, and you must be great with your hands.

Me: Okay, ignore that comment. It was a joke.

Theo: I just laughed out loud. Thank you for that. Are you

sure it was a joke, or are you curious? I'd love to show you what my hands can do in the near future.

Me: Ha-ha funny. Don't push it, Theo.

Theo: What?? I was talking about trimming your shrubs at no cost.

Me: Uh huh sure lol. Depending on how this beach trip goes, I may take you up on the free shrub trimming. Btw I don't personally own shrubs, but the apartment complex I live in may appreciate the gesture.

Theo: You call, and I'll be there, ready to work magic with these talented hands. I'll let them know I'm a close friend of yours. Maybe they'll knock some off your rent. So, where is my fun fact for the day?

Me: Lol, how kind of you. There's nothing fun about me to share.

Theo: I find that hard to believe. Come on… you agreed.

Me: Fine. Um, I work at a call center.

Theo: Now that's not very fun…

Me: It's a fact though?! UGH. OK. I like to read books.

Theo: What kind of books?

Me: All kinds of books. Romance, Fantasy, Thrillers. EVERYTHING.

Theo: So you like reading porn?

Me: Sir, those genres are not all about sex. But I don't mind when it is.

Theo: You're a little perve… I like that.

Me: Wbu Theo? What's a fun fact?

Theo: I've already given mine.

Me: Which was?

Theo: That I'm extremely talented with my hands.

Me: That's just coming from your own mouth. So It's not exactly a fact.

Theo: Test the waters and I'll show you just how good I am, Olive.

Me: You are quite confident in yourself I see… maybe even a little cocky.

Theo: Being confident doesn't automatically mean someone is cocky. Again, maybe I can show you a few things next time I see you.

Me: Maybe you can ;) Danielle just got home. We're having a girls' night. I enjoyed talking to you. Text tomorrow?

Theo: I like that answer. Is it crazy that I haven't stopped thinking about you? As short as our conversation was, I can still remember your voice, your face. I don't know, Olive. It's doing something to me. I look forward to Friday.

Me: I don't think it's crazy. And maybe I haven't stopped thinking about you, either. I don't know what this all means. But I'm okay with the unknown. Goodnight, Theo.

Theo: I think we're going to find out what this is sooner than we think. Sweet dreams, Olive.

I set my phone down on my nightstand. These last few days, I've thought something was wrong with me. I've tried fighting this urge that unapologetically swallows me whole. Now, knowing that Theo has similar feelings has me even more curious about this "unknown."

What is this between us? This is something I've never encountered before. It scares me to my core but it also ignites something deep within my bleeding soul. He feels so familiar in a way, almost like our souls knew each other in a different lifetime. Tonight, I am looking forward to talking to Danielle about our conversations with Theo and me. Friday can't get here quickly enough.

I feel a strong grip on my upper thighs. I look down and see thick, dirty blond hair; the slightly curled ends tickle my legs. I can't move. All I can do is watch. Who is this mystery man lying between my legs?

On a normal day, this would scare the shit out of me, and whoever this person is would lie on the floor with a swollen lip. But I am intrigued by the way his massive hands hold my thighs steady. It's like they were molded just for me. He slowly looks up.

Holy shit, I know those fucking eyes. Theo is shirtless on my bed, between my legs.

Our eyes stay locked. I can't pull away from his dominating stare. It's so dark in here, but Theo's punishing eyes are glowing with want. Just by how he's fixed on me, I can tell he refuses to take no for an answer. I am his prey, and he came to feast.

Within seconds, his vivid blue eyes became somber. A sinful grin plays across his gorgeous mouth. My legs shake with anticipation.

In one smooth movement, he lifts my legs onto his broad shoulders. He places a gentle kiss on my left thigh. His plump lips are warm yet cold as ice. It sends a pleasurable sting through my stomach.

I can already feel pressure in all the right places. My

breathing is deep and heavy. And as if he senses what he's doing to me, he trails his fingers down my stomach, inches away from where I want him next. Theo then spreads my legs a little further, keeping them propped and secured. He gently runs his thumb around my clit.

My back immediately arches without my doing. My hands find their way into his soft blond locks. I have no control over my reflexes right now. Theo is the pilot of my entire body, and he's causing me to accelerate at a high speed. I can't do anything but allow him to drive me into oblivion.

And just like that, he plants one finger inside me, slowly pumping back and forth. I can't hold back the moan that escapes my lips. I look back down, catching Theo staring at me with so much hunger in his eyes. Before I can process the pleasure coursing through me, he places another finger inside me. He curls his fingers up, hitting that intense G-spot that Noah could never seem to locate.

While fucking me with his fingers, he places his thumb on my clit and plays small circles in a perfect rhythm. I can see his muscles tensing with each pump.

The pressure is building at an almost unbearable rate. It's like a volcano ready to erupt at any moment. If this man does one more thing, it will be my undoing. I can't help but close my eyes and cover my mouth, trying to shove the moans back down my throat. Theo was right; he knew what he was doing with his hands.

My pussy was an abandoned garden needing attention. He came in without permission. And planted flowers in all the right places. Call it landscaping or whatever you like. This man is a professional, and I'm ready to give him all my money.

He bites down on a sensitive spot on my thigh while sucking it into his mouth. My inner walls expand, this is a high I never want to stop chasing. Just as I begin to orgasm, everything goes black. I am spiraling in unexplainable pleasure.

I look back down. Theo is gone. I can feel my center pulsating viciously. I'm here in my room all alone, with a puddle between my legs. Which instantly tells me I just orgasmed in my sleep. I feel like a moron right now. I will definitely keep this to myself. I am so drained from my finger fucking dream I can't even get out of bed to clean up.

I reach for my phone on the nightstand. It's 4:30 in the morning. I need to be up in two hours to prepare for work. I'm instantly annoyed with myself. I fumble around and locate a shirt beside my bed to wipe away the evidence of my embarrassing release.

I can't believe that happened. This man hasn't physically touched me and has that effect. I close my eyes and curl up into a ball. I rub my inner thigh. It's almost as if I can feel a sore sensation on the spot where he bit me in my dream. My mind wanders off. I'm so exhausted that I don't even realize I've fallen back into a deep sleep.

CHAPTER 10

I'm trying to ignore the fact that I woke up around 4:30 this morning with a full hard-on. There's a first for everything. I've never been one to have vivid dreams, but I guess I left out the part where, since meeting Olive, I've dreamed about her often. It's almost like my mind wants to physically brand my memory with every stunning feature she's gifted with. And last night's dream tops them all.

I don't know if I should be embarrassed or thankful for the pleasurable experience. Olive would probably have nothing to do with me if she knew the details of my dream. I can still remember her soft skin beneath my fingertips. The feel of my hands wrapped around her perfectly shaped thighs, molding well in their place.

Her legs are quaking, begging for my touch. In one swift movement, her legs were resting on my shoulders. I placed one kiss on her left thigh; her body trembled beneath my grip. I was now in control of her sacred body. And respectfully, I wasn't stopping until her undoing had us both gasping for air.

The look of lust and desire played across her face. Almost as if she had never experienced that kind of touch before. Seeing her need for me only fueled my burning desire for her. I trail my fingers down her smooth, toned stomach, goosebumps rising with each touch.

Both of us wanted, no, needed this moment. I swear she was in that same dream with me for a split second. Together, like our souls had already met in a past life.

Her eyes were so telling, letting me know what she wanted at that moment. I gently twirled small circles around her clit. She instantly hitched her back; it was so fucking hard not to cum from her body's reaction to me. Her delicate hands found their way into my hair, gently tugging. I then, without hesitation, slid a finger inside of her. She was so tight around my finger and already wet for me. An enticing moan escaped her delicious lips.

This told me she wanted more, so I placed another finger deep inside her. I could feel her strong inner walls expand and tighten around my fingers. It took all of me not to remove my sweats and fuck her like a proper gentleman.

But right then, I wanted to watch every movement of her brilliant body while I pumped in and out of her. I desired to continue feeling her tight pussy beg for more. I so badly wanted to taste her on my lips. God, I know she tastes so fucking good. I stopped myself by lightly biting her inner thigh. Her skin was silky and smelled of coconut.

I could sense her climax approaching with every thrust I gave her. If she only knew the things, I could make her feel. I couldn't help but to delicately suck and bite her thigh. I wanted to bite down harder. Honestly, I think she would have loved it if I did.

She quickly covered her mouth as muffled moans seeped through her fingertips. Holy fuck, just her cries alone could have made me crash in pleasure. Just as I felt her inner walls collapse around my thick fingers, I woke up and realized it was nothing more than a dream. I was left in my bed with a rock-hard dick and blue balls.

Maybe I'm a little ashamed to admit that I replayed the dream in my head while jerking one out. It's a piss poor excuse, but I wouldn't have been able to go back to sleep if I didn't finish the deed. And I plan to take that to the grave with me.

The fucked-up thing is that I'll never be able to look at a girl the same since Olive crept into not only my life but my dreams. At least, not until I see her again. She doesn't realize the imprint she has already left in my mind. I won't stop until I know more about her. I want to touch her and hold her.

This desperate need for her presence is scaring the fuck out of me. I haven't felt whole since meeting her at that party. Like she unintentionally snatched a piece of my soul and took it with her.

Friday needs to show its face; the waiting is eating me alive. It doesn't help that she's a tough cookie to break. Something tells me she's been through unimaginable events in her life. It sounds crazy that I hardly know this girl and want to be there for her in ways she's never known. The thought of someone hurting her awakens a raging beast that sleeps deep within my soul. There's a reason we found each other, and I'm determined to claim what's mine.

Olive

CHAPTER 11

I never understood why people chant "Happy Monday." Mondays are by far my least favorite day of the week. Which in return doesn't make me happy. Maybe it's because I dwell on its arrival on the weekends that I have off. Or it could be the fact that I am currently fifteen minutes away from my job right now.

I struggled to get ready this morning, replaying my wild dream repeatedly. It felt so fucking real. Weirdly, I felt disappointed when I realized it was just a silly dream. *Right, it was so silly that it left my panties and bedsheet wet.*

Danielle kept staring at me this morning while we were eating breakfast. She said there was a strange glow about me, and I was too quiet. I told her without hesitation that I had been having crazy dreams all night, which woke me up. But I didn't remember what they were about, so it wasn't a full lie. I mean, I very much remember every little detail. I am still blown away by it. I didn't mind it, though. It's been months since I've pressure washed my clit with the removable shower head. So it was a much-needed release, for sure.

My phone rings, and it's Nora. I'm so happy to see her name flash across the screen that I don't hesitate to answer. "Good morning, Olive Oil," she says in a tired voice.

I can't help but smile. "Can we please move past that nickname, sis? I no longer look like an awkward noodle with arms and legs."

I hear her quietly snort. "Sorry, lil sis, you're stuck with it for eternity." Oh well, at least I tried.

"How are you doing, Nora?"

The phone goes silent for a moment. "I'm doing the best I can. Nothing more."

I nod my head as if she can actually see me.

"I just hope you know that I'm here for you, and you can talk to me about anything," I say with genuine intent.

"I know, Olive. And I love you for it." I can almost hear the sadness in her tone.

"I've been lucky to have you as my big sister. I want to be there for you like you've always been for me."

She lets out a long sigh. "That's what big sisters are for, and I wouldn't change it for anything."

I can't help but smile. "I know you wouldn't. Let's take one of our random beach trips soon, please. I'm pulling into work now. I love you, big sister."

She lets out a small laugh. "Hell yes! With Stevie Nicks blasting on the radio the whole way. I love you most. Talk soon."

My smile fades when our call ends. It was hard to keep quiet about my visit yesterday, but I knew it wasn't the right time. I just hope whatever she is struggling with is short-lived. I miss seeing her happy and vibrant.

Knowing she's hurting from fresh and past wounds tears me apart. Not having the ability to make it go away for her is what pains me most. She's been so much to me my whole life, and here I am, the useless little sister. I know grief plays a huge role in her struggles, but there is something else lingering in the shadows. And I have a feeling it will show its ugly face sooner than later.

Today has been dragging by, with at least 5 to 10 minutes between every call. On an average day, calls come in every twenty seconds. It sounds draining, but my day is much quicker when busy. I think some of my problem is that I'm eager to reach Friday, but also, who enjoys working thirty to forty hours a week? Not me.

I won't deny that I'm excited to finally bury my feet in the sand or that I'm impatiently waiting to see Theo so that I can figure out what this is between us. I have felt numb in certain areas for a long time. And somehow, Theo has sparked my sensory receptors. His existence alone rejuvenates me, like a nerve terminal restoring life to my cells.

My heart is still hiding in the shadows of my chest cavity. With the history of distress and trauma, it will take an army of good to persuade it into believing in anything more than failure because defeat and brokenness have secured their thick chains around my once whole heart. I'm nothing more than remnants of my being.

I take my lunch break at two instead of eleven. Now, my stomach is protesting against me. I need calories in my system. My work friend, Vanessa, is on her break as well. So, we agree to go to the little sub shop in the strip mall across the road from work. Honestly, I could eat anything edible. My mistake was picking at my breakfast this morning and daydreaming about this hot Theo guy finger-pounding me. It didn't help to have Danielle watch my every move like a hawk. The moral of the story is that Monday is "Mondaying" and I'm fucking over it.

I demolished an eight-inch Italian Sub, and I'm pretty sure I didn't even breathe while gobbling up its deliciousness. I can feel the crankiness subside from my mood. I don't know what it is, but the older I get, the more my irritability levels rise when I am hungry. I can't function correctly on an empty stomach.

The fact that I often feel anxious and worried probably explains why I need to keep food in my system most days. My overworking body is burning up every bit of nutrition I give it.

Vanessa and I discuss some changes at work. She tells me about her boyfriend and how she's 95% sure that he's going to propose to her soon. They have been dating for around six months, so that seems oddly early to assume such a thing. But I am happy for her. I admire others' happiness and sometimes wonder if I, too, will one day feel genuine contentment.

I'm not saying it's impossible. All things are possible. Well, I don't know about "all." I must emphasize that nineteen years of my existence have been rather unstable in some aspects.

I won't get my hopes up, but I refuse to give up fully. The child version of myself is clinging to the depths of my frayed soul. Hoping, praying, and yearning for affection. Sometimes, I can feel her crying out for someone to save her. And I can't help but feel remorse. As a young adult now, I can manage. But how the fuck did a child survive neglect for so many years?

I wish I could hold her tightly and take the burdens away. I can't, though, because that little girl is me. So, for now, all I can do is keep myself composed on the outside and suppress the inner demons that attempt to surface.

I completely forget that Vanessa is sitting directly across from me, babbling about who knows what. God, I love her; she's sweet as can be. But this girl always has something to gossip about. Most times, I sit and listen while nodding my head. Thankfully, she didn't notice me drifting off in my thoughts. If she quizzes me right now, I would fail miserably. I've got to work on sitting in my thoughts. Somebody's going to call me out one day. Which, I have Danielle for that.

The day continues to drag on, taking its sweet time. I won't lie and say that I haven't checked my phone over and over hoping to hear from *someone*. I have about forty-five minutes left until my shift is finally over. And fuck, am I ready for it.

Just as I'm about to give in and shoot a text over to Theo, I receive a text from him. No one notices the smile that takes over my whole face. Even if someone did, I would scowl at them heavily.

Theo: Happy Monday. How has your workday been?

Me: Hello, Mondays are never happy for me. It's going. I leave at five. And I can't freaking wait. WBU Theo? How is your workday going?

Theo: As expected. We had six jobs today, so we took a late lunch break. Still, there are two to go, and then I will be free. It's fun fact time, ma'am.

Me: You and these fun facts… Hmm, okay. Well, I have a tiny dog. Her name is Lottie, and she has 94% hair.

Theo: So basically, a rodent with hair? Suits you I suppose.

Me: Psh. She is a princess, and if you're lucky enough, you'll get to meet her. Where's my fun fact, sir?

Theo: How did I become so lucky to potentially have the honor of meeting a rat with a name? Since we are discussing pets, I have an actual dog. His name is Leo, and he is a black Lab.

Me: Leo… seriously. Don't you think the similarities in your names are a bit much?

Theo: Technically, my name is Theodore. He was born in August, and so was I. So I don't know; it seemed fitting.

Me: Okay, I see the sentiment behind it. Maybe he and Lottie can be friends one day.

Theo: To me, it sounds like you're thinking of the near future, and I like the sound of it so far.

Me: You'll turn anything into something, won't you, lol?

Theo: If it's fitting, hell yes!

Me: There's so much I need to figure out about you.

Theo: Need is a strong word, Olive. And your curiosity ignites something inside me. I want you to pry and explore every inch of me if you must.

Me: Wow, that was deep. Have you always mastered

swooning women?

Theo: No, but there are other things I've mastered with ease.

Me: You have a dirty mind. I caught onto that early on.

Theo: Dirty minds think alike. And whether you want to tell me. Deep in your bones, I know that you enjoy our bantering. And I wouldn't be surprised if you've had dreams about me.

Me: That's a strong assumption, Theo. But yes, I won't lie to you. I do like the shit-talking back and forth. Who doesn't?

Theo: All I care about is that you like it. Fuck everyone else.

Me: I learn more about you every day. I hate to cut this short, but my shift is almost over, and I have to log out of everything. Talk soon?

Theo: My phone is always on me. Just don't turn into one of those crazy girls who blows my phone up every hour of the day. I may question things then.

Me: I would never. And I think you know that.

Theo: I'm fucking with you. You are the only person I'd allow to stalk me every minute of the day.

Me: Lol, okay, Theo, calm down. Enjoy your day :) Until next time.

Theo: Until next time.

I don't know how I would have handled that conversation in person. I can't deny that some of his comments have me sweating in areas I don't want to admit to.

The way he uses his words, even through text, makes me feel every single word. One thing I've learned about Theo is that he is well-spoken. And I feel there is genuine intent behind everything he says. I will be in alert mode this weekend. This seems too good to be true.

Once I'm in my car, I give my mom a call. Of course, she doesn't answer. I planned to stop by before heading home. Something tells me I should go by and check on her either way. I need to make sure she's still breathing and has access to food.

I don't think Nora has been over to see her in a while. Do I blame her? No, not at all. Most would disown their parents if they went through half of what we did. However, even if I keep a distance between us, I can't leave her all alone with no one. It's only the three of us. We are in contact with no other relatives. And it's been that way my whole life. I refuse to lose another person in my life.

Pulling into the trailer park gives me a sense of "home," but it also makes my stomach turn in unimaginable ways. This is where I grew up. From the start until the day I moved out years ago, I have some of the best memories and others that haunt my dreams.

There are parts of this place that are the same as I remember it as a child. But since then, there have also been changes. I felt a tinge of sadness when Danielle's parents' old trailer was torn down years ago and replaced with a newer model just because her house was my break away from the chaos at home. Sometimes, when mom would leave me by myself for days, I would run to Danielle's, and her parents would always welcome me with open arms.

As far as I know, my mom is the only person who has lived here for a decade. She has no choice but to. No one has the money to move her elsewhere. Times have changed tremendously. Rentals now require background checks and good credit. Let's not forget that mom lives off a disability check. She doesn't even meet one requirement. She's very inconsistent with her life choices. So this is what it'll have to be, at least for now.

Pulling into the driveway, overgrown grass and weeds invade the ground. Wispy vines are weaved and wrapped into the vinyl of the house. They creep up to the roof and cling onto the neglected gutters. This place looks abandoned. Guess I'll need to find someone to come and take care of the lawn again. This is the reason my visits have space in between them.

I can't deal with this shit all the time. I feel I was robbed of having a mother and, in return, forced to be the mother figure to the one who birthed me. It's a fucked-up situation, but here I am, playing mom.

Walking to the front door is a challenge. It's like I am walking through an undiscovered jungle. The long blades of grass and thick weeds harass my legs. By the time I reach the stairs, my legs are itchy, and I bear scratches from my short travels. The door is cracked open, so why knock? Stepping inside, I scope out the living room.

It looks the same as it always has. Mom's dusty chestnut-washed china cabinet still holds the small porcelain figures my mom used to love to collect. When I was little, I used to love carefully playing with them. I close my eyes for a moment and take a deep breath. Do you know how certain smells stick with you for a lifetime? It's the realest thing. This place has a distinct smell that lingers with flashbacks. I can picture little me and Nora Ray sitting on the floor playing

Crash Bandicoot together. My heart aches with the good memories of this house.

I can tell Mom has cleaned very little, which is still weird to me. She once was a cleaning fanatic. This place was always spotless, with not one speck of dust to be found. Nora and I had daily chores to keep this place in tip-top shape.

Now, I look around and see a disaster. There are piled dishes that have probably been there for weeks. Dirt piles and hand-length dust bunnies latched onto things. I let out a long, agitated sigh. I might as well get this place in decent condition before it turns into something more. I can't afford to hire someone to come tidy this place up especially since I'm already needing the weed infestation taken care of.

First, I need to figure out where Mom is. I know she's here somewhere. My first guess is her bedroom. She's always spent most of her time in there, well, when she's home. Since her DWI years ago, she doesn't go anywhere anymore. But if Jewels need to go somewhere, she will find a way.

I walk towards the hallway and glance at the bathroom. I instantly feel chills run up and down my spine. Unwanted visions throw themselves into my thoughts.

I close my eyes and rub my temples. *Not today, Olive, not today.* I walk across the small hall and peek into my old bedroom. It looks the same from the day I moved out, untouched and flooded with nostalgia. My two Backstreet Boys posters still hang on the aqua-blue wall behind my old, unused bed. The memories ambush my mind every time I step into this room.

I walk over to my small, battered dresser and pick up origami notes between Danielle and me. They're still folded to perfection. And I can't help but smile, thinking back to those adored moments with my best friend.

I close my bedroom door and head towards Mom's room. Sure enough, I find her lying on her stomach on top of the bedcovers. Her room reeks of alcohol. Beside her lays an empty pint of Tito's vodka. I'm assuming she passed out and forgot to put the lid back on the bottle. There is a small spill circling the opening of the bottle. Mom isn't one to leave a bottle half full. Which tells me she drank the entire pint in one sitting. And now she's intoxicated and passed out.

Me being me; I grab the small, quilted blanket hanging on the bedpost and quietly cover her. She's probably not waking up anytime soon. When she gets in these drunken states, she normally sleeps it off, just to start again as soon as her eyes fly open.

Her head barely rests on the pillow, and her thick curls wrap around her face like a protective cocoon. Seeing her so vulnerable reminds me that she is a human and humans make mistakes. But it still doesn't make it okay. I never asked to be born into such heartbreak. Nora and I deserved better. But didn't our mother deserve it, too? I glance at her one last time before shutting her bedroom door.

After straightening the living room and kitchen up, I locate a pen and scrap mail. I leave Mom a note letting her know I stopped by. I stick a fifty dollar bill with the note. In the back of my mind, I know she will most likely spend it on something I don't agree with. I can't control every action made by Jewels. If she wants to waste it, that's on her.

But at least I can say I helped. I can't live with the racing thoughts and guilt that ambush my brain. I've done my part, even though I shouldn't have to.

I lock the doors and head out the side door. There's one more thing I want to do before leaving. Walking through the backyard brings back young summers here. Those were days I cherished as a child. Because smiles and happiness were far in between, those sweet moments have stuck with me.

Even with the yard being overgrown with tall greenery, I spot the small trail at the edge of the yard line. Walking through, I get hints of honeysuckle and pine. I feel a sense of security being here on this trail.

And there it still sits high off the ground, "The treehouse." The only fatherly thing our dad ever did for us. Aside from the overgrown vines that caress its wilted boards, it hasn't changed much. This place holds a huge piece of my childhood. Memories begin to flow endlessly through my mind. There were times when mom would be fighting with one of her flings or, in a drunken rage, high on drugs.

Nora's bedroom window faced the backyard. We would climb out and run straight for the treehouse. Nora and I made a pact that anytime we got scared, this is where we'd go together.

I climb the wooden ladder, careful not to get a splinter. At the top, I unclasp the small lock on the uneven door. Crawling inside, I finally stand and look around.

Ancient cobwebs are formed in every corner of the four walls. I can't help but smile being up here. This was my favorite place, my safe haven. My and Nora's little plastic table with chairs still sits in the same place we last left it. The little drawings we created are all over the table, faded but still visible.

I run my fingers over the words in the center of the table. "Nora Ray and Olive Oil, sisters forever." The corner of my eyes fills with tears. I still remember that day.

It's bittersweet thinking that long ago, Nora and I were in here with our wondrous imaginations. We did not know that it would be our very last. Because life got in the way, we grew up and left behind the very place that made our childhood worth remembering.

I walk over to the cutout window, which holds no glass or frame. I always loved it because we could hear the crickets chirp at night. And even from time to time, we'd catch a small forest-scented breeze.

Our dad knew what he was doing when he picked where to cut out the window. You'd never guess that there would be views worth seeing while living in a trailer park. I stare off into the endless forest beyond the window. Nora and I used to love coming up here at night and watching the moon. We had the best view of it. There was something about the moon that would draw Nora in. Sometimes, I'd watch her instead.

I think she would have stayed up here all night just to watch the moon illuminate the night sky. Every night around 10 p.m., the moon's natural gleam would shine through the forest and cast its glow into our treehouse window. It was a beautiful thing to see.

And what made it even more special was seeing a content smile on Nora's face while she stalked the moon. She was so beautiful in the moonlight. The way its light magnified her dazzling facial features. It's as if they were connected. Or maybe the moonlight healed her each time. Nora never wanted me to see her vulnerable side.

When I was younger, I didn't comprehend how she held it together so well. But as I grew, I understood why. She was the big sister, and she felt she needed to be strong for me. She was taking on a role that wasn't meant to be hers. I've always admired her strength.

I'd give anything to be young again in this treehouse with Nora. Just one last visit as kids. Those childhood memories are what I cling to. I hold on to them so tightly. Because in those little kernels were happiness. We could forget how fucked-up our lives were. We could pretend that we weren't born into a never-ending shit cycle of blood genetics.

Yeah, maybe it was only for a moment. But it was just enough to keep my splintered heart beating. I take one last look at the place that helped me fight for my once-tender life. One day, Nora and I will come here again and watch the moon together. One last time.

Olive

CHAPTER 12

Age eight

"Nora, Nora, wake up!" *I scream out in a panic. Nora frantically jumps out of the bed. "Olive, what the heck is going on?"*

I am so worked up that I struggle to voice to her what I just witnessed. I stumble on my words. Nora quickly crouches in front of me and grabs my face, forcing me to focus only on her.

And in the calmest manner, she says to me, "It's okay, Olive Oil. I'm right here. Tell me what is wrong." She then gently swipes sweaty strands of hair from my face, ensuring each piece rests behind my ears. I slow my breathing and concentrate.

Once I finally find the words, I speak. " I, uh, went to use the bathroom. And when I cut the light on, I saw Mom naked in the bathtub. There was white, foamy stuff coming out of her mouth. I got scared and ran out to get you! I don't know if I was dreaming."

Tears flood my worried eyes. Nora's face turns ghost white, which tells me I may not be dreaming this. Before I can say anything else, she picks me up and sits me on her bed. "I need you to stay right here and do not move. Do you understand me?" she says sternly. I nod my head.

Nora rushes out of the room. And now I am left with my pounding heart. There is a weird, heavy feeling in my chest, which is making it hard for me to breathe.

Please be a nightmare, please be a nightmare. Nora runs back into the room and stands me up. She is trying to stay calm, but panic is written all over her face. Her voice rattles out a response. "Listen to me, Olive; I need you to be strong for me, okay? We do not have time. We have to be quick!"

She grabs my hand before I can ask what's happening and charges towards the bathroom.

This is very much real. Mom is lying inside the tub, naked in the fetal position. She doesn't look like she's breathing. Her skin is discolored and almost lifeless. My stomach rapidly turns to hot lava, acid makes its way into my throat threatening to exit my insides.

I take a few deep breaths. I have to be strong for Mom and my big sister. I can do this. I nervously rub my hands together so aggressively that I could probably start a fire. Nora finds Mom's purse beside the toilet and dumps its contents on the bath rug. I noticed that she carefully picked through the random items. I spot syringes, a dirty spoon, lighters, and a crumbled-up pack of spearmint gum "mom's favorite".

Nora grabs something in a small clear package; whatever is inside is white and looks like plastic. She quickly sits it on the toilet. The labeling has a small fine print that reads Narcan.

She turns back to me. I can see the angst in her eyes. "I need you to help me get Mom on her back. We have to be quick, Olive." I can't fully process what is happening right now, but I give her a slow nod.

Nora and I climb into the tub. Nora gets above her head, and I get below Mom's legs and feet.

Nora quickly instructs, "Grab around her legs, and I will count to three!"

She then grabs underneath Mom's arms. Nora and I make eye contact. "One... two... THREE!"

Mom is dead weight. We lift with all our might and somehow get her rolled over into position.

Nora snatches the strange item from the toilet and rips it open with her bare teeth. She swiftly drops to her knees, picks Mom's lifeless head up, and places it on her lap. She then sticks the white object into both of Mom's nostrils.

It nestles perfectly like it's made for just that. She pushes up on it, and I hear a faint spraying sound. Did she shoot nasal spray into her nose? She throws the object onto the bathroom floor and tilts Mom's head back. Why does it look like she's done this before? How did she know to look in Mom's purse? And how'd she know how to use that weird white thing?

I sit frozen, staring at Mom's unconscious body. She's still not moving or opening her eyes. Panic invades my nervous system once again. I jump out of the tub and run for the door.

Nora shouts at me. "Olive, where are you going?"

I fumble in my words but answer quickly, "I'm going to find the house phone and call 911!"

Nora looks down at Mom and then back at me. "NO! Olive! We can't call 911." She is shaking profusely, and I'm trying to comprehend what she just said.

Our mother is unconscious and may be dead or seriously hurt.

I go from all but whispering to yelling, "What do you mean, Nora? We need help, MOM NEEDS HELP!"

Nora rubs the hair back from Mom's forehead. She shakes her head and sternly shouts, "Do you understand what will happen if the cops come here? They will take us away, Olive. We have no family outside of Mom. We'll end up in foster care and probably be separated. I won't fucking allow it!"

My mouth falls open. How would I survive without Nora? The thought of being placed in a system where I have no control over who my family may be makes me tremble to my core.

They wouldn't hesitate to take us from Mom if they could be a fly on the wall and witness what we endure. I massage my temples and let out a long, shaky breath. "Is Mom going to wake up?" I ask nervously.

She grabs Mom's wrist and checks her pulse. Her shoulders instantly relax a little, and a look of relief hits her face. "It may take some time, but yes, she should."

Nora looks beyond exhausted, and I feel horrible that I had to wake her up to something so traumatic. I had so many questions for her, but I decided to wait another day. Tonight has been a real-life nightmare. I don't know if I'll ever be able to recover from this.

If Nora hadn't been here, Mom would most likely be dead. And the thought of that causes my insides to sting through every nerve ending in my body. I finally plop down on the bathroom floor and rest my head against the wall. We both just sit in silence and patiently wait.

Olive
CHAPTER 13

It felt like an eternity, but Friday is finally here! Holy shit, I never thought we'd make it. I was supposed to work until four today. But one employee from work took over my shift. He was looking for extra hours, so it worked out in both our favors.

I woke up feeling super positive at seven. We will ignore the minor panic attack I had while packing. When I get in my head, it can turn into a whirlwind of anxiety. I have so many emotions trying to make an appearance today. I don't know what to expect for this short beach trip. I was face-to-face with Theo for maybe five to ten minutes at Taylor's party, and we barely spoke because my dumbass ran off like a scared little puppy.

Now I'm spontaneously meeting him at the beach to stay a couple nights. Life can be a strange ride, let me tell you. Danielle attempted to pack the entire apartment in her suitcase. After tackling her on her bed, I talked some sense into her hard-headed ass.

We are opposites with packing. I plan my outfit for each day and bring one emergency outfit. That's not including the bare minimum of essentials needed. I fucking despise coming back from a vacation and having to spend an hour putting things away I didn't even touch.

We've been on the road for nearly an hour now and should arrive around lunchtime or shortly after. I ended up asking Theo if Chase would mind Lottie tagging along. It took me staying up late Wednesday night overthinking the situation before I finally mustered up the courage to text and ask him. I'm pretty sure I wasted the worry on nothing.

He seemed cool with it and let me know Leo would be there, too. Originally, I was going to ask Nora to keep her. But with everything that's been going on with her, I didn't want to bother with it. I'd much rather Lottie be with me, anyway. You never know, she just might make a new doggy friend.

I haven't even told Nora about Theo yet. Honestly, I wanted to wait to see how this trip would go. I'd hate to make a big deal out of it, and then this trip be a huge fail, and I never see or speak to him again.

She knows that Danielle and I are going to the beach and meeting a couple of people there, but she didn't ask too many questions. Theo told me I could invite her, but I knew what her answer would be. She would rather it be the two of us taking one of our day trips, jamming to her favorite musician, Stevie Nicks.

Danielle made sure she primped to perfection before we left home. Which she doesn't need, since she is naturally a looker. Her raven-tinted hair falls just a little over her shoulders. Her dark, thick lashes make her deep blue eyes pop, and sometimes I catch myself staring into them. Minus when she pisses me off, which is every other day.

But I love her for it; she is my best friend. She doesn't want to admit it, but I know she's looking forward to meeting Chase. I pray he has a decent personality. The last thing I want is her pouting about the guy with a dull sense of humor.

The GPS shows we're getting close to the beach house. I'm trying not to freak, but I can't deny that I'm nervous. I try distracting my mind by rolling my window down and gazing at the endless rows of palm trees. There is something about them that warms my veins. I take a deep breath, soaking the salty air into my lungs. The sky is an aqua blue; big cotton-like clouds dance across the open sky.

This is my happy place; a temporary healing session if you will. And I'm thankful to be here with Danielle, I adore our mini adventures together. But I can't help but wish Nora was here with us. I miss her.

My nerves are getting the best of me as we get closer to our destination. I'm feeling so many emotions right now. The eagerness to actually meet Theo hits me, but also an unsettling sensation crawls through me.

This trip can only go two ways. Either we hit it off and become friends and figure out whatever this is, or we realize this was all a joke and a waste of precious time, then we part ways and pretend we never met. Even considering that as a possibility almost makes me sad.

We pull up to a two-story coral-painted beach house; the shutters are a pretty shell-creamed color. There are Dwarf Date Palm trees on each side of the front stairs. Chinese Fan Palms sit left and right of the house wrapped with cream stone. I notice different shapes and sizes of seashells sitting along the stones in a variety of colors. Probably all plucked from the sand near the ocean.

This place is so cute and gives the best beachy vibes. I can already picture how the inside will look just by the well-nurtured yard and the appearance of the outside.

I shoot Theo a quick text to let him know we are here. We haven't even exited the car yet, and within seconds I spot two males walking up from the backyard. I instantly glue my eyes to Theo.

He is wearing a plain black t-shirt with grey and black swim trunks. How can such a simple outfit look so damn good on a human? He is even more stunning in the daylight. His luscious dirty blond hair glimmers as the sun's rays naturally highlight each strand. His flawless skin exudes a golden glow, blessed by the sun's affectionate embrace.

I'm going to assume that Chase is the one walking in sync beside Theo. They stride towards us, both tall and strong. He looks to be maybe an inch taller and slightly thinner than Theo. Danielle and I look at each other before getting out of the car.

A huge sneaky grin spreads across her face. "Girl, shit is about to get wild."

I smile back and playfully roll my eyes. I can't help but

feel excited about what's to come for the weekend. We are at the beach with two hot-ass guys. At this moment, I feel utterly content.

The boys help get our things out of the trunk, which is mainly Danielle's ridiculous amount of luggage. Even the boys seemed surprised, noticing I only had one suitcase, and the rest was Danielle's. I catch Chase looking her up and down while she gathers a couple of bags to carry in. I wonder if he finds her attractive. I would be shocked if not.

Danielle's had no trouble getting what she wants from boys. She's been a beauty since she was a child. I always envied her confidence in herself. It's something I have lacked growing up. Being bullied in grade school didn't help the shame I already felt towards my appearance.

Chase has chestnut-colored hair that lays long enough to almost cover his ears. His deep hazel eyes are easy to look at. He has a burly jawline, not quite as chiseled as Theo's, but just enough to have any girl crawling. And I think Danielle likes what she sees. I know her taste pretty well, and I can see the two of them having some fun together. Which knocks a weight off my shoulder. I can't enjoy myself if she's feeling some type of way, so things are looking good so far.

I smile at my thoughts and focus back on my task, not knowing that Theo is staring at me. *Here we go.* How long had he been hawking me while I was having a conversation in my head? I've tried to avoid lengthy eye contact with him.

I have not forgotten the trance he had me in at Taylor's party. I just got here; it's too early for this shit. I squint my eyes at him and give him a cute smile. "What are you staring at?"

He doesn't break eye contact while biting his bottom lip slightly, which sends a sting through my insides. "You, obviously. No hello?"

I roll my eyes dramatically. "Oh, forgive me, Theo. Hello. Is that better?"

He shrugs his shoulders "It'll do for now."

I glance over his shoulder and see that Chase and Danielle are having a conversation. That's a good sign, I think. Danielle is doing her little flirty giggles while twirling the ends of her hair, so I already know she's feeling what she sees.

I decide to walk over to introduce myself. I try to shake his hand, but he pulls me in for a quick side hug. He seems very welcoming and laid back. Not to mention, he has the cutest ear-to-ear smile; I know she's going to eat that up.

Lottie confidently trots over to Theo and vigorously licks his leg. "Ah, there's that little fluffy rodent you call a dog," he laughs.

"Watch it now!" I say through a snicker. She has a good sense of people, and I can tell she approves of him. I'd say we're off to a good start so far.

We finally make it into the house. And just as I expected, the inside welcomes you with vibrant beach decor. The walls hold different shades of white with small hanging trinkets. The furniture is a mix of navy and light blues. The decorative pillows on the cream-tinged couch are the same bright coral color that paints the outside of the house. Seahorse statues stand tall on either side of the front door.

The end table holds an oval-crafted lamp that has different varieties of seashells dangling from the lampshade. The style is simple and cozy. I can picture Chase and his family holding many special memories in this place. Something I've never gotten to experience.

Chase seems like a real gentleman. And I can see why he and Theo are good friends. They give us a quick tour of the house. Chase is staying in the downstairs primary bedroom, while Theo left us the bigger guest bedroom upstairs across from his room. There is a full bath downstairs, and the upstairs restroom is at the end of the hall, which has a walk-in shower.

This whole house is so clean and well cared for. Lottie jumps up on the bed, wagging her tail back and forth. I'm so happy she is here; she loves little adventures with me.

Danielle flops down on the bed, playfully kicking her feet. I settle down right beside her and give her squinted eyes. "What are you thinking about, bestie?"

She slowly looks at me with an enormous grin stretched across her face. "I'm thinking I can finally throw out my nun outfit. Things just might get hot and heavy tonight!"

Without thinking, I slap her arm. "Oh my gosh, you freaking perve!" I can't help but bust out laughing.

"At least one of us might get some action finally. I'm still rocking cobwebs down there." Danielle snorts loudly. "I saw how Theo was ogling you when unloading the car. That man is feeling you, Olive."

Before I go to speak, someone clears their throat near the door. I pop up from the bed, seeing Theo standing in the doorway. His face is slightly flushed, and he's rubbing the back of his neck.

Holy fuck he heard everything, or at least the parts he didn't need to hear.

"I wanted to see if you were hungry or wanted to meet us in the backyard. Chase has some hamburgers on the grill. I'd also like you to bring the rodent down to meet Leo."

I nervously clear my throat while rubbing my hands together. "Uh, yes, sure we'll be right down."

One side of his mouth quirks up. "No, please take all the time you need. I didn't mean to interrupt your conversation. It sounded pretty action-packed."

Before I can respond, he gives me a quick wink, then turns on his heel to go downstairs. I immediately look at Danielle, and we both bust out laughing.

We walk out the back door into a small, enclosed deck with wicker patio furniture. On the deck's right side, there is a hot tub that can accommodate up to four people. The backyard is fairly small and fenced-in, which is relieving since I have Lottie with me.

In the corner of the lot sits a small fire pit with a few lawn chairs. My eyes light up when I see the two big palm trees with a hammock resting between them. I will spend some time in that hammock while here.

As soon as Leo spots Lottie and me, he trots over to us. I decided before coming downstairs to carry her just in case. Their size difference is by a lot. Once Lottie notices Leo, she barks a few times, and he cocks his head from left to right like he's trying to figure her out.

Theo reassures me that Leo is just a big harmless teddy bear. I believe him, as I'm pretty good at reading animals' demeanor. I gently place Lottie down on the ground. They immediately start circling each other, sniffing their rear ends. A typical meet and greet for dogs, if you will.

Within a couple of minutes, they are chasing each other around the fenced yard. Lottie hasn't been around another dog in a while, so it makes me happy to see her run around and play with one of her kind. The size difference is sort of funny. I've never pictured a Pomeranian and a Lab playing together.

Chase made some pretty good cheeseburgers. Theo was a little concerned that I asked for mayo. I don't see any other way to eat a cheeseburger, and everyone else seems to play it safe with ketchup and mustard. *Fucking gross.*

After we finish eating and chatting with the boys for a bit, Danielle and I head upstairs to get our bathing suits on. The boys asked if we wanted to head out to the beach. I may or may not have yelled *yes* out of sheer excitement. I am eager to get my feet in the sand. I haven't been here since the fall of last year with Nora.

This is my first official beach trip of the year. Never would I have thought I'd be here with a man I hardly know. This is so unlike me. I just hope I haven't made a mistake coming here.

I ended up picking my new cheetah print two-piece; it was on sale during the fall months. I've only gotten to wear it once. It's a little revealing, but not too extreme. Danielle is wearing a hot pink one-piece that shows her every curve. It compliments her body type very well. I've never been able to wear them because of my long torso. My ass either eats the back end, or it aggressively rides up my lady parts.

It took me a long time to appreciate my body, and the curves finally given to me. I think with being a female we're hard on ourselves in different areas. Social media constantly reminds us we have imperfections and will never be happy with our natural bodies. It's a sick generation we've grown up in. Females compete with their image, instead of lifting each other up.

I've gotten a lot better at loving myself in certain ways. It took many years to get past the bullying and body shaming. Broken things can't be repaired in a day. And truthfully, I don't think they can ever be fully whole again.

Coming down the stairs, we catch the boys waiting on the living room couch. Sitting in the kitchen area is an oversized cooler for the beach I'm assuming. Probably packed with beer and snacks. We brought two cases of White Claws, but they insisted we save them. Since we're guests, they're supposed to host for us.

Before reaching the last stair, I catch Theo scanning me from head to toe. I keep my eyes on the floor and try not to hold eye contact for too long. This man can take one look at me and my body temperature immediately skyrockets. *This can't be normal. Noah never made me feel this way.*

Chase lets a drawn-out whistle leave his mouth. "Damn, I think hot pink is my new favorite color." Danielle and I look at each other, and I give her a dramatic wink.

She's going to eat the fuck out of his compliments all weekend. She tells him thank you and gives him a small playful curtsy. These two are going to be trouble, I can already sense it. Theo heavily shakes his head at Chase's attempt to flirt with Danielle.

I can't help but let out a small giggle at his reaction. So far, I feel pretty damn comfortable with the four of us spending time together.

I give Lottie and Leo generous amounts of head rubs and kisses before we walk out the door. "You'd assume they've known each other for years." It gives me another reason to continue down the road of exploring Theo. Maybe now I'm fishing for any reason to be around him more. I can't help that I'm drawn to him, and I refuse to back away without knowing what this is between us.

I did not realize we were that close to the ocean. Chase says we're only two streets back. We could have walked and made it there within ten to fifteen minutes. But with the huge cooler, and Danielle's human-sized beach bag, the boys decided we should take his grandparents' golf cart.

Danielle and I hop on the back together. I feel like a kid right now, excited to get on the beach to build sandcastles and run after seagulls. As broken on the inside as I am, being here gives me a sense of peace.

Riding along the streets, I gape at all the colorful beach houses. The streets are adorned with vibrant shades of blue, pink, and green. People here really take care of their properties. I love how every yard has its own unique characteristics. But each represents the qualities of this place. The gentle breeze tousles my loose ponytail, lightly whipping small strands around my face. Passing cars with their windows down, fill the air with upbeat music.

In this moment, happiness courses through me, but in the back of my mind, I know these feelings will be overshadowed once this temporary paradise ends.

We arrive at the beach in minutes. Chase parks in public access where other golf carts and cars line up. I can already hear the waves crashing; it sends a thrill deep inside my bones. After gathering our items, we walk along the pier; seagulls fly ahead in sync. It's such a beautiful day, and there is hardly anyone out here, which is nice.

It takes no time to find a spot for us to set up. I brought my favorite beach blanket, which is big enough for at least six people to sit on. I like to keep it in the trunk of my car just in case I want to run away to the beach.

I dig my toes into the wet, cool sand, tiny broken seashells gently poking at my heels. The ocean is looking noticeably blue today; giant waves continuously dance along the shoreline. I watch Chase and Danielle walk side by side looking for shells. They seem to hit it off so far, and I couldn't be any happier for her. Even if this is nothing more than a brief affair, I believe they complement each other well.

I watch Theo as he walks back from testing the ocean's temperature. Even this man's walk is gorgeous. What the fuck is wrong with me? I try not to peer at him for too long. I can't have him thinking I'm some desperate, broken girl needing attention from someone I barely know. As I turn to look away, he removes his shirt while approaching me.

I watch as his impressive muscles flex with every slick movement. His upper body is just as I pictured it in my dream. This man was molded close to perfection. Even though he's wearing sunglasses, I know he is watching me stalk him. I see a smirk form on his charming mouth. He knows exactly what he's doing, and he's enjoying every second.

He sits down right beside me, his broad shoulder grazing my arm. A tingle runs straight through me, similar to what I felt after my explicit dream. Why does he make me feel nervous but calm and comfortable all at the same time? I can sense him looking at me from my peripheral.

"What are you thinking about, beautiful?" he asks with ease. I can't help but look over at him and take in the stunning scenery of Theo Rivers.

Seeing him here at my favorite place, looking like a whole damn snack. I put my arm down between us, close enough to where our arms are brushing against one another. Somehow, my body lets me know in this moment that I need his touch. The hairs on my arm instantly rise with every brush of our skin.

Theo takes his sunglasses off and holds my stare. I let out a slow breath before responding, "Nothing much."

He squints at me like he's trying to figure me out on a deeper level. "That's all you've got? I can tell that you're in your head, so it's hard for me to believe that. I want more." He gives me a light arm bump, which gets me a little off balance.

I give a dramatic sigh. "Okay, Theo, I want to know who you are. I hardly know you, yet here I am sitting on the beach beside a stranger wondering what the fuck I'm doing here."

"There's my spicy Olive," he lightly chuckles. "You are like an onion with endless layers, and I'm intent on peeling you until I reach the center."

I make sure he sees me roll my eyes at his reply. "You'd tire of me before even starting," I say in annoyance.

He gently grabs my chin and tilts my face in his direction. His ocean eyes instantly burn through me. "You may not have confidence in others, and I can't change that. But when I say something, I fucking mean it."

The air leaves my chest for a moment. This is one thing

that sparks my curiosity about him. In the most peculiar way, I genuinely believe him and his words and I'm desperate to let him in.

Theo softly runs his thumb along the side of my jawline. His strong, calloused hand could easily wrap around my petite face. I can't help but close my eyes and allow us this moment. Though it may seem like a small gesture, I've never experienced such an affectionate touch by a man.

I slowly open my eyes, not wanting this physical interaction to end. Theo's expression almost holds empathy behind it. But within seconds, his eyes grow cold. "I don't know who hurt you, but they better hope our paths never cross." His words knock the breath out of me, all I can do is give him a slow nod. I'm not ready to dive into the debacle called my life just yet.

The day has been pretty great, which is a lot coming from me. Theo and I end up joining Danielle and Chase in the ocean. The water is freezing at first, which has me slowly inching in. Theo makes sure I don't hesitate any longer by picking me up and tossing me into a wave. *The audacity*. I so badly want to be mad at his actions, but seeing Danielle's contagious laughter and the four of us together, I can't help but join in.

It feels incredibly satisfying to genuinely laugh for once. It's been a long time since I've felt this giddy on the inside. Today has been one of the best days I've had in a long time.

Olive

CHAPTER 14

There's nothing more stimulating than shooting out of a bed that's not yours because of a shitty night terror. The confusion hit me first, along with a pounding heart. I don't know how the heck I didn't wake Danielle up.

Oh, wait a minute, she's not even in the bed. She must have snuck out last night and joined Chase downstairs. I think it's funny how she sees me as a mother figure in ways. There's so much irony behind that, considering my personal experiences in life. They must have hit it off very well yesterday. I won't deny that I thoroughly enjoyed our entire day with the boys.

I try my hardest to go back to sleep. But I'm tossing from side to side, and my mind won't rest after that fricking dream.

Fuck it, I'm going downstairs. I give Lottie a couple of head rubs and tell her to stay on the bed like she understands me.

Honestly, I think she really does. I shut the door just in case she wasn't listening.

Stopping outside the bedroom door, I notice Theo's door open. The moon is shining onto the bed where his peaceful sleeping body lays. Theo is lying on his stomach with his arms wrapped around a pillow. He's shirtless with nothing but his boxers on.

With the moon's help, I can see every curve and cut from his back muscles. Thank you for the steamy view, moon.

I wonder how it would feel to lie next to him. It's been so long since I've had a man's touch. If I'm being honest, Noah was nothing close to a man. He was an immature boy that didn't give two shits about my emotions. Theo is so much more. He carries himself well, and I see a gentleman when I look at him.

So badly I want to crawl into his bed and feel his warmth against my bare skin. How thrilling it would be to trace every curve and muscle that runs along his sculptured back. Or to lay my head against his chest and feel his tender heart beating with life. Sometimes I wonder how mine is still beating with all the battle wounds it bears.

Just as I realize that I've been staring at Theo in the doorway for too long, in the dark, in nothing but an oversized t-shirt and panties, he shifts in the bed. I panic and try to B line it down the hall, but before I make it to the stairs, I hear Theo call my name.

His voice is so deep and filled with sleep. I rest my head on the wall beside the stairs for a moment. *What a fucking creep you are, Olive.*

I slowly walk back to his room, preparing to explain why I was hawking him in the dark like a weirdo. Just as I turn to walk into the room, I slam straight into a shirtless Theo. Not only do our bodies collide, but so do our heads. *Great work, Olive.*

I definitely won't be going back to sleep for a while now. I don't even know what time it is, but so much has happened and all I can do right now is say sorry repeatedly.

Theo seems to get a kick out of this. How the hell does someone laugh after waking up to a strange figure standing in a dark hallway? And then knocking noggins with that same creep immediately after. *The creep being me, of course.*

Theo grabs my face and rubs close to where our heads had collided. "Olive, what the hell are you doing?" he says with amusement behind his eyes. His hands are so big, I can feel small calluses on his palms, which show how well he works with his hands.

Before I can answer, he realizes he's still holding my face and pulls away quickly.

Without thinking, I reach up and place my hands where his once were. "I uh, had a bad dream," I say barely above a whisper.

The moon is the only form of light in this room, but I can easily make out his facial expressions. His appearance softens as he examines my body language. "So, what brought you to my doorway?"

Fuck. I was hoping he'd forgotten that part, after our head-butt connection. There's no real answer to that question, so I just run with it. "Just couldn't go back to sleep. I was heading downstairs, and you just, I don't know, looked so relaxed. I'm sorry for startling you." I give him a weak smile.

He gives a sleepy grin in return. "You're forgiven, Olive. But you interrupted a pretty good dream."

I squint my eyes at him. "Oh, was it about me?" I say jokingly.

For a moment he does nothing but slowly look me up and down. His eyes seem to grow hungry. "Mmm, maybe it was. Nice sleepwear, by the way."

I quickly grab the bottom of my shirt, trying to pull it down further; it reaches close to my mid-thigh. But if I were to bend over, he'd see that I have nothing more than a thin piece of cloth covering down there.

Theo catches me pulling at my shirt anxiously. He inches towards me and softly wraps his massive hands around my shoulders. "Olive, I'm just messing with you. I think you look rather cute in nothing but a t-shirt." I watch him trail his toxic eyes down below my waist.

I slap his hands away in a playful but serious manner and scoff. "How dare you, I am wearing something under my shirt, just so you know." Before thinking, I yank my shirt up exposing my thin black lace panties. So dumbfounded by my actions, I turn on my heel to run out the door.

But before I can escape my embarrassment, Theo grabs my arm and twirls me around. I look up and see him gaping down at me. Our mouths are only a couple of inches apart. His breathing has changed course.

We both stand quietly, just two hearts beating at a rapid pace. I look between his eyes and his mouth. His full lips are slightly parted. The sight of it causes me to bite my bottom lip. His grip tightens on my arm slightly.

He lets out a long exhale. "You can't do things like that in front of me and expect me to be good, Olive." His words cause me to sway back. He doesn't let go of my arm, which prevents me from stumbling backyards. He speaks again before I can process what he just growled at me. "Come sit with me."

He finally releases my arm, and the disconnection from his touch makes my chest ache. Theo gives me a reassuring look before heading for the bed.

A tiny piece of me whispers turn around and go back to my room, but a big part of me screams, "Girl get in that damn bed with him!" Which takes little to no convincing.

I awkwardly climb on the bed beside him, trying to hold my shirt down so that I don't foolishly show my panties again. I sit close but ensure there's distance between us. I'm still baffled at everything that has occurred in the last hour. How the hell did I end up in this bed beside him?

We sit in silence for a while, gazing out the window at the moon. Theo asks questions about my family, hobbies I like, and so on. I ask the same of him. I briefly mention Mom and her battles. I even talk about my childhood and some things Nora and I endured. I share a lot about Nora and how much she means to me and give small details about Jake and how it's affected her.

It's refreshing to get things off my chest, even if they are only the breadcrumbs of my life. Theo sits quietly, soaking in every word. I feel safe and comfortable having this deep conversation with him.

There is a sliver of me that wants to tell him about Noah.

He needs to know where my hesitation emerges from, but every time I go to speak on it, the words won't form. Maybe I'm worried about how he'll react to it. What if he looks at me differently? I already feel shame towards myself. I'm unsure if I can accept him potentially judging me for my past decisions that I'm still trying to move on from.

Fuck Noah, but the wounds he created will always hover. I understand that if Theo and I continue this, I must let him know. For now, it'll have to wait. The right time will come.

We talk about his family a lot. His parents were high school sweethearts and have been together since. He has one adopted sister, and her name is Emma. She just turned nine recently. She's his cousin on his dad's side. Unfortunately, her biological mom and dad are in active addiction, in and out of jail and rehab. They didn't hesitate to sign their rights over to Theo's parents when she was only four.

I feel so much for that little girl; her experiences remind me a lot of myself and my past battles. Thank goodness his parents saved her. Theo seems so proud when he talks about her; it warms my heart to see the love he has for that girl. Maybe I'll get the chance to meet her one day.

Aside from Danielle, I've never had someone want to hear about me or my life. And I've never been much for opening up to people, but Theo makes it easy to let go. He's soaked in every word, and I think he'd listen to me talk for hours longer if he could have it his way. Never in a million years would I have guessed I'd be here in this moment with this man.

Let's not forget his good looks and catching features. He has been shirtless the entire time, and I've caught myself staring at his toned chest different times. Theo is all man. Point. Blank. Fucking period.

Thump, thump, thump. I squint my eyes open; it's so bright in this room. I wonder what time it is. Or when I went to sleep finally? *Thump, thump, thump.* What the hell is that loud pounding in my ear?

I take a moment to process the sound and orient myself. Whoa, somehow, I fell asleep on Theo's chest. My left arm is resting across his stomach. I turn my head and look up; he is still slightly sitting up on his pillow. His arm is gripping around my bare waist. Mind you, my shirt is bunched up to just right under my breast. Okay, now I'm panicking.

How in the hell did I get myself in this position? Last night, we sat together in this bed and delved into an in-depth discussion about many aspects of our lives. We shared stories, exchanged thoughts, and explored various perspectives. Neither of us asked or checked what time it was; time meant nothing. It was the two of us exploring each other's thoughts. Most guys would rather jump to business and get their dick wet. But not for one second did I think that was Theo's intention.

His body is so warm against mine. His heart beats strong and steady. It's what I imagine a pure unbroken heart sounds like. I could stay in this position forever. This intimate feeling is so new to me that I would be okay with it sticking around for a while. His muscular arm rests along my side, while his hand secures my waist tightly.

Shit, this feels too intimate. This is moving faster than it needs to. This man doesn't understand what he's potentially getting himself into. My life is toxic and depressing, and anyone who tries nudging their way in ends up poisoned by it.

I gently grab his forearm, and his grip on my waist loosens. I slowly slide his arm from my side, but he doesn't budge. *Thank goodness.* I feel like a ninja on a mission to escape my enemy's territory. I finally make it off the bed and tiptoe towards the door. I'm so glad he didn't just witness my pathetic attempt.

Just as my hand grabs the door frame, I hear Theo shift in the bed. I hesitantly look over my shoulder. What are the odds that he's now sitting on the edge of the bed. His disheveled hair is so adorable, indicating that he had a good night's rest.

I turn fully around and rub my hands together nervously. He grips the mattress on either side of him. I watch his shoulders and chest flex, showing off how fit he is. I can still feel my head laying against his impressive pecks.

Theo gives me a sly look. "Those were great bailing skills, Olive," he says teasingly.

Pinching the bridge of my nose, I whisper in response, "Sorry, I needed to use the restroom and didn't want to wake you. You seemed so comfortable."

He gives me a nod and runs his hand through his blond locks. " I was, thanks to you."

My cheeks become warm and tinted with pink. Surely, he doesn't notice the way his words impact my body. As if reading each other's minds, we say nothing more. Things are about to get insanely interesting.

Olive
CHAPTER 15

Danielle dives onto the bed directly beside me. She matches my posture and lies on her stomach propped on her elbows. I give her my most annoyed expression. I know exactly what she's doing and what she's about to ask me.

Danielle kicks her feet in the air like an excited schoolgirl ready for some tea to be spilled. *Here we go, in three.. two..* "So, is it big?" she exclaims.

I want to slap the shit out of her right now. "Oh my gosh, Danielle, shut the fuck up!" I say behind my teeth.

She has the nerve to roll her eyes, "What? I genuinely want to know. Does it scream eggplant emoji?"

My mouth gapes open in disbelief, but would I expect anything less out of my best friend? Instead of responding, I grab the pillow I've been using and chunk it at her head. One thing about me is that I have an exceptional aim. The pillow connects beautifully with her face and moves in slow motion for a moment. The impact causes Danielle's sunglasses to fly off her head.

If she had a wig on, it would have gone with the glasses. She slowly turns and looks at me with her mouth wide open. I try to hurry and squeeze my lips together trying not to laugh, but it's too late, I bust out in laughter. *Serves her right.*

"You're lucky you're my best friend, you bitch," Danielle belts out while throwing the pillow back at me. "You owe me an answer."

I let out a small sigh and lightly massage my temples. "Danielle, I don't know what his dick looks like because I did not see it."

She gives a dramatic gasp. "You looked extremely comfortable when I passed by his room this morning though."

Now my resting bitch face is in full effect with this conversation. "Yes, Danielle, people are allowed to fall asleep together without the fucking part. Also, I recall waking up in the middle of the night and you being gone. Would you care to elaborate on that?" I ask with a teasing smile.

Danielle twirls a strand of hair around her finger, which tells me something went down. "If you must know, we didn't fuck, but there was definitely some heavy foreplay." She looks at me and almost winces like she's expecting me to scold her. Now I feel like the giddy schoolgirl who found out her best friend had her first kiss.

A giant smile dances across my face. "Oh my gosh, girl!" I shout a little louder than I want. I instantly lower my voice "How good was it?"

Danielle covers her face with her hands and then peeks at me through her fingers. "Um, so good that it may have gone on for hours."

My eyebrows shoot up in a surprised manner "I freaking knew it!"

Danielle rolls her eyes at me playfully. She then gives me a sly grin. "This scenario reminds me of another time, don't you think, bestie?"

I lightly swat at her arm. "Don't you even dare bring that up!"

We both fall back on the bed laughing like teenagers. Honestly, I wouldn't want to experience this time here with anyone but Danielle. This will be another memory for the books.

I wonder if the boys are downstairs or out back having a similar discussion? Something tells me they're not like most guys. Well, I'm unsure about Chase, but I don't see Theo being one to tell his or others' business. It makes me appreciate him more. Even if last night was nothing, and we don't see each other again after this trip.

It will always mean something to me, and I'll never forget how comfortable we were, just to sit and talk. Most skip the talking part and jump straight into intercourse. This seems like so much more than a simple fling. I often catch myself reaching for more of him.

The four of us ride the golf cart to a little breakfast bar a few blocks over from the beach house. This place is simple but charming. It's getting close to lunchtime, but breakfast food sounds amazing.

It doesn't take me long to choose over-medium eggs, bacon, and crispy hash browns. There is a small stone patio area on the back side of the joint. It has an enclosed three-foot-tall rock wall built around it, overlooking the ocean. The view is breathtaking. Danielle and I pick a table closest to the ocean view, which is exactly what I wanted.

The food and the view are amazing. I easily get lost in watching the waves, growing and crashing in unison. Almost forgetting that I am accompanied by three friends. I can hear their conversations beginning to fade out, and for a moment everything around me becomes mute.

It's just me and the ocean's natural melody. It dances around me, lifting the weight of my lingering traumas. If only this feeling could be permanent, maybe then I could be whole again.

I shake my head breaking from my mini daydream episode. Danielle and Chase are bickering over how bacon should be cooked. One thinks extra crispy where you almost break a tooth, the other thinks it should be flimsy and chewy. Watching them go back and forth about something so silly, causes a smile to appear on my face.

I look over at Theo wondering what his thoughts are on this pointless banter, but he's not listening to them. He's quietly studying my face. When our eyes find each other, he doesn't look away, and neither do I.

Theo's stare can be very intimidating sometimes, but his eyes are giving a soft, intimate feel right now. Looking into his blue-hued eyes almost feels like I never stopped watching the ocean from this very patio. His waves are crashing all around me, trapping me into something fascinating.

No one has ever looked at me the way he does. Butterflies swarm in circles in my lower abdomen, causing me to search for salty air. In this effortless exchange, I truly see Theo for the beautiful man he is.

After our late breakfast, we take a nice stroll checking out the surrounding beach shops. I've always loved all the little trinkets and beach-inspired gifts. I could spend hours walking through looking at them.

Picking through different earrings, rings, and necklaces, I find the perfect gift for Nora Ray. It's a dainty sterling silver wristlet with a moon pendant on it, showing the moon reflecting on the ocean. I got us matching ones since we both love the beach and the moon. I hope she likes them just as much as I do.

We make it back to the beach house around two. Leo and Lottie greet us at the door with tail wags and leg kisses. The two of them have become inseparable pals in such a short time. Never would I have thought Lottie would run around with a dog the size of a small bear, but here we are and I'm not mad at it.

Chase and Theo had told us this morning that there'd be a band playing at the pier this evening. The band plays one Saturday out of each month during the spring and summer seasons. We plan to hang out here and leave around six to go grab a bite to eat, then check the band out.

Theo tells me there is a little seafood joint and tiki bar all on the pier where the band will be playing. I'm looking forward to listening to some music by the ocean, something I've never done before besides bringing a boombox on me and Nora's day trips. I picture there being a light breeze, and the waves moving to the band's instruments. It sounds so peaceful.

While we're just hanging around the house, I choose to take Lottie for a walk on the beach. She hasn't gotten to since getting here yesterday afternoon. Theo wants to tag along with me so Leo and Lottie can play on the beach. We ask Chase and Danielle to join us, but they are both quick to say how they'd like to just chill at the house and take it easy. Theo and I both look at each other, trying to hold back smiles.

When Chase and Theo aren't looking, I give Danielle a quick wink and motion my index going in and out of a hole that I created with my other hand. Danielle's mouth all but falls to the floor. She flashes me a quick "up yours" hand motion. *I bet you it's going to get nasty in this beach house.*

Another beautiful day. The waves are violent, crashing with force against the shore. We walk just close enough to where the water runs over our feet. The sand is cool and slick against my toes. Currently, I am wearing my bathing suit underneath a white knitted pullover that comes down just underneath my ass. The breeze caresses my skin keeping me cool from the sun's beaming rays.

There is something about the sun hitting my olive-kissed skin. Since being here my body has become a rich golden color. There's nothing like getting a tan at your favorite spot.

After walking at least half a mile, we pick an area to sit down and let the dogs run and play. They're having the time of their puppy lives. Leo chases Lottie in circles. I love when she tucks her tail and playfully runs from him. I am truly embracing every little moment here. My life has been robbed of many things, so when a speck of happiness creeps into my day, I soak in every ounce.

I contently stare off at the horizon, and I imagine where it starts and where it ends. The ocean is a beautiful mystery filled with secrets. I can't help but close my eyes and listen closely, hoping it'll share one with me.

When I open my eyes, I tilt my head to look at Theo. There he is watching me again. He does this frequently. If I'm not crazy, I'd say he almost has a look of admiration on his face. Which is fucking weird because what is there to admire about me? I catch myself before asking him why and instead watch the pups frolic alongside the shore.

Theo takes a deep breath beside me and rasps out, "I truly hope I get to see you again. This trip has honestly been exhilarating with you so far. And I would like to continue exploring whatever this is with us," he utters with sheer confidence.

His effective words catch me off guard, and my mouth speaks before processing them. "My life is far from roses and cheerful smiles, Theo, and from our recent conversations, yours seems to be the polar opposite. And as much as I've appreciated our time here together, I'd hate to be a nuisance in your close-to-perfect life."

Abort. Destructive Olive is here. Fuck, why do I do this? I look away and decide to stay silent after my mini outburst.

I can sense him studying me for what feels like an eternity, I regretfully turn to look back at him, and his expression hardens.

He then speaks roughly. "No one's life is perfect, I can promise you that. It's what makes our time here so individually unique." *If he only knew how absurdly unique mine was.*

Just as I drift off into my overworking mind, Theo puts his hand on my thigh and stills me with his piercing glare.

"Our lives may not align perfectly together, but damn it, Olive, I know our souls were destined to dance." My breath hitches in my achy throat—such *a poetic bastard.*

Every time this man speaks, it has this magnetic effect on me. In this moment I can feel our souls desperately reaching toward each other like they are preparing to sing a beautiful song in harmony. I slowly pull from his gaze and rub my hands together repetitively. *A nervous tick I've had since I was a small child.*

I pull back into his stare and say with all but a whisper, "And what makes you so sure of that?"

Theo's delicious lips purse together, and I hear a modest sigh escape them. "Because the second our eyes found each other at that party, I felt it. And I know you did too." The corner of his mouth quirks up. "You may not know this, but your eyes tell everything, Olive. It's one of the many things I love about you."

I let out a small gasp. Did he just use the word *love?* And damn do I admire the sound of my name rolling off his slick tongue. Mm, I can only imagine the performance that tongue could give.

"Olive, you're doing that spacing out thing again," he says with a faint chuckle.

I quickly snap out of it. "Ugh, sorry," I say with reddened

cheeks. All I can do in this heated moment is give him a genuine smile. He returns the small gesture with the cutest crooked grin. I catch myself wanting to touch his beautiful face, but I quickly refrain.

I almost feel my guarded walls give out. He's a determined cannon ready to aim and fire. Theodore Ace Rivers is going to be the death of me, I just know it.

Theo and I barely talk on the walk back to the house. Everything is fine, but I think I just needed a second to process the interaction on the beach. I am not used to someone being so straightforward about what they want. And most importantly what they want, being me. This is different. Most douchebags just want to get in your pants.

Theo has clarified that he is feeling something more. He hasn't disrespected me or attempted anything other than to know more about me. It makes me feel giddy and terrified at the same time.

Chase and Danielle are in the kitchen when we walk in. Her black hair is sticking up in different places, showing signs of possible foreplay. What gives it away is the red mark on Chase's neck. I slant my eyes at Danielle, who then snatches her head towards Chase.

I curiously need to know, so I ask, "Um, is that a hickey on your neck Chase?"

Without thinking, he reaches up and rubs his neck like he's able to feel it with his fingers. He opens his mouth but pauses and cuts his eyes to Danielle as if trying to find the answer to my question.

Danielle's snaps back at me. "Maybe it is!"

I can't help but snicker under my breath. "Cool, I didn't

know those were still a thing. Nice work, Danielle." She scoffs at me immediately in response.

I give both the boys a quick wink and head for the stairs.

Once I am about halfway up, I yell out, "Looks like you got to straddle someone after all, Danielle!"

She lets out a loud huff and runs towards the stairs shouting, "Bitch!" I can't help but laugh like a little kid. I haul ass towards our guest room with Danielle on my heels.

Thank goodness for long legs. I make it to the room before she catches me. I faintly hear the boys laughing downstairs, which tells me they're getting a kick out of our banter. This is the first time they've really seen our playful side.

I lightly pat my cheekbones with a pink blush while staring at my reflection in the bathroom mirror. I went with a more natural look for this evening. I've never cared to cake makeup on my face. For one, it is too much work. Second, I hate the taking it off part. And to be honest, if I'm only appealing with my face covered in toxic products, I'd much rather be invisible and unnoticed.

My ashy brown hair falls below my breasts, holding crinkled beach curls. I love the way the salty air works its magic on each strand. I see so much of my mother when my hair is like this. The mother she once was long ago.

After trying on a few outfits I bought before this trip, I go with a sage green flowy summer dress. The straps are around an inch thick, and the front cuts down into a V. It reveals a small amount of cleavage, but just enough to keep it classy. The length reaches right above my ankles with a high front leg slit. I adore all things sage. Different shades of green make me feel at home. How ironic considering my name. I don't know how my mom came up with it, but I've always admired the uniqueness of my first and middle name. See, there are some things I like about myself.

Danielle went all out for tonight, as she should. She did loose curls on her hair, bringing it right above her shoulders. She's wearing a pink floral crop top with high-waisted denim shorts. Her makeup is flawless as always. My best friend is stunning from head to toe. Chase is most definitely going to choke when he sees her.

We find the boys sitting by the firepit waiting for us. Once we exit off the back deck, they both become mute and turn to look at us. I'm pretty sure Chase has eaten at least three bugs with how wide open he's holding his mouth. I hear Danielle snicker beside me. Glancing at Theo, I notice him running his tongue along his bottom lip, while making it known that he's eye fucking me.

It shoots jolts of pleasure through my entire body. Dirty thoughts creep into my mind. I quickly shove them away and lock them out. *Get ahold of yourself, Olive.*

"Wow, you ladies look fucking hot!" Chase croons at us both.

"The two of you look pretty dapper yourselves," I say behind a dramatic wink.

Chase is wearing a mint green button-up with khaki shorts. Theo, on the other hand, is in his normal attire. A plain navy blue t-shirt with cream-tinted shorts. I love that he doesn't even try to dress to impress. He could make any outfit look good. Honestly, all four of us are looking rather lovely this evening.

We park at a different entrance this time, where cars and

golf carts line each side of the parking lot. I instantly get a whiff of fresh seafood and a hint of hushpuppies.

My stomach growls at the smell of it. I can't wait to get my hands on something tasty. The restaurant is swarming with people. The server guides us to the back side of the restaurant to an outside seating area, which is connected to the entrance to the pier. We can hear the band perfectly from here. Right now, they're playing a mixture of classic blues and rock music.

Either I was close to malnourishment, or the food was that damn good. I cleared my entire plate within minutes. I haven't had flounder that good in a really long time. Once everyone finished their plates, Theo insisted on paying for our food. I fought him on it and finally gave up—stubborn *ass*.

The pier is much longer than I expected it to be. The band has set up under an awning near the middle. Chairs wrap around in rows for people to sit and enjoy the music. There's even a cleared-out area where some are dancing together and swaying to the music. A small tiki bar is situated near the band, making me crave a refreshing lime margarita. And of course, I'm the youngest one in the group and will have to depend on one of them to get me an alcoholic beverage.

Just when I'm planning to ask Danielle, Theo walks up behind me and places his hand on my lower back, which catches me off guard. He leans in close to my ear. I can feel his warm, minty breath hit my neck. "What would you like to drink, my little underage criminal?" he softly whispers in my ear. I barely hear him because of the band's loud instruments.

I turn my head slightly to look back at him. I reach my arm back, running my hand along his belt loop while making eye contact. I take two fingers and slide them into his pocket just enough to place a twenty-dollar bill in them. I give him a testy grin and lean back to where I am gently pressed against his hard body.

I tilt my head up. My lips are so close to his ear that I picture gently biting his earlobe. Focusing back on his question, I let him know what beverage I'd like to have.

I don't know what Theo and I are doing to each other, but it feels exhilarating with a taste of danger. And right now, I am enjoying the body high it's generously feeding me. Something has significantly shifted between us, ever since our talk on the beach earlier today. I'm trying hard to be good. It's difficult for me to open up when I've been deeply betrayed by those I once trusted.

I'm trying to give him the benefit of the doubt. There have been no red flags thus far. If anyone has given red flags, it's me. Baby steps are in the works, so that's progress, right?

Whoever is working the tiki bar must want me drunk because I can taste the generous amounts of tequila with each sip. I can already feel the alcohol soaking into my bloodstream, sending warmth through every vein. One thing is that I'm a lightweight, and I drink very little. I got all that out of my system during my teenage years. It's a very occasional thing for me now. This one drink will probably be enough to have me slurring my words slightly, I'm going to do my best to pace myself.

But damn, this margarita is good, and now I'm vibing with the music that my body sways along with each note.

The worries that normally pick and pry are subsiding with every gulp.

I don't remember the last time I felt this *free*. I glance over at the three people I've been spending the last couple of days with. They're all smiling, talking amongst each other while watching the small band perform. Danielle is freaking glowing with contentment. I love seeing how giddy she is around Chase. Something tells me their story has just begun.

Olive

CHAPTER 16

The crowd has tripled since being on the pier. There are people all over dancing and cutting up with friends and I presume loved ones. The night is still young, and I am slightly buzzed from my stout drink. Danielle tried to get me another one, but I'm quite pleased with where I'm at, and I don't want to push my limits. I get Theo's attention and point towards the end of the pier. I need to break away from all these people for a moment.

As I approach the end of the pier, I inhale slowly and exhale through my mouth. Calming the tingly sensation of nerves that try to surface. This view is remarkably beautiful.

The moon is full and reflecting on the ocean, shining a path to the pier. I grasp the pendant wristlet I got for Nora and me. The waves have calmed since earlier today when we brought the pups out for their walk. I imagine myself floating far from land, the moonlight shining on my body as I drift further away from the shore. Most would find that daunting but for me, it sounds so peaceful.

Theo appears beside me gripping the wooden railing along the pier. I watch him for a moment as he stares out at the horizon. His pronounced side profile could put anyone to shame. I truly appreciate the view of Theo Rivers. Watching how the ocean breeze fondles his golden locks makes me want to reach up and slowly run my fingers through it. My dream pops back up into my head, and it makes me wonder if that's how his hair really feels.

"Come on, Let's go," Theo demands politely.

I shoot him a confused look. "Where are we going?"

He grabs my hand and leads me back towards the direction of the band, looking back at me with excitement in his eyes. "Away from all these people."

As we pass by the seating area near the band, I spot Chase and Danielle dancing around each other. They are goofing off and laughing hysterically. Danielle looks my way and blows me a kiss. Theo must have told them what we were doing.

We soon reach the pier's entrance by the seafood joint where we ate dinner. We walk down alongside the pier. Once my feet hit the sand, I quickly remove my sandals and dig my toes in. There's no one near us on the beach; I'm pretty sure most are on the pier listening to the band. Theo leads me down underneath the pier area.

I can hear the music perfectly above us, minus the crowds of people. Don't get me wrong, I enjoy the atmosphere of people dancing and laughing, but sometimes my anxiety gets the best of me, and I need to break away and breathe.

The moon's reflection is beaming under the pier, showcasing a path. Without hesitating, I throw my sandals and bag down, grab my dress, and sprint to the water's edge like I'm a kid again seeing the ocean for the first time. The salty water feels cool against my feet, I take a few deep breaths and take in my surroundings.

Tonight has been everything I've needed for such a long time. It's been going so well that I'm waiting for a huge boulder to fall out of the sky and crush me along with my happy moments because this weekend has been too good to be true.

The wind blows in my direction, and the smell of oak hits my nasal passages. I instantly know that Theo is right behind me. A smile curls along my mouth.

Twirling around like a ballerina, I face him and give him a wobbly curtsy. Theo shakes his head and snickers at me but follows up with a slow, respectful bow. We both giggle at one another. I inch towards him and reach up to tap the tip of his nose.

"You're surprisingly okay to hang out with. I'm shocked," I tease him.

Theo furrows his brow at me and quickly chimes back, "I was thinking the same thing. Here I thought you were some jailbird out looking for trouble. You know, considering your lengthy criminal record. But come to find out, you're just a lightweight."

I give him my most dramatic eye roll followed by a firm middle finger.

I turn to walk back to the water, but Theo grabs my wrist and whips me around so quickly that our bodies collide. Letting go of my wrist, he softly runs two fingers along my forearm.

Goosebumps trail up my body with every gentle connection. I close my eyes for a second to embrace what his simple touch does to me mentally and physically. I place my other hand on his chest near his shoulder, lifting my head to look up at him.

His expression is almost unreadable, but a hunger behind his stare causes me to shiver. *I swear, this man could fuck me good with just his eyes.*

His heart is thrashing against me at a rapid speed, and my heart seems to follow suit soon after. Within seconds, our hearts are in sync, beating as one. Blood is aggressively pumping through every vein from the intensity of things, and heartbeats pound in my head causing me to feel slightly lightheaded. As if Theo senses my unsteadiness, in one swift movement, he slides both hands to where my back arches, using them and his firm body to keep me upright.

He gives me a questioning look, almost like he's asking for permission to touch me there. *How fucking polite of him.* I give a tiny nod, letting him know it's okay.

Our bodies fit perfectly together like they're made for each other. So much has happened in these last few minutes that I had forgotten the band was still playing above us on the pier. There is a sudden moment of silence where all I hear is the ocean's natural melody and the steady beats of our two hearts. I swear time stood still in that silence; the weight of its absence causing me to forget anything but the man standing before me.

The band starts back up, and I quickly recognize the song they're covering, Iris by the Goo Goo Dolls. I love this damn song. I remember when it first came out. Danielle had just recently gotten her driver's license, and anytime it came on the radio we'd crank up the volume and roll the windows down singing our hearts out to the world.

I think we both had hoped one day that the lyrics would have real meaning in our lives. It makes me wonder if her and Chase are dancing to it now.

The thought slips my mind, thanks to Theo tightening his grip on my lower back. I hadn't realized that we started slowly swaying to the beat of the music. Like I'm in a trance with no control over my body or mind. Even if I wanted to break free, I couldn't; there's something irresistibly magnetic pulling our souls closer to one another.

The lyrics are resonating down to my bones, every word flowing effortlessly through my body. I wonder if he sees me for who I truly am. I've yearned for this experience with him; to escape the hardships of my past, my mother's struggles, Nora's pain, and my own. I want it all to dissolve from my mind so my heart and soul can rest. Even if only just temporary, I will greedily take what I can get. Because this right here with Theo feels like a forbidden antidote. *My antidote.*

My arms gravitate around his neck, and I lay my head against his solid chest. His body emits a comforting warmth beneath my cheek, enveloping me in a sense of safety. He runs his fingers up my spine, caressing every nerve through my body. How can a simple touch ignite so much inside me?

The band reaches the chorus, and our body movement picks up speed, synchronizing with every note. I sway my hips, allowing the music to enter my body and take control. His securing hands run along my lower back in a pleasurable pattern, trailing just above my ass.

I tenderly rub his neck, touching the hairs forming his hairline. I can hear his staggered breathing. Does my sensual touch do the same for him as his does for me?

Theo rubs his hands along my hips, all the way until he reaches the nape of my neck, his hands clasp around it reaching into the hair behind my ears, and his thumbs rest perfectly underneath my jawline tilting my face up to look at him. His gorgeous mouth is slightly parted. Warm, minty breath invades my senses as our eyes bore into each other. We are opposite souls, no longer reaching but intertwined.

So many emotions are racing through me, causing me to bite down hard on my bottom lip. Theo's eyes shift before I can even pinpoint what I've triggered. He lets out a muffled groan. "Damn it, Olive, I've wanted to do this for so fucking long."

He grips my hair pulling my head back. Leaning down, he tenderly bites my bottom lip, and I can't hold back the moan that escapes my throat. Within seconds our mouths clash together, tasting one another.

No more holding back or rejecting what's been gifted to me on a silver platter; Theo is currently nourishing my starving soul. My hands desperately make their way into his thick wavy locks. Our tongues passionately explore each other, never stopping for air. Fuck breathing; all I need are our lips and bodies as close as possible.

He pulls from my mouth, causing me to let out a small whimper from our disconnect. Before I can catch my breath, I am whipped around to face the ocean. Theo grabs around my stomach and pulls me against his body. The music has long since stopped, but our bodies continue moving with the rhythm of our souls. With every smooth motion, I can feel the emptiness within myself slowly filling with something *euphoric.* His pureness bleeds into my tethered being, bringing it back to life.

I grind up against him. In return, Theo groans into my neck, sending butterflies through my stomach. He kisses up my neck until his warm breath reaches my earlobe. He then pants in my ear, "Do you feel what your presence does to me, Olive?"

I let out a rigid gasp. His hard length rubs against my ass, letting me know just how intense this is.

Pressure is quickly building in my mid-section. I need him closer; I crave more of him. I hike my dress up near the front split and grab his hand, guiding it up my thigh. Thanking myself for not wearing panties tonight, I place his hand near my sensitive spot, permitting him to explore how he pleases.

Without hesitation, he runs two fingers over my center, triggering my back to arch. I lean my head back and rest my lips against his neck, unable to control my breathing.

He runs small circles right where I want him.

"Do you feel how my body reacts for you, Theo?" I moan, barely able to form words.

He answers my question by pushing one finger inside me. My head falls back on his chest. I pull my arm up over his shoulder and grab onto the back of his neck. Then I take my other hand and grip his forearm, feeling his muscles tighten with every pleasurable plunge he feeds my pussy. *Fuck, this is too good.*

Theo with no regret slides in a second finger, curling both inside me. Pure ecstasy builds from my inner walls. I have no control over my body right now, Theo has ruthlessly taken over every nerve that consumes my nervous system by continuing to finger fuck me.

I buck my ass against him wanting to feel friction anywhere I can between us. I'm trying my damnedest to fight the release that is building in my core. I don't want this consuming rapture to end.

Without warning, he slowly pulls his fingers from inside me. Looking up, I study as Theo lifts his hand to his mouth. Cutting his eyes to mine, he licks the two fingers that have evidence of my arousal all over them. Watching him thoroughly enjoy the taste of me almost causes me to orgasm.

Theo grips my chin with urgency, bringing our mouths together he mumbles deeply into my lips, "I want you to taste just how fucking delicious you are." *Holy shit.*

He takes his middle finger and runs it across my swollen lips, never taking his gaze from mine. And as if he was starving for more of my taste, he latches onto my bottom lip sucking it into his mouth. A pleasurable yelp slides from my lips, and Theo lets out a heavy moan in return.

"I'm ready for you to cum for me, Olive," he grits out. God, I want no other man to say my name but Theo.

He yanks my sundress back up and begins rubbing small circles around my wet, achy clit, adding pressure behind each motion. In one quick movement, Theo's fingers find their way back inside me, pumping with relentless force.

Lust-filled kisses plant along my exposed neck. Heaviness forms around my sensitive spot, causing my breaths to become unhinged. I can't hold back any longer; my undoing is ready to surface.

My vision becomes blurry as I ride out an unexplainable high that I don't want to come down from. *Theo is a drug worth craving.* His pumps grow faster and harder, with no breaks in between. The intensity of my orgasm leads me to cry out.

I crash so hard like the waves that my legs give out on me. Theo wraps his free arm around my upper stomach, right under my breast saving me from collapsing in the sand.

I give myself a moment to gain back full consciousness. I know how cliche that sounds, but I'm not bullshitting you when I tell you, it was that damn delicious. You know it was a good climax when it feels like your heart is pounding its way out of your vagina. And to be honest, I'm a little embarrassed at how intense it was.

It makes me wonder how sex is with Theo, like holy shit would I be able to survive it? Or would that be what takes me out of this sick world? I can picture it now on my gravestone. *Olive Sage Landers passed from intercourse.*

"Is everything okay, Olive?" Theo asks with concern in his voice.

I snap my eyes back up to him, realizing I was in my own little world for a second. I give him a genuine smile. "Yes, no, everything is good."

He offers me his best smile before placing a single, sensual kiss on my cheek. "What are you thinking about in that cute little head of yours?"

I let out a long sigh. "I think you weren't lying when you said you were good with your hands." I feel my cheeks warm up from my answer.

He lets out the cutest laugh, but then his expression morphs into something sort of intimidating. Theo leans into me, gently locking his hand into the back of my hair. He brings his lips to my ear and whispers, "Wait until I show you what else I'm good at."

Theo

CHAPTER 17

I could sit here all night under this pier, watching her. How can someone masking so much be this beautiful? She's caught me countless times staring at her, and I refuse to look away. I want her to see what I see when looking at her. Her admiration of all the simple things is hypnotizing. She's like an old soul trapped in a corrupt world.

Most people come to the beach to sit and stare at their phones or to snap pictures to post on social media, not even enjoying their surroundings. Olive is different. Observing her the last couple of days, I've noticed how she takes each moment down to every breath.

Seeing her like this excites me, and I am fortunate to know her and to have the chance to dig deeper. Fuck the ocean; she is a view worth exploring.

A smile creeps across my lips, watching her stare at the moon. I notice her fidgeting with the bracelet she bought at the beach shop. She's holding the small moon pendant between her fingers. I first spotted it when we were standing at the end of the pier. I wonder what value it has; it seems sentimental to her.

I clear my throat before blurting out, "May I ask what the bracelet means to you?"

She quickly looks down at it, rubbing her thumb over the front of the pendant. I see a smile appear along her soft lips.

She focuses back on the moon and responds, "Growing up, my sister Nora and I had a treehouse that we'd play in. We often watched the moon together from our little window; it became our little tradition in a way. We've always had a fascination with the moon, Nora especially.

"And as cliche as it sounds, those small memories in my childhood were some of the best. And in some scenarios, they are the only good ones." Her expression hardens for a moment, and then she relaxes, almost like she had memories surface that she wanted to keep at bay.

From the bits of information she gave me during our conversation the other night, I quickly gathered that she has been through unimaginable things, starting as young as a child.

Which breaks my fucking heart. You have people out here in the world, spoiled since birth. They grow up filled with greed and hate in their heart, competing for luxury. Then you have Olive, a beautifully broken human searching for peace. She deserves the goddamn world. And I have this deep desire to provide her with everything the world offers.

But how do I tell the girl I just met weeks ago that I want to fill the missing pieces of her heart with pieces of mine? How do I explain that when our eyes found one another, I knew my life would never be whole without her? I know she feels something for me, but will she let me in? I don't blame her for guarding her heart; she has every reason to.

And I will do everything I can to earn her trust and heal the wounds I didn't cause because that's what you do when you *love* someone. Holy shit, that's deep. Never did I think I'd fall for someone like this.

Olive stands and brushes the back of her dress before heading to the shore. I carefully watch her enter the water, inching further in. I quickly stand and move towards the water's edge. "What the hell are you doing?" I say with slight concern.

She slowly looks back at me, her hair blowing perfectly around her petite face. A testy grin appears. "Get in with me."

I immediately cross my arms and retort, "You're not supposed to swim in the ocean in the middle of the night. Get out of the water."

Now her arms are crossed, and she's laughing at me. "Are you worried you'll get caught, Theo?" She's waist-deep now, and before I can respond, she slowly removes her dress from her shoulders, revealing nothing but her lace bra.

I'm speechless now; all I can do is keep my eyes on her. She pulls it down past her stomach. There's no way she's about to take her dress completely off. As the thought crosses my mind, Olive tosses her drenched dress onto the shore beside my feet.

She is in nothing but a bra now—my *spicy little criminal.*

She's testing me, and I don't think she understands the thrill I get from bending the rules.

One thing about me is that I'm a rule breaker; the feeling of almost getting caught is exhilarating. And the thought of breaking one with her is causing my dick to twitch in my shorts right now.

Without breaking eye contact, I remove my shirt and shorts, quickly throwing them beside her dress.

I watch as Olive scans me up and down, shaking her head. "You realize I have nothing on but a bra, right?" she says teasingly. She's feisty tonight, and I fucking love it.

I stop in my tracks, looking down at my boxers. I confidently chime back, "And you realize I'm only in boxers, right?"

She scoffs at me.

I can't help but laugh. "If you expect me to get fully unclothed, I expect the same from you, ma'am." I see her hesitate with my question; honestly, I expect her to brush it off.

She brings her eyes back to mine, and I hungrily watch as she unclasps her bra and throws it to shore. Whoa, her breasts are perfect. I clench my fist tight on either side of me.

The moon is our only light source; thankfully, it's enough to see how beautifully shaped she is.

She pulls her lips into her mouth before chiming, "Is that better, sir?"

I run my tongue along my top teeth. She likes this between us, and just the thought of that makes my dick throb for her even more.

She wants to play a dangerous game with me, and I'm ready to deal the cards. In one quick movement, my boxers are at my feet.

I slowly edge into the water, keeping her in my clear view. Holy shit, the water is cold. I do my best to hold my composure and let nothing show on my face but curiosity. Her stare moves up and down my body. I watch as her eyes finally focus on my dick, her mouth parting open.

I hope she likes what she sees. I've replayed in my head over and over what it would feel like to be inside her. I can only imagine how good it would feel the way she wrapped around my fingers so tightly, but I refuse to rush anything or expect her to want that with me. If that day were to come, I'd like it to be special and private for our first time.

After what happened between us earlier, I can't get the intimate thoughts out of my head. Never have I experienced something so natural with someone before. Nothing will ever be the same for me again, not after meeting her.

And I swear, her reaction to my touch told me she's never experienced touch affectionately. How has she not had men begging for her attention? It infuriates me but also gives me a sense of relief. I don't want to picture another man near her. I want to be the only one close to her, touching every inch of her body and making her call out my name. I don't care how crazy it sounds; I will indent a mother fucker's face if they even think about touching her.

I've never felt territorial over a woman, but Olive brings out a side of me I never knew existed, like a lion protecting his mate. I know her natural beauty has something to do with it, but it's much deeper than that.

She's strong, and her walls are sturdy. She's bandaged her invisible scars all by herself. And most people turn cold after experiencing hurt. Not her, though; she carries the world's weight and still finds beauty in everything. I hope she can see the beauty from within herself. She makes me want to be a better person, but she also makes me want to rip anyone's head off who tries to place harm in her direction.

I stop in front of her and crouch down into the blistering, salty water to be at eye level with her. Olive gives me a devilish grin. "Is that thing tamed?" she blurts out.

I squint my eyes at her in confusion. "Is what ta..?" Okay, so now she's a little comedian. Two can play this game. I lightly chuckle at her playfulness, then quickly retort, "Only if you want it to be."

Her grin dissipates, and I watch her drag her teeth along her bottom lip. A grunt flees from my throat.

I pull her closer, keeping a little distance between us considering our nonexistent attire. I use my fingers to comb back her wet locks. How can a face be this stunning? I feel honored to touch and admire it. It almost feels forbidden, like a lost treasure hidden from humanity. Her eyes are mesmerizing, even in the dark, and I can see a battle within them. What is she thinking about?

She places her delicate hands on my chest, and I watch her as she runs them around my pecs and up to my neck in a sensual motion. I feel goosebumps all over my body; having her hands on me feels so damn good. I only want her touch, and I can't even fathom another woman doing what she is doing to me mentally and physically. I'm currently frozen, only able to watch as she controls the sensation raging through me.

She slowly trails her hands below my chest, reaching my stomach under the water. Out of nowhere, her caressing touch comes to a halt. I bring my hands down, wrapping them over the top of hers, keeping them pressed to my stomach. She brings her eyes back to mine; I can tell she has something on her mind. I lightly squeeze her hands. "What is it?"

She stalls for a moment before answering me. "Stand up, Theo." Her voice quivers but also holds demand behind it. What is she up to?

I won't argue with her, though. She could tell me to bark, and I probably would right now. Never has a female gained control over me like this. I keep my expression steady while slowly standing. My guy is already rock hard just from Olive's hands touching me. My dick emerges from the water, looking like the damn loch ness monster coming up for air.

Olive is now almost perfectly at eye level with it. I can't help but look down and take in her kneeling in front of me, bare. She looks so hot. Her breasts sit naturally above the water, glistening with wet kisses from the ocean. She slides her hands from my stomach, gliding them slowly down to my lower waist, and then pauses.

I watch as she eyes my cock, almost like she's taking in its length. She then looks up at me; her lips are wet and pouty. I'll never fucking forget this view of her staring up at me, her eyes glazed with desire.

My heart feels like it is seconds from fleeing from my chest. The anticipation is eating me alive, and I sense it's doing the same for her.

Olive blows out a deep breath. "I want to do this for you. Can I.." Before she finishes her question that I already had the answer to, I grab her left hand and wrap it around my dick.

We both let out a rigid gasp. God, her hand fits deliciously around me. I try to calm my breathing because I can't have her thinking I have no control now.

I grunt out, "Look at me, Olive." She pulls her attention back up to me. "You never have to ask to touch me. You don't understand how often I've imagined this moment with you or dreamed about it. And just the view of you gripping me right now makes me want to cum."

I see something flicker in her eyes, and before I can process it, Olive runs her tongue over her top lip. I groan at the sight of it.

She inches closer to me, then slowly runs her tongue on the tip of my dick, causing it to jerk in her hand. I hear a soft moan come from deep within her. She wraps her other hand around me tightly, running her tongue up and down, making sure it's soaked with her saliva.

She slides her hands up and down in perfect motion, squeezing me just enough to cause me to throw my head back. Fuck this is too good.

I can hear every inhale and exhale leave her gorgeous body. She looks back up at me with a naughty grin. "I don't think you understand how many times I've pictured what it would be like to have you in my mouth." Her words seep into my skin.

I place my right hand behind her head and gently grasp

her hair. "Show me then, Olive," I growl out.

She gives me a playful look, almost like saying "brace yourself". She doesn't wait a second longer. Her needy mouth slides onto me, sucking down until her lips meet where her hands grip me. She creates a flawless motion of sucking, tugging, and licking.

This right here feels like pure ecstasy. Everything I envisioned it would be with her is playing out in front of me in the ocean right now; it's everything and more.

Her consistent moans tell me she is enjoying this just as much as me, and witnessing it turns me the fuck on. I am enjoying this very much. I don't know if I can hold off much longer. Pressure is building at the base of my dick, and I already know that when I release, it's going to be intense.

Continuing to suck the life out of me, Olive removes both of her hands, using one to cup my balls while taking the other to grip my thigh. Without warning, she shoves her mouth down, and the tip of my dick hits the back of her throat.

My grip tightens on her hair. This girl is talented and doesn't know what a gag reflex is. I don't even care; I let heavy moans leave my lips. "Shit, you feel so good wrapped around me."

Olive looks up at me; tears stain her cheeks and swollen lips.

I'm trying to keep control, but I'm seconds from filling her mouth with my seed.

She picks up speed, squeezing my balls every time my dick hits the back of her throat. She then takes her hand from my thigh and places it over the top of my hand, which is grasping her hair. She pushes it with hers, causing her head to bob back and forth. Taking both her hands, she places them on the back of my legs, like she's bracing herself.

She's giving me the control to finish this good deed; she's such a good girl. I gently wrap my fingers through her hair and begin slow motions, pushing her tight mouth to the bottom of my dick. Deep moans leave her body; I follow suit.

I take deep breaths, trying to steady myself, but this is just too fucking good. Spit is streaming down the sides of her mouth, and I stop for a second to make sure she is okay.

Olive latches onto my legs and forcefully slams my dick down her throat. "Holy fuck, Olive!"

She's now clarified that she can handle this. There is no turning back now. I start slowly using her hair as leverage to push her head forward and back.

I feel like I am about to combust into a million pieces.

The time is fucking now. I begin forcefully slamming her head onto me with no remorse.

She quickly wraps both hands around me and jerks along with my fast motion. My dick is pulsating from the pleasure building inside me. In one quick movement, I thrust my hips forward, and I feel the tip of my dick slide down her tight throat. "Oh my Go—" I release myself into her throat. My legs shake from the intensity of it all. I tilt my head back and gaze at the night sky; the stars illuminate the darkness.

Once I catch my breath, my vision loses that fuzzy feeling. I look down at Olive; she is wiping my remains off of her mouth. I bring myself back down in the water and pull her into my chest.

All I want to do now is to be close to her. It's the weirdest feeling. I've never wanted to do this with a girl; honestly,

I never have. I've never disrespected a girl, but anytime I hooked up with someone, that's all it ever was. Olive has snatched my soul right out of my dick and claimed it.

Olive lifts her head from my shoulder, looking behind me. She begins quietly laughing. What the hell is she laughing at? "Theo, we are naked, and there are people headed this way with flashlights."

I quickly turn and look over my shoulder. Oh shit! They're getting close.

I urge her, "Come on, we've got to go now!" She is laughing hysterically now. And I can't help but join her as we run out of the water butt ass naked. This girl is trouble but in a damn good way.

Olive

CHAPTER 18

I don't think I've laughed that hard in a long time. We barely made it off the beach in clothes before the family of five passed through with their flashlights. I don't think they saw anything, but I can't be so sure about that. It was challenging to slip my fully soaked dress back on. Mind you, it was also covered in gritty ass sand. Theo had his shorts on in no time immediately after exiting the water. He was frantically trying to hurry, and I couldn't help but pick at him just a little.

It took us around thirty minutes to walk back to the beach house because we may or may not have stopped at someone's random condo to use their outdoor shower. So, by the time we returned to the beach house, it was after three in the morning. What a night it's been. I haven't felt this alive in a very long time. Thanks to Theo.

I don't know how long Chase and Danielle have been asleep. I had gone upstairs to get Lottie, but she must be rooming with them tonight. Leo was lying in front of the bedroom door, almost as if he was guarding it. I love how quickly he and Lottie took to each other.

I don't feel a wink of tiredness. So much has happened tonight that I think my body and mind are trying to process it all. This is all very new to me, a high I didn't know existed. Never has a man made me feel what Theo has. The way he caressed me with every single touch. Noah never touched me in that way, because I was an object to him, nothing more.

It's already almost time to head back home, which means reality is waiting at my doorstep. I dread the shit out of it. I have no words to express the time I've had here with the four of us. It's everything I've needed and more. I have felt at home while here, thanks to Chase and Theo being so welcoming.

Life works in mysterious ways, and even though I feel very grateful for the memories and people brought into my life, it also terrifies me. Most good things get snatched away from me, or just merely do not exist.

And the thought of letting someone break those internal barriers scares the shit out of me.

I won't deny there is something there with Theo. My body alerted me when I first saw him at Taylor's party. I've played multiple scenarios in my head, and my soul tells me he came into my life for a reason. Like the cure to my brokenness, the way he made me feel tonight continues to replay in my head. Our dance, the intimacy, the connection. It's almost too good to be true.

As we sit here facing each other in this hammock, I know I need to tell him about Noah. How he takes in the information will tell me if this is something worth fighting for.

I've fought all my life, trying to stay above the water that continuously tries to pull me under. I won't give up so easily on this, not after the reassurance Theo has continued to give me. But will he accept things from my past?

"I could sleep right here in this hammock tonight," I say, looking up at the two palm trees holding us up. I look back at Theo. Of course, he's staring at me like he's soaking me in. I gently slap at his leg. "What is your fascination with my face, sir?"

He gives me a cute grin. "If I had your face, I'd stare at myself in the mirror all the time."

I let out a loud snort. "Ha, okay!"

He encircles my leg with small, tantalizing movements, causing the familiar goosebumps to appear once more. "I'm serious, Olive. You are absolutely beautiful."

I must remember what he told me on the beach about being serious when he says something. I won't argue with him on this one. I smile at him. "You're not bad to look at yourself, Theo."

He lets out a deep breath. "Seriously, quit being so hard on yourself. There is no one quite like you, and it draws me to you." He always has such a way with words.

"I'm sorry; I know I can be negative sometimes; it's just something I've done for a long time." I pick at my fingernails nervously.

He gives my leg a squeeze. "Because someone stole your confidence at some point?" he says with understanding.

I nod my head. "Something like that, I guess you could say."

Theo sits quietly, waiting for a more detailed answer. Do I tell him that Noah wasn't the start of my insecurities? Do I tell him a kid bullied me into thinking I was nothing more than walking trash? Do I leave out the fact that I've never had a father figure?

This is my moment to bring up the uncomfortable subjects I've been avoiding.

I take a slow, deep breath. "A boy who received everything in life bullied me throughout grade school. I was trash in his eyes, and he ensured I felt the same about myself. It wasn't until I was older that maturity grabbed ahold of me and slowly built my confidence in physical areas, but it didn't change how I felt on the inside."

I pause for a moment to see how Theo is taking in the information. He nods at me, almost like telling me to continue, like he knows there's more to this story.

"I've been in a relationship before. His name was Noah. I was young and naïve, desperate for someone to love me. And he was a good actor. He skillfully manipulated my emotions, knowing I was in a fragile state. There was no hiding that from him. When he had the opportunity, he took the one thing I had control over: my innocence. Once he claimed what he wanted, I was nothing more than a toy, and I allowed it for a long time.

"Until I caught him screwing one of my friends in his precious Mustang, and that was it for me. I never saw him again after that. But I can't blame him or the bully from school. It's not Noah's fault I stuck around for as long as I did. I stayed because I felt like I deserved nothing better. And if it was so easy for my father to abandon me and Nora when I was only five, then surely I was worthless to most."

Shit, this is the moment where Theo is about to jump out of this hammock and make a run for it because who the hell wants to hear those things or even deal with someone who has such a depressing background.

I would understand if he's done with me and this conversation. Who am I to judge?

I nervously look up at him. There is pain in his expression but also rage. He quickly looks away while running his hand through his hair. "I'm so fucking sorry you had to go through that, Olive. The thought of someone taking advantage of you burns me to my core. Honestly, all of this. I can't wrap my head around it. Fuck all of them. If only I could have come into your life first, never would you have had to question your worth, ever."

His words are so comforting, and I know them to be true. There is no judging, just understanding. He makes it so easy to confide in him. We sit quietly momentarily, listening to the breeze blow through the palm trees.

A weight has lifted from my shoulders. And truthfully, I don't want this night to end.

"How do you do it?" Theo asks with genuine curiosity in his tone.

I tilt my head at him. "How do I do what?"

He pauses for a moment, scanning my expression. "How do you keep going with everything you've been through?"

No one has ever cared to ask me that before.

I look away for a second to pick at imaginary threads on the side of the hammock, soaking in his question; I then let out a soft sigh. "Giving up has crossed my mind a few times. Right now, saying the words out loud feels so peaceful. I know how easy it would be just to let go, but I can't bring myself to do it. The little version of me deserves better. She deserves the world, and I keep telling myself that even if I am eighty years old, withering away in my bed.

"One day, she will hold the world in her hands for the first time, and she will know what love and acceptance are. But if that day never comes and I am on my deathbed, I will hold that little broken girl so tight, and I will tell her she is worthy, she is loved, and I will hold her until my last breath."

Wow, I can't believe I just said all that. I'm sure it sounded very morbid and depressing. Strangely, it felt good to vocalize it with someone listening. And I meant every word. Hopefully, he doesn't think I'm crazy, but I couldn't blame him otherwise.

Worried about how he may look at me now, I finally bring my eyes back up to his. Theo's eyebrows are deeply furrowed, and I'm almost certain that his eyes are glazed over. Ugh, I should have kept my damn mouth shut. The last thing I want is for someone to feel pity for me.

Before I'm able to form words to apologize, Theo sits up in the hammock, placing his long legs on either side for support. He leans in and grabs my face, combing his fingers through my partially ocean-drenched hair. Our eyes meet again. There is a fire burning behind his stare.

His breathing becomes heavy before he grits out, "That

little girl was you, Olive, and it's you that deserves nothing fucking less than the universe."

Whoa, that was deep. His words pulsate through my guarded heart, causing an ache that almost hurts my chest.

"What do you even see in me, Theo?" My words come out shaky.

He brings his eyes to my mouth, then quickly locks them back with mine. "I see a girl that was robbed of so many things and forced to grow up too soon. I see a woman who has gone through the deepest trenches and made it out stronger. I see a beautifully broken human who sees the world through kind eyes. I see love when I look at you.

"So much that it seeps from your pores and into this sick world. Because I see you, Olive. The good, the broken, the little girl that craves affection. I want to fill that void you've lived in for so long. Let me in. Let me find the scattered pieces of your soul and hold them close. I can't promise you the Universe, but I can promise you a piece, a piece that is filled with all of me."

His words wrap around me, cradling me tight. Theo gently wipes warm tears I didn't realize were trickling down my face. I can't control their release, and just as another makes its way down my cheek, he leans in and kisses my jaw, taking the salty tear with him.

I watch as his lips slightly curl up. "You're even beautiful when you cry, and that is intriguing in itself." He runs his thumb over my quivering, tear-soaked lips.

Without warning, he caresses them with his, stealing my tears with every kiss. Within seconds, he parts my lips with his tongue, and our mouths become one. Our tongues clash together, creating a perfect rhythm. Butterflies dance around in my stomach.

Everything with Theo feels genuinely real, and I've tried my hardest to fight the spark that ignited in my soul the night I first laid eyes on this beautiful man in front of me. Just having him near me makes me feel safe. I don't even care right now; letting him in feels right. It took me a while to realize that my walls had already crumbled with each interaction we shared. This is me choosing to let him into my heart. And if this ends up being a failed attempt at happiness, I can at least say I fucking tried.

Olive

CHAPTER 19

Here I am, stuck back in dreadful reality, and this work week has gone by so slowly. Two weeks have long passed since the beach trip, and it's all I've been able to think about. All that transpired Saturday night. Theo and I stayed up until around 5 a.m. Sunday morning. We explored each other's minds, and eventually, each other's bodies. We went from deep conversations lying in the hammock to deep foreplay in the hot tub. And that man had electricity running through every nerve in my body, so much that I could have jump-started a damn car if necessary.

All it takes is him touching my skin, and it feels like a defibrillator sending electric charges to my soul, putting pieces of life back into its darkness. But once his touch left me, I could sense the darkness overshadowing the light again. It's like Theo is my life support, and without him near, I can feel my existence shutting down breath by breath. I imagine the hospital monitor beeping in my ear, my pulse slowing drastically.

I didn't want the beach trip to end. After staying up so late, we finally made our way to the guest bedroom Theo was staying in. It was the best sleep I've had in a decade. He held me flush against him, and I didn't have one bad dream. In the strangest way, I can still sense his strong arms wrapped around me, caressing me, holding me close.

There was a second before I drifted away into a deep sleep, where I felt a lump in my throat; tears fought their way to the corners of my eyes. It was an overwhelming emotion that clouded my mind.

Maybe just the thought of knowing that in my nineteen years of living, I had never known what it felt like to be held by a man affectionately, never experiencing a father that adored his little girl. And just plain and simple, I'll never know what that feels like. Theo willingly gave me a piece of that comfort, the feeling of security quickly blanketed those undesired emotions and shoved them out of my mind. And for that I am so thankful to know him and witness the person he is.

Chase and Danielle are the absolute cutest. I have seen a new side to Danielle, a very giddy Danielle. Normally, she takes the lead, and it's a short-lived fling that burns out quicker than a lit match. But these two can't keep their damn hands off each other.

Only two weeks since the trip, and they've seen each other

at least three times since. He's come to the apartment to hang out after work, and she stayed with him at his place one night. I'm genuinely happy for them, and I really like him for her. She needed him more than she wants to admit.

As far as Theo and I go, we're just going with the flow. New things take time, right? And I'm not exaggerating when I say this is extremely new and unexpected for me. No one but myself understands the constant battle in my head. *You are not good enough, Olive; no one will ever love you.* It took me maturing before I truly understood the damage that trauma causes in the human brain.

Will I be able to handle another heartbreak? Is Theo capable of tearing me down?

I don't think so, anyway. He's continuously shown me that his intentions are pure, but time will tell. And I'm not ashamed to admit that I fucking miss him when he's not near me.

After almost five days of no response, I finally got Nora on the phone. She had me so worried that I reached out to Jake's mom. I can tell something is bothering Michelle, or she knows something I don't. I decided not to interrogate her. It's best I wait and have a conversation with Nora myself.

It took me nearly begging her into coming over this evening. Danielle will be with Chase, so it felt like the perfect opportunity to spend some quality time with my sister and hopefully figure out what's going on with her.

After seeing the items in her bag last week, it's been extremely hard not to assume the worst. I always worried that one of us would fall down the same generational path of drug addiction. Honestly, I initially thought it would be me, but upon reflection, I realized it was something I couldn't continue. The guilt and disappointment outweighed the temporary numbness I felt when trying them.

I'm damned if I do and damned if I don't. Either way, I am suffering somehow. It's me, myself, and I against my fucked-up brain every single day. It makes me wonder what Nora is battling silently. I want her to confide in me so badly. I cannot lose her too.

Family-wise, she is all I have left aside from our dysfunctional mother. I just want her to be happy and healthy. And I miss spending time with her, seeing her smile and contagious laugh.

My Thursday workday has finally ended, and I'm excited because Nora is supposed to arrive within the next couple of hours. To kick off our evening together, I'm treating us to a delicious New York-style pizza. It was always our go-to choice on nights when Mom didn't come home; Nora and I would gather enough change and crumpled dollars to order one pizza.

By the time the delivery person handed us the pizza, we couldn't wait any longer. A slice was already in our hands, tempting us to indulge in its mouthwatering flavor. And we did just that each time, indulged until there was nothing left in the box but the grease stain where the pizza once was.

I made a quick stop by the grocery store for a few things; I plan to mix up some refreshing margaritas, the perfect accompaniment to the pizza we'll be consuming. Once I received the green light that Nora would come over, I had Danielle pick up the tequila for me last night, ensuring I'd have everything needed for tonight.

Arriving at our two-story brick apartments, I happily clutch the bags filled with the goodies I purchased from the store. As I ascend to our second-floor sanctuary, I am grateful to Danielle for securing this tranquil spot, free from late-night noise above. I sense our downstairs neighbors appreciate our quiet lifestyle, especially since there have been no complaints.

As I reach the door, I pause to listen for Lottie's little feet tapping against the floor. It's our routine on the days I come home from work; she usually runs to the door and barks to let me know to open it. I wait for a moment, but she doesn't come to the door. What's going on? I enter our door code and swing the door open. Immediately, I spot Lottie sitting on her small dog bed in the living room, chewing on something.

Quickly I run over to see what she has. It's a cookie-shaped dog treat, and she's eaten over half of it. Where the hell did she get that? I scan around the apartment, and my eyes freeze on two vases sitting on the kitchen island. Confusion swarms my thoughts. I walk over to peek at the items. Each vase has at least twelve lovely varieties of roses. Wait, roses?

I spot a small card sitting between the vases, written on the front. *To my very spicy Olive.* I open the card to find written on the inside. *You once told me that your life didn't possess roses or happy smiles. So, I thought I'd bring some into your life. Hopefully, these put a smile on your beautiful face. I almost chose all red, but then I thought you deserve every color. And before you wonder, I individually picked each one for you. There are perks to running a landscaping company. And you should know that I got my fingers pricked at least three times. I will need you to kiss my wounds tomorrow when I see you. Only you can make them feel better.*

P.S. I hope your fluffy rodent enjoyed her treat.

-Theo

A warm smile spreads across my face at his simple yet thoughtful gesture. I run my fingertips along the silk petals, admiring the colorful mix of reds, lavenders, whites, and even some salmon-tinted ones I've never seen before.

They are breathtaking. If he's trying to find more ways into my heart, he has succeeded. I leave one vase on the kitchen island and place the other on my bedroom dresser.

Basking in Theo's sweet gifts, it slipped my mind that he has been here. Chase is the only one that has been here before. How in the hell did he get in? And did he drive an hour just to bring me flowers? I pull my phone from my back pocket and send a text.

Me: First, thank you for the gorgeous variety of roses; I love them. And Lottie left no remains from the treat you gave her. You didn't have to do all of that.

Theo: There's my girl. You are so welcome. I wouldn't have done it if I didn't want to, you know. I'm glad she enjoyed it. I was concerned that she wouldn't be able to finish it, considering it was almost the same size as her.

Me: That's so dramatic. Well, I appreciate it, and I want you to know it did, in fact, put a smile on my face.

Theo: I can't wait to see that damning smile tomorrow. Also excited about you tending to my wounds.

Me: Don't worry—I'll take good care of them for you. :) I must ask, though, how the hell did you get into the apartment?

Theo: I broke in. I'm kidding. Danielle gave me the code. I was passing through on my way to clients out your way, so it worked out perfectly.

Me: Damn, looks like I need to get our code changed now. Joking. Again, thank you. I can't wait to see you tomorrow. Believe it or not, I will be all dressed up for our little dinner date.

Theo: Mmm. I already know no matter what you're in, all I'll be able to think about is your body bare beneath your clothes.

Me: Well, if you're a good boy, I might just let you help me undress before the night is over.

Theo: I'll be on my very best behavior. You have my word.

Me: Good :) I will see you soon. Nora should be on the way here soon. I'll talk to you later. Have a good night, Theo.

Theo: Have a good time with your sister. Talk soon, beautiful.

Damn, this man makes me want to do very dirty things to him. Not only is he nice to look at, but he's thoughtful. So thoughtful that he kindly finger fucked me on the beach the other day.

Warm chills run up my spine just thinking about everything that transpired that night. It makes me wonder how good he is in bed. And something tells me he is talented in many other areas. It makes me nervous about tomorrow.

After refusing to let me drive and meet him tomorrow at the restaurant he's taking me to, we finally agreed on him picking me up. Danielle and Chase will stay at the apartment with Lottie, and I will stay with Theo at his house after dinner. This is the part that terrifies me. It has been over a year since

Noah and I last slept together, and that was my last time.

I've been uninterested in seeking men until Theo snuck up on me. I have this strong feeling that I won't be able to keep my hands to myself. And the last thing I want to do is make a fucking fool out of myself.

Danielle begged me to let her pick my outfit and do my makeup and hair for tomorrow's festivities. I didn't have it in me to tell her no; plus, I already knew she was going to make sure I looked classy but fuckable. Normally, I would protest against it; I've never wanted that kind of attention on me. But something inside me wants to see Theo's ocean eyes spark a flame when he sees me tomorrow night.

I want him hungry for me. And I know that when I see the switch in his eyes flip, it'll take all my willpower to be good. I will do my best to keep my hands to myself and let Theo take the lead on everything.

Olive
CHAPTER 20

Nora and I happily devour the entire pizza while watching our favorite childhood movie, "The Never-Ending Story." It's just as delightful as it was when we first saw it as kids—so much so that we could easily reenact the entire film if we wanted to, having watched it countless times.

The nostalgia I experienced tonight brought me comfort, and having Nora here with me has made it even better.

Spending time with her tonight has meant the world to me; I've missed having quality time with her. Our relationship has shifted since Jake passed away, but not in a negative way. It's not that it has changed; I think it has more to do with how Nora has changed.

Even tonight, I can sense that something is off with her. While we've shared some great laughs since she arrived, I've noticed her body language during the moments when she doesn't realize I'm watching.

I fidget with my moon bracelet, twirling it around my wrist. "Oh, I almost forgot!" I jump up from the couch and head towards my room.

"What is it?" Nora shouts.

I quickly return and plop back down. "Let me see your wrist."

Nora glances at my enclosed hand before extending her arm my way. I clasp on the moon bracelet and watch as her eyes light up. She runs her thumb over the moon pendant, a genuine smile stretching across her face. *There's my beautiful Nora Ray.*

"Where did you get this? I love it!" she chirps.

I throw my wrist up and jingle my bracelet for her to see. "From a gift shop at the beach. We're matching now."

Nora continues staring at the pendant. "It's perfect, Olive. Thank you."

"I'm so glad you like it. It makes me think of all those nights in the treehouse watching the moon when we were kids."

Nora smiles a little, and I watch as it slowly melts from her face. "Those same nights, our mother was high as a kite or nowhere to be found." She lets out a short, dramatic laugh.

Grabbing my watered-down margarita from the coffee table, I take a huge gulp to flush down the ache that claws up my throat. "It's not a childhood I would wish on anyone, but I can only be thankful that we had one another," I reply.

Nora stares forward blankly, nodding her head.

We both sit in our dreary silence for what feels like an eternity.

There's more to this conversation to be had. My mind trails back to the day I stopped by to visit her. I can't hold back anymore; I need to know if what I saw in her purse was what I've prayed it wasn't. It has not left my mind since.

Now my stomach is turning into knots just thinking about where this will lead and the fact that I'm potentially stirring some shit up when we've had a great night so far.

I brace myself and turn back towards her on the couch. "I need to know if you're okay, Nora. Please, I'm an adult, and I can handle whatever it is. I'm worried about you!" I anxiously watch Nora's expression fall into a deeper frown.

She was not prepared to have this discussion with me. The last thing I want to do is put her on the spot and upset her, but I love and care about her; I need to know if she is battling something alone.

We sit silently for a few seconds before she turns towards me. Her gorgeous brown eyes are hazy, and I can see the pain behind them. I feel tears building in my eyes, but I hold myself together; I can't fuck this up. I have to show her I can take whatever she tells me as an adult.

Her lip quivers slightly as she speaks. "Since you must know, Olive, no, I'm not okay. Every day, I have no choice but to wake up and be reminded that Jake is never coming back. I sleep in a bed where he once slept beside me. A bed where we laughed, cried, and had intimate moments together for so many years."

Tears are streaming down her face, and I can't stop the

ones now streaming down mine.

I hear a sob leave her throat before she speaks again. "He saved me, Olive, don't you know that? He loved me despite my brokenness. I had to leave that house; I stayed for you until I couldn't stay any longer. And it was Jake who brought me into his family and was patient with me. He let me cry many nights in his arms while he reminded me he'd always be there. And now he's gone."

This hurts me so fucking bad. She's bottled this all up and has dealt with it all alone. I feel like the shittiest sister ever. My voice is shaky. "Nora, I'm so—"

She quickly cuts me off before I can finish. "No, let me say this, please. I need you to know that I tried; I tried so goddamn hard to cope with the grief. It has haunted me since the day he died. Sleeping was my friend at first until his death crept into my dreams every single night to the point I'd wake up crying or gasping for air that wasn't there."

She sucks in a shaky breath.

"Olive, I had to numb the pain because nothing else was working. That's when an acquaintance at my old job had heard about Jake's death and offered me some of her pain medication from when she broke her arm months prior.

"At first, I was skeptical about it, but she reassured me it was okay and would help calm my nerves. It took me a week to muster up the courage to try them. The first time made me sick; I puked my guts up, but by the second time, I felt relaxed in a way, my anxiety subsided, and I felt like I could breathe again."

She takes a deep breath and waits for me to respond. That was a lot to take in, and I'm trying to hold it together. I need her to trust me and confide in me, but I also want her to know that I'm concerned.

I finally muster out, "Are you still taking them?"

She looks away and begins rubbing her forearm. "Yes, but I promise you it's just temporary. You know Jake's twenty-sixth birthday is coming up soon, and I need to get past that. It's his first birthday gone, and I won't get to spend it with him."

I slowly nod my head in understanding. "I'm so sorry that you have felt alone in this. I wish I could have been more for you, Nora." I can't help the rattle behind my words.

She turns and wraps her arms around me. "Olive, you are everything to me and more. This isn't your fault or your problem to fix. I love you dearly, and nothing will ever change that."

I lay my head on her shoulder, closing my eyes while she gently rubs my back. For a split second, I feel like we're kids again. I picture Nora as only a child, too, trying her best to calm me, letting me know she's right here. She had no one to comfort her like that. She has had to be strong for me, herself, and our mom all these years. And the thought of it strikes my heart. I put my arms around her and lightly squeeze. I don't want to let her go.

Tears flood my face again. "I can't lose you, Nora; you're my sister."

I hear a deep breath leave her wobbling mouth. "I'm not going anywhere, I promise. I'm going to get out of this. I love you so damn much, Olive Oil," she chokes out.

And I know with every fiber in me she does. "I love you too, big sister."

CHAPTER 21

*F*ucking breathtaking. Those two words run through my mind as I lean against the hood of my car, watching Olive emerge from the apartment stairs.

She outdid herself this evening. Her hair is halfway up; two wavy strands lay in the front, framing her gorgeous face. She wears a red cocktail dress that hugs her figure impeccably, its length reaching right above the knee. The front cuts down into a V, showing a tasteful amount of her immaculate cleavage.

Her lips are adorned with a rose stain that complements her blush-dusted cheeks. However, what draws me in the most are her eyes. They make my knees weak, which probably makes me sound like a little bitch, but it's the truth. She has applied a smoky color on her eyelids that makes her eyes stand out even more. They almost seem to glow, highlighting the hint of green beautifully present in her honey-brown irises.

It's easy to imagine slipping that dress right off her and even easier to feel her absence when we are away from each other. This is my first time seeing her since we left the beach. Our work schedules have prevented us from being able to see each other sooner, but I've enjoyed our little text banters back and forth since. It's what has kept me going every day.

She strolls over to me, her damning eyes never leaving mine, sliding her body in between my legs. I wrap my arms around her waist, running my hands along the curve of her ass.

She smells like sweet coconut with hints of peony; she always smells so delicious. It's amazing how certain aromas stick with you. It could be of a place or a person. And there is something about her scent that drives me fucking mad.

She places her arms around my shoulders, resting her hands behind my neck, giving me the cutest lazy smile. I love that her little cheek dimple appears even when giving the slightest smile. I take my thumb and run it along her dimple, watching as her warm honey eyes shut from my touch, causing me to grin instantly.

"I sure have missed your beautiful face," I purr.

She feeds me a wicked grin while twirling her fingers around my hair. "So, that's all you've missed?" I slant my eyes at her and match her grin.

I quickly cup the back of her head, locking my fingers into her thick strands, careful not to mess up her updo. *I'll save that for later tonight.* Forcing my mouth on hers, she doesn't fight back, parting her lips so that our tongues can dance in sweet, tasteful circles.

I've craved her mouth since last seeing her. And no matter how hard I try to savor the taste of her smooth tongue, I can never get enough to satisfy the hunger inside me.

When I pull away, I gently nip her bottom lip, and a small whimper leaves her throat. My dick is already throbbing for her. And I'd love, more than anything, to pick her up and lay her on the hood of my Corvette. I picture sliding her red dress up and finding that she isn't wearing anything underneath. So many dirty thoughts run through my head.

I rest my forehead against hers, caressing her cheek with my thumb. "We would be late for dinner if I went through everything I've missed about you."

She closes her eyes for a moment and replies with so much desire in her tone. "Maybe you can show me how much you've missed me after dinner."

Fuck, I can't wait to show her physically just what she's doing to me. I growl back, " Yes, my little spicy Olive, we'll save dessert for later tonight."

We arrived at our 6 p.m. reservation just in time, and luckily, the dinner traffic hadn't affected us yet. The server collected our menus and guided us to the table I had requested at the back of the restaurant. From there, we have a perfect view of the chefs. My parents used to bring me here as a child, and we always sat at the same table so I could watch them cook our food. And after they adopted sweet Emma, we continued this little tradition for many years.

I watch Olive as she scans the room, always paying

attention to her surroundings. I hope she likes the food here, as this has always been one of my favorite hibachi grills near home. I might sound biased, but I truly believe they serve the best sushi around. I'm eager for her to try it, as I doubt she has experienced anything better.

"So, what do you usually order?" she asks playfully, peering out from behind her menu with a curious glint in her eyes.

I smile and reply, "I was thinking about getting sushi. I really hope you'll try it—I'll be amazed if it's not the best you've ever had."

A flicker of surprise crosses her face, followed by a soft laugh as she shakes her head, clearly skeptical.

"I've actually never tried sushi. It always looked unappetizing to me," she admits, her nose wrinkling slightly. "I think I'll just stick with teriyaki steak, rice, and vegetables. You really can't go wrong with that."

With a playful grin, I shake my head. "That's fine, but you have to at least try a piece for me, okay? Just one little bite!"

Her eyes twinkle with amusement at my enthusiasm, and after a brief pause, she nods in agreement, a smile spreading across her face. It's clear she knows I won't let this go easily, and I can't wait to share this experience with her.

Our server eventually brought out the sushi; I ordered several California rolls. I wanted to stick with simple since this would be her first time trying it. Olive spends a good minute examining the rolls on the long dish.

I can't help but let out a small chuckle. "There's no backing down now," I say with determination.

She wrinkles her cute little nose at me. "Fine, just one

bite."

She picks up a roll and smells it before I can warn her not to. Her expression makes me laugh again.

"Theo, how do you eat these? They smell awful!"

I quickly grab one, dip it in shrimp sauce, and pop the whole roll into my mouth. Then, I gesture for her to do the same. Finally, she follows my lead, dipping the roll in the sauce before putting it in her mouth.

I sit back and patiently watch as she slowly chews, holding a napkin near her stained lips.

She mumbles, "Okay, it's not that bad, but I don't see myself eating it again. I'll let you handle the other several rolls on your plate." Then she gives me a half-hearted grin. She looks so cute, even with one side of her cheek bulging from stuffing a whole roll in her mouth. The sushi might have been a failure, but dinner has gone well so far.

As we drive to my house with the top down, the night breeze feels refreshing. Olive asks to listen to Sublime, and I'm more than happy to oblige. I can't help but glance at her as her hair dances around her face, gently framing her high cheekbones.

She sings along with the band, her smile proving to be contagious. For once, I notice she isn't lost in her thoughts. As silly as it may sound, seeing her like this makes my heart skip a beat.

And seeing her in my passenger seat makes me so fucking happy; her presence makes my car look good. I give her smooth thigh a light squeeze, and in return, she squeezes my hand, giving me that lazy smile I've grown to love.

As we near my neighborhood, Olive turns down the radio.

"How long have you lived here?" she asks curiously.

"I started working in the landscaping business with my dad when I was thirteen. I saved up every penny I could. When I turned eighteen, he gave me partial ownership of the business. Since then, I've focused on building my credit, and I bought my place about two years ago."

We pull into the driveway, and I park the car, leaving the headlights on. I turn towards her, placing my hand back on her thigh. She gazes at me for a moment before looking towards the house.

"That is really impressive, Theo. You should be proud of yourself."

I let out a long breath. "I appreciate that. Truthfully, my parents are the reason. It was working hard and building something for myself or failing and figuring it out on my own." I let out a short laugh. "But I'm glad they stuck with it because I probably would have turned out to be a fuckhead otherwise."

I watch Olive's expression fall to her lap while she rubs her hands together.

Maybe bringing my parents into the conversation wasn't the smartest idea. She never had the guidance and support that I had while growing up, and I can never fully understand what she has been through and what she missed out on.

All I can do is be there for her and remind her just how special she is to me and to others.

I quickly place my hand over the top of hers while taking my right hand and gently turning her head to face me. I admire her natural beauty momentarily before pulling her chin towards me and placing my lips against hers. Our tongues reunite, desperately swirling around one another. I never want this to end with her. *She is my addiction.*

I pull away, giving her lips another peck, still holding firmly to her chin. Her eyes stay locked on my parted lips. "Hey, look at me." She slowly brings her eyes to mine. "Look at the life you've created for yourself, Olive. You did it all on your own. Few can say that."

She lays her face on my hand, closing her eyes. "I didn't have a choice." Her voice cracks.

Gods, I want to hold her right here in this car and never let go. I recline my seat back and motion for her to climb over to me. "Come here," I demand.

She looks at my lap, taking her heels off before climbing over. I watch as she straddles me, her red dress riding up to just below her ass. I place my hands on either side of her hip. It's hard not to appreciate the view of her straddling me.

A view so pleasant that I couldn't control what was going on in my jeans, and I'm positive she felt it beneath her. *Remember, he's far from shy.*

Our breathing becomes staggered, and our eyes lock back to one another.

I reply, "You had a choice. You changed the path of your family's bloodline. You are stronger than you think, and so many admire you—including me."

She runs her hands above my chest, her fingers tracing along my neck. A smile graces her face. " I appreciate you so much, Theo. You don't understand how much I needed you in my chaotic life."

I give her ass a light squeeze. "I needed you just as bad, if not more, my little criminal."

She reaches around, grabs my hands, and pulls them to the front of her. She then places a single kiss on the palm of my left hand, never breaking eye contact. "Now show me the fingers that you pricked yesterday," she commands.

I lift my index and middle finger, never saying a word. I observe as she runs her fingertips over the small red spots, giving each one a quick, sensual peck. Her lips are so soft against my skin. I run my fingers over her bottom lip, feeling her warm, staggered breath against them.

Her mouth opens, and she slides her tongue across my index. Before I can process what she's physically doing to me, she sticks both fingers in her mouth, sucking them in an up-and-down motion.

Holy shit, this is hot. She keeps her half-lidded eyes on me as she runs her tongue around my fingers. I'm seconds from taking her right here in this car; this is torture.

A wicked smile plays along her face as she removes my fingers and then leans in, putting her mouth against my ear and whispering, "As badly as I want you right here, I'm dying for you to show me your bedroom." A deep growl resonates from within my throat, echoing the primal instinct that has awakened in me.

We are two desperate flames, flickering with intensity, each filled with the potential to ignite an entire house, consuming everything in an inferno of passion and chaos.

Theo

CHAPTER 22

Leo greets us at the door when we walk in, his tail hitting everything in his path. He's so happy to see Olive again. I watch him as he circles around her, searching for Lottie.

Olive gives him generous head pats before scoping out the living room. Her eyes trail around until they reach me. I can see the determination in her expression. No more waiting; this is it. I have dreamed about this for a long time, and we are here in the moment now.

I lead her to my bedroom, fully shutting the door behind us. Olive slowly walks over to the bed, running her fingers along the linens. She turns to face me as she sits on the end of the bed, patting beside her for me to join. I walk towards the bed, unbuttoning my shirt. Her eyes trail down my body, then back up, watching as I slowly remove each button.

She runs her teeth over her bottom lip. "I've admired how pleasant you look in your plain t-shirts but seeing you tonight in a black button-up really caused dirty thoughts to run through my mind."

I click my tongue, unable to control the grin her comment gave me. "I'm thrilled to know that I'm not the only one having dirty thoughts." I pause right in front of her. She leans back on the bed, propping up on her hands.

She scans my body until her eyes meet mine.

"My question for you, Olive, is, what about your dreams?"

She tilts her head up at me and replies, "What about them?"

I lean down, placing my hands on her thighs, sliding them up to where the bottom of her dress now sits right below her ass. "Do you ever dream about me?" I growl.

Her cheeks slightly redden against her tan complexion. She hesitates at first, then admits, "Yes, often." I instantly feel my dick harden beneath my jeans. *No more waiting.*

I motion for her to scoot back onto the bed; she doesn't ask questions as she slides back, now lying flat.

I remove my shirt and throw it on the floor. Her lips are slightly parted as I climb onto the bed, hovering over her. I lean down, using my hands for support, and kiss her exposed neck. I can feel her pulse increasing beneath my lips.

I bring my mouth to her ear and whisper, "I have dreamed about you since the night I met you. And touched myself to the thought of you." She lets out a long, breathy exhale. I bring my gaze back to her just inches away. "What do you think about that, my spicy Olive?"

She slides her tongue across her top teeth and lip. "I think I need you to show me," she rasps.

I laugh through my nose. "Good answer, darling."

I trail kisses down her neck, stopping below her collarbone. I twirl my finger around the straps of her red dress before clenching them with my fingers. "May I?"

Without a verbal response, she places her hands on top of mine and slowly pulls the straps down, over her shoulders, and down to her stomach. She then lifts her ass, allowing me to slide the dress completely off of her. I pause momentarily, taking in the naked view of Olive Sage Landers. *She's so fucking perfect, from head to toe.*

And just as I had imagined, she isn't wearing panties. I watch her chest rise and fall, long, wavy, ash-brown hair resting on her chest, reaching down below her perky breasts. She is a masterpiece that became my obsession. *And to think she is all mine.*

My mind goes back to our intimate moment under the pier, the taste of her on my fingers, and how it made me crave her even more. I hover over the top of her, planting sensual kisses along her collarbone, moving down to her breasts. I start at her left nipple, circling it with my tongue; I feel it quickly harden beneath my touch. Her breaths come in quick gasps now. I lift my gaze to meet hers; she watches me closely, her mouth slightly agape.

I continue my path further down, her smooth, toned stomach covered in goosebumps with each kiss I left behind. I reach down to her inner thigh, giving a gentle nip; she lets out a hiss. I position myself so that I am on my stomach, between her thighs. I wrap my arms around her legs. This feels very familiar and is exactly where I want to be.

Seeing her bare and vulnerable before me sends sheer pleasure through my veins. I need to taste her because this is no longer a dream I'm living in, and the anticipation is building at my core. I sense that it's building for her too. I kiss right above her lady parts, looking up as I do.

Olive's head falls back on the bed. The way she reacts to my every touch makes me wonder if fuckface ever focused on making her feel good. I quickly remove the thought of him touching her.

That's okay; I have every intention of making sure her sexual desires are met tonight.

I position myself just where I want to be. I've never considered a female's sex to be beautiful, but goddamn, Olives is perfect. I lick my lips, preparing to devour her.

I bring my eyes back up to hers. "Can I taste you, Olive?"

She looks down at me nervously, sucking in her bottom lip. Then she gives me a slow, approving nod. I no longer hesitate. I slide my tongue up her center, and she instantly bucks her hips upward, letting out a loud yelp.

I grip her legs tighter to keep her lower half positioned. Once again, I run my tongue through her center, hitting right where intended. Loud moans flow from her lips, which in return causes me to grunt against her sex. *Tonight is about her.*

I continue to caress her with my tongue, applying pressure with each fixed stroke, sucking her throbbing clit into my mouth. I feel her body shudder. *She's already so close to coming undone for me.*

Boys often create a façade to please girls, proclaiming their ability to meet any female sexual needs. Meanwhile, those same girls are laughing with their best friends about how so and so failed miserably in the pleasure department. Not all, but most women fake their orgasm. Either out of feeling a sliver of pity for the cocky fuck that just raw dogged all the wrong places or just to avoid an awkward conversation afterward.

Learning a woman's body is quite simple, really. There are three things to focus on: body language, pace, and location. Once you grasp the concept of each and their importance to the female body, you'll gain access to all their sexual needs. If you go into it only thinking about your pleasure, you'll surely get a woman who's a good actor in the bedroom.

I can't enjoy myself if my partner is faking it through. I need her in it with me. And a real man makes his girl feel good, and right now, all I'm focused on is catering to Olive. I want her entire body convulsing when I'm done with her. And I am confident that I'll get her there.

Olive's hands move to my hair as I continue to ravish her clit with my tongue. I remove my right arm from her thigh, curling my middle finger inside her. Her tight pussy clenches to my finger. I start with slow, deep pumps, clicking my tongue on her center in a beautiful rhythm. Her breathing pattern is fully unhinged now; I look up, witnessing her eyes rolling back as she chews her bottom lip aggressively. *I could cum from the sight of it.*

I can feel her tightening around my finger, showing she is close to her release. I slowly slide my finger out, and a small whimper escapes her lips. I sit up on my knees, maintaining eye contact with her. She observes as I unbutton my jeans. I can't wait any longer; I need to feel her around my dick.

I slide off the bed, walking over to my nightstand to retrieve a condom. Olive props up on her arms, still out of breath. "We don't need one of those," she states hoarsely.

I peer over to her with a questionable look.

"I got on birth control a couple of weeks ago. I wanted to be prepared for if we ever made it to this point. I-I wanted our first time to be real." *Gods, this woman makes my knees weak.*

I can't hide the devilish grin that stretches across my lips. That means she got on it before the beach trip. *My little sneaky girl.*

"Are you sure?" I murmur, brows furrowing.

She looks up at me, and the fire in her eyes almost steals my breath. "I have never felt so sure in my life, Theo." With those words, all I feel is starvation deep in my bones.

My pants and boxers fall to the floor beneath my feet. I wrap my hand around my hardened length, stroking it gently as I approach the bed.

Olive keeps her eyes on my movement, sucking in her swollen bottom lip as I climb onto the bed. Sitting up on my knees, I spread her legs, coming in between them. I hover over her once more, cupping her ample breast in my palms before stealing her mouth and sliding my tongue between her lips. She moans heavily in my mouth as we steal each other's air.

My dick rubs along her sensitive bud, causing her to arch her lower back. I can feel that she is soaked for me. When our lips are released, our eyes bore into each other, and I see a reflection of us both. There is so much lust, but mostly, I see love. We both have wanted this for so long.

"Are you ready for me, Olive?" I breathe.

She anxiously nods her head before placing her hands on either side of her head. I position my dick at her entrance, then brace my arms on the bed. I slowly thrust forward, feeling my tip stretch her entrance. She throws her hand over her mouth, muffling a cry.

I push in a little further, already feeling pressure down there. *Holy fuck, she's so tight.*

She keeps her hand over her mouth with her eyes sealed shut. I steady myself and grab her hand, removing it from her mouth. She opens her eyes to look up at me.

"I want to hear you scream for me, Olive," I murmur.

I then pin both of her hands together above her head and thrust all the way in, stretching her more. She screams out. A loud howl fumbles from my throat. She follows suit, not holding back the pleasure she is enduring.

I continuously roll my hips, giving her my full length, ensuring I hit every wall inside of her. "Fuck, you're so tight around me," I grunt out.

Olive wraps her legs around my back, thrusting her hips into mine. *She is so captivating.* I increase my speed, pounding in and out of her greedily. Every nerve throughout my body has heightened. I let her hands go and wrapped mine around her petite waist, slamming myself into her repeatedly.

"Oh my God, Theo," she mewls. Her legs shake vigorously around me, and I feel the pressure building inside me. My vision is getting fuzzy; this is pure ecstasy with her.

"You are mine, baby. Do you understand?" She nods her

head up and down. "Say it," I growl.

She breathlessly retorts, "I am yours."

I quickly grab her and sit back on my knees, bringing her to my lap, never pulling out of her. Her arms naturally wrap around my neck.

I love the way her hips dip and meet her plump ass. I'm savoring every second with her. I grab her bottom with my hands and start rolling her hips back and forth. We both moan in sync. The way her pussy has me in a chokehold it feels too damn good. I could live inside of her forever.

Olive throws her head back, sweat beading along her hairline. Sliding my hands up the sides of her stomach, I dig my fingers in slightly, and with no remorse, I bounce her up and down. Olive adds more weight and follows along, slamming her ass onto me.

The sound of our heated bodies molding together sends me over the edge. I feel her body trembling, her insides pulsating around my throbbing dick.

"Fuck, Theo!" she moans, her orgasm crashing through her. Pleasure consumes me entirely, and I let out a low, heavy growl as I come undone inside her.

We ride out our rapture together like two avalanches, growing stronger and destroying everything in their path. She eventually slumps over in my lap, her lungs needing air. My dick jerks inside her as we both climb down from the highest mountaintop. My vision slowly clears as I come back to level ground.

I rub her back softly, placing her long, sweat-drenched hair over one of her shoulders. I kiss her shoulder blade, feeling her fire-hot skin against my lips. I slowly fall back on the bed, pulling her against my chest. Our hearts pound viciously against one another. I hold her tightly, never wanting to let her go.

I don't know how much time passes, but we say nothing; we just lay in silence, reminiscing what we both know was more than just a fuck. We made love to each other. And it's the realest fucking thing I've ever felt.

Olive
CHAPTER 23

"Okay, so how big was it?" Danielle chimes as she jumps onto the couch like an overly excited toddler.

"Oh my God, Danielle! Why are you so obsessed with dick size?"

She looks at me like I just kicked her dog. "Um, Hello! Because size matters, bitch!"

I roll my eyes dramatically, making sure she sees them roll to the back of my head.

She huffs at me intently. "I'm already pissed that you waited this long to come clean about all of your scandalous pleasures. So spit it out, Olive Sage."

I cut my eyes at her before responding, "Okay, I won't

lie; his size was intimidating. I definitely felt like a virgin again, but I took it like a champ," I finally confess. I stick my tongue on the inside of my cheek, trying to suppress the smile tempting to form.

Danielle scoffs at me. "You little slut bag!"

I playfully swat at her arm. A guilty grin covers my face. "He definitely made Noah's look equivalent to a pinky toe."

Her eyes bulge before she lifts her chin, nodding profusely. "Well, we lucked up with two friends carrying full arms between their legs. GO US!"

My mouth almost falls to the floor. I, on instinct, shove Danielle's arm, causing her to fumble off the couch onto the living room floor.

"You mother fuck, you!" she yells. I don't even attempt to hide my face.

Laughter fills my lungs and pours out from deep in the pit of my stomach. Before I can stop her, she reaches up, yanking my arm and causing me to roll onto the floor beside her. Actually, knocking the breath out of me. We both join in together; loud belly laughter echoes through our apartment. Lottie runs over, taking turns licking our faces. How did I get so lucky to have this annoying bitch as my best friend?

Another week has passed, and yes, I hesitated to tell Danielle. Why? Because I knew she would have a trillion questions to drill me with. And I just wanted to soak in it for a little. I may have also enjoyed Theo and I having our own little secrets.

I figured it was best to tell her everything in one sitting. Maybe that was the wrong thing to do, considering she's my best friend, but she actually handled it better than I expected.

And for that, I am fucking thankful.

Last weekend has been heavy on my mind. Theo exceeded my expectations in the bedroom; the experience still blows me away. I hate to bring up Noah because, well, fuck him, but seriously the comparison is the polar opposite. Something changed inside of me that night with Theo. I felt it deep in the vessels of my fragile heart. He showed me what I think to be passion, as bat shit as that may sound.

It wasn't just a hookup for us. And when it was over, we held each other in silence. And I swear to you, places that were empty inside me bit by bit filled with pieces of him. I could have laid on his chest all night.

Theo called me earlier this week, saying his mom was dying to meet me. As wonderful as that sounded, my stomach dropped to my ass. I became a stuttering mess, and it took him calming me down over the phone and reminding me it wasn't a big deal. He let me know they had invited us for dinner this weekend, which only increased my anxiety. But I didn't have it in me to say no. So here I am now, sitting in front of my full-body mirror, letting my mind self-sabotage.

So many racing thoughts storm through my mind. What if they don't like me? Will that end things between Theo and me? What if his mom senses my brokenness and refuses to have me around Emma? That would cut me deep. *Okay, deep breaths, Olive.*

Everything is going to be fine. I breathe in and out, slowly focusing back on my task.

My outfit is simple but classy. I didn't want to overdress, but I also didn't want to look like I just crawled out of bed. I want them to see that I can be presentable but also come as me, nothing more. I'm wearing a mauve button blouse with a pair of my favorite faded high-waisted jeans that slightly flare at the bottom. Lastly, I pair it with my white sneakers.

My hair is down, but its natural wave didn't want to cooperate with me, so I added some loose beach curls to give it more volume. My makeup is subtle; I applied a small amount of mascara and a dab of brown eyeshadow to enhance my eyes. My cheekbones are lightly dusted with a neutral pink blush, and my lips have a slight gloss.

Just as I'm walking out of my room, I hear my phone pinging on the bed. It's an incoming call from my mom. I haven't talked to her in a while; the last I heard from her, she sounded belligerent on the phone. It took all of me not to curse at her, but I held back and let her finish her slurred sentence.

Closing my eyes, I take a deep breath, preparing myself for whatever she's calling for because rarely does she just check in on her youngest daughter.

"Hey, Mom," I say dully.

"Hey baby, how are you?"

"I'm doing alright, how about you?"

"Oh, well, I'm okay. I tried to call Nora a couple of times, but she's not answering my calls."

"What were you calling her for?"

"Well, I-I wanted to check in on her, but also uh… my power is off."

"How long has your power been off?"

"Just for a few days. Is there anyway you could get it back on for me? I just didn't have the funds this month."

"Okay, Mom, yeah, I'll do that now."

"Oh honey, thank you so much. I promise it won't happen again."

"Sounds good, Mom."

"I love you, baby. Come see me soon, okay?"

"I will. I love you, too."

I hang up quickly, letting out a dramatic huff. I swear I can feel steam shooting from the top of my head like a burning teakettle on the stove. I aggressively toss my phone back onto the bed and head for the kitchen.

Danielle is already waiting there with two shots of tequila in her hand. Her lips are pressed into a firm line. She definitely heard the conversation with Mom. She quickly extends her hand out, offering me a shot. *Don't need to ask me twice.*

I grab the shot glass and throw it back like it's 1990 again. The warm liquid travels down my throat, giving a delicious burn as it seeps into my pulsing bloodstream.

I can sense the tension in my shoulders slowly dwindling.

"Nothing an ole shot can't fix, right, bestie?" Danielle blurts out.

I purse my lips. "I don't know if anything can fix the headache that woman gives me."

Danielle looks at me with understanding written on her face. "I know, just don't let it ruin your dinner with Theo's family."

I give her an agreeable nod.

Danielle's lips curl up. "And maybe a good twiddle of the bean later will ease some tension, too."

I scoff loudly at her comment. Danielle tries to hurry, pouring her shot into her mouth. Her mistake is immediately looking back at me. I burn a hole between her eyes with my fiery glare.

Danielle's cheeks blow out with the liquid still in her mouth. She seals her lips tight but gags from the taste of the tequila. Within seconds, tequila shoots out of her mouth onto the kitchen island. I laugh under my breath, "Serves you right."

Danielle says nothing but doesn't hesitate to throw up her middle finger.

I admire the property as we pull into Theo's parents' driveway. Every tree, bush, and plant has been meticulously cared for. Various flowers bloom around the foundation, while green vines elegantly twist around the beams that support the porch and roof. Woven hand baskets hang from the porch, each overflowing with colorful flowers.

I spot a cherrywood swing on the left side of the porch. It's clear that they have a strong sense of landscaping; their yard is immaculate. And I can only imagine how beautiful the inside is.

We park the car near the garage entrance. And now my nerves are kicking in again, and I can't stop myself from rubbing my hands together profusely. My heart is sucker punching against my heavy chest. If Theo listened closely enough, he could probably hear how aggressively my heart is pounding.

He adjusts in his seat and faces me, reaching over to clench my moving hands. Within seconds, I can already feel my nervous system ease off.

I swivel my head in his direction, catching him staring at me with an admirable glare. Gosh, this man is beautiful to look at. Just a glance at him calms my rapid heart. It almost makes me eager to get in this house and meet the two who created this masterpiece they call their son.

He actually changed up his attire today. To be honest, I love his plain T's, but today, his dirty blond locks sit neatly under a tan ball cap, swooping across his forehead and reaching above his brow. He's wearing a thin, short-sleeved tan flannel with white pinstripes. He has it completely unbuttoned, showing off a white tank underneath. I can see his tasty muscles flexing beneath it, which causes me to squeeze my legs together multiple times on the ride here.

I'm tempted to reach over and unbutton his pants to show him what he's doing to my insides. But that would be extremely rude to do in his parent's driveway, and it definitely would not be the first impression I'm hoping for.

Theo grabs my chin, stealing my attention back from my intrusive thoughts. He smirks at me. "You can't stay out of that pretty little head of yours, can you?"

I look into his stunning eyes, pondering on my response. "No," I admit.

He chuckles. "You're going to be fine, babe; you're easy to love," he croons.

Butterflies flap their wings viciously in my stomach. *Damn, this man and his effective words.*

He guides me through the garage area and up the stairs to the door. Before we enter, Theo turns to me and kisses my flushed cheek. "Just be yourself, babe," he says calmly.

I give him a forced smile, realizing that just maybe I'm panicking for no reason. What could go wrong?

As we step into his parents' home, a delightful aroma fills the air, making my stomach growl in response. Something smells absolutely delicious. We walk through a small hallway, and I notice a bathroom on the right. Just a little further ahead, there is a staircase on the left leading up to another level, and at the end of the hall, there looks to be a bedroom. Finally, we make a right leading into the kitchen area.

A petite woman, whom I assume is Theo's mother, stands in the kitchen, tending to several pots on the stove. The delicious aroma of her cooking fills the air.

She quickly notices us. "Oh, here's the beautiful girl that Theo can't stop raving about!" she exclaims as she walks toward us. I glance at Theo, his lips pressed together.

He murmurs with a tight smile, "Hey, Mom."

She gives him a loving hug, followed by a kiss on the cheek.

Before I can react, she pulls me in for a warm hug and gently rubs my back. To my surprise, I accepted her warmth and returned the gesture.

Eventually, she pulls back, her hands resting on the tops of my arms. "It is so nice to meet you, Olive. I've heard wonderful things about you. I'm sure Theo has mentioned my name—I'm Ruby, but you can call me Momma Rivers if you'd like!" she says, her smile genuine.

"Yes, I'm happy to be here and meet you all," I reply.

Ruby is stunning, and I can see where Theo gets some of his good looks. Her hair is almost the same color as his, though maybe a shade lighter. Her curly blonde hair falls just above her shoulders, and she wears a turquoise blouse that complements her lovely greenish-blue eyes.

Ruby leads me into the living room area, with Theo following behind us. Sitting in a recliner is a man who I believe is Theo's dad.

The resemblance is striking. His short dark brown hair is peppered with gray, and when he stands up, he's slightly shorter than Theo. I could have sworn Theo resembled his mother, but now that I see his dad, apart from the dark hair, it feels like I'm staring at an older version of him. The Rivers clearly have good fucking genes.

"Hey, old man!" Theo calls out as they pull each other into a bear hug. I can see that they share a close father-son bond, and it warms my heart. Theo's dad turns to me with the same crooked grin that his son has. "You must be the gorgeous Olive we've heard so much about?"

I return his smile and nod in agreement. "That's me."

"We're glad to have you over for dinner. My name is Lucas, and believe it or not, I'm Theo's dad," he says, his sarcastic comment making me chuckle. I now see where Theo gets his sarcasm from. So far, things are going well, and honestly, the anxiousness I felt prior to walking in has subsided tremendously. His family has made me feel comfortable being here thus far.

I don't know why I worked myself up over nothing. I was mainly worried that his parents wouldn't accept me. I have no idea what Theo has told them about my family, and I hope they don't ask because that could make things really awkward for me. It's obvious that this is a well-put-together family filled with love and calmness—the literal opposite of what I have.

"Is Emma in the bonus room?" Theo asks.

Ruby nods in response. "She has been really excited to meet you, Olive!"

Just those simple words bring a smile to my face. Although I was nervous about this visit, I was genuinely looking forward to meeting little Emma.

As we head up the stairs to the bonus room, I pause for a moment to look at the photos lined up along the cream-colored walls. I spot a picture of Theo wearing a red Christmas sweater. He appears to be around three or four. His hair was once snow-blond and perfectly combed over on his little head. He was the cutest little towhead.

Next to it, I see a picture of a little girl with straight, silky, auburn hair that reaches just below her ears. She wears a small blue bow paired with a cream sequin dress. Her eyes are an emerald green, and tiny freckles dot her cheeks and the bridge of her nose. She is absolutely adorable. This must have been Emma when she was younger.

Upstairs, we spot her lying on the floor on her stomach, focused on her task, while a movie plays on the TV. Colored pencils and markers were scattered all around her. She doesn't notice us, which gives Theo the perfect opportunity to scare her.

I stand nearby with a smirk, watching as he sneaks up behind her and grabs her legs. She screams loudly, flailing her legs in every direction. I cover my mouth to stifle the laugh that escapes my throat.

"Theo!" she squeals. She jumps up from the floor, and he scoops her up, squeezing her tightly in his arms.

"There's my little squirt," he murmurs. I can tell he really loves that little girl.

Emma peeks over his shoulder at me, and something in her eyes lights up. I give an awkward wave, followed by a wide smile. She has grown a lot since the picture I just looked at; her hair now reaches a little below her shoulders.

She finally wriggles her way out of Theo's strong arms, sticking her tongue out at him as she paces towards me. My nerves are kicking in again, and I don't know what to do with my hands, so I plant them flat on the sides of my legs.

She stands in front of me, staring into my eyes. At first, I wondered if we were having a staring contest, so I continued our stare-off, never blinking.

After a minute of silence, hearing nothing but my heart beating, she finally opens her mouth to speak. "Hi, I'm Emma. You are really pretty, " she chirps.

I can't hide the ear-to-ear smile her comment gives me. "Well, hi, Emma. My name is Olive, and you're really pretty, too." Her eyes sparkle with joy.

She lunges forward, grabbing me in a hug, with my arms still pinned on either side of me.

"Do you want to see my drawings?" she exclaims excitedly.

I look at Theo, who is wearing a smug look. I can tell this moment means the most to him. It makes me want to run over to him and give him the deepest, most passionate kiss. That will have to wait until later, though.

I look back, down at little Emma. "I would love to see your drawings!"

Spending time with Emma gives me hope for her future. Theo and his parents rescued her early on from a life filled with trauma and heartbreak. I know that one day if she hasn't already, she will have questions about her biological parents. No matter how well the Rivers treat her, it's human nature to want to know. She will probably wonder why they didn't love her enough to get better. Those same thoughts echo in my mind. Even at nineteen, I still don't have answers regarding my own, and I doubt I ever will.

I believe the Rivers will provide her with the answers she needs and deserves. They will be there to comfort her whenever she needs it and will also give her the space to process her feelings. Most importantly, she will be in the place that has been her home for as long as she can remember. For that, I am truly thankful.

After our late dinner, Ruby and Lucas walked with us to Theo's car; the evening, to my surprise, went very well. Ruby had prepared the most delicious chicken and dumplings. I felt embarrassed asking for seconds, but thankfully, I wasn't the only one who did. Theo mentioned that chicken and dumplings were his mom's specialty and that she wanted to make them for me to hopefully "seal the deal," which made me laugh.

Sitting at their dining room table was a real eye-opener. It was so normal for them to share a thoughtful meal together. You could tell it was something they had done as a family for many years. What felt traditional to them seemed out of place for me, but they made me feel welcome. It was as if I had known them for years, and I felt like a part of the family for the first time in a long while.

Ruby showed a lot of interest in getting to know Nora; she even begged me to bring her over for dinner soon so that she could meet her. I let her know I would talk to her about it. But I left out the part where I hadn't told Nora about Theo yet. I swear I'll have the conversation with her soon. I know Nora would adore Emma just as I do now.

We all exchange hugs and say our goodbyes. Ruby squeezes me extra tight while reminding me I can come over and visit anytime I want. I appreciate her. She has a beautiful soul, and she and Lucas have raised two good humans. And I can see why Theo is such a gentleman.

As my hand reaches for the car door, I hear Emma yelling my name. She runs out of the garage with something in her hand. "Here, I made this for you!" she strains out from running so fast. She hands me a piece of paper.

I flip it over to find what looks like a picture of me and Theo holding hands, with a big heart over our heads.

I feel a slight ache in my throat and maybe even tears building behind my corneas. I don't know what emotion is taking over me right now, but I think it's a mixture of the wholesome his family has made me feel and how Emma has shown that maybe I'm not so bad of a person after all.

Emma gestures for me to lean down. She puts her hands around her mouth, blocking so no one can see. "I can tell Theodore really likes you," she whispers.

I purse my lips, fighting the urge to smile, knowing this moment is too precious. With a burst of warmth in my chest, I pull her in for a brief, tight hug, whispering my gratitude for the sweet picture she made me. It's a small gesture, but it means so much.

As we make our way out of their driveway, I take a moment to glance back. The three of them stand there, waving their goodbyes with bright smiles. It's a heartwarming scene that makes me feel surprisingly light.

In that fleeting moment, a wave of emotion washes over me. For the first time, I sense that life is gently returning the kindness I've longed for after enduring so much pain and hardship. It's a refreshing feeling as if the universe finally acknowledges my struggles and offers me a glimmer of hope. I needed Theo and his family in my life.

Olive
CHAPTER 24

"See, that wasn't so bad, was it?" Theo teases, squeezing my leg. I run my eyes along his forearm up to his bicep, watching his muscles tighten. My legs instantly squeeze shut. It's a new reflex I've unintentionally created for myself called the "Theo effect."

And I don't know. There is something about a man kicked back, driving onehanded with their other hand lax on a female's leg. And this is not just any man. It's Theo Ace fucking Rivers. I'm in a live movie right now, cruising in a hot guy's Corvette with music playing and the night sky swallowing us whole.

Sometimes, I doubt myself, wondering how a man of his stature could be so interested in me. I'm not saying I'm some hideous creature, but there are so many beautiful women out there. It still baffles me he has chosen someone like me—the girl who grew up too fast in a small trailer with a dysfunctional mother and a protective big sister.

I may never fully understand, but I must show him how much I appreciate him and his presence. Never have I wanted to jump a man's bones like I want to right now. Ignoring Theo's comment, I take my seat belt off and angle my body to face him.

"What are you doing?" he asks. I choose to stay silent and not give him an answer.

I focus on my task, leaning over the middle console. I run my left hand up his leg; even with his jeans on, I can feel his length resting along his thigh under the fabric. I can feel it jerk beneath my touch when my hand grazes over where it lays. It sends shivers up my arms, causing the hair on the back of my neck to rise.

Theo keeps his focus on the road, gripping the steering wheel so tight that I can see the white of his knuckles even in the dark. His right hand has now moved from my thigh to behind my lower back.

I finally stop at the zipper of his jeans, looking up at him. He tilts his head towards me, his expression firm. But when I glimpse at his sexy, light eyes, it's almost as if they're daring me to continue. And one thing about me is that I've never been one to back down from a dare.

I bring my attention back to his lap, carefully unzipping his jeans. Theo pulls his hand from my lower back, and I examine it as he reaches between the openings of his jeans. He leans forward while adjusting his jeans and boxers. My mouth fills with saliva, and I am ready to pounce and claim him in my mouth.

His impressive length springs out of his jeans, causing my pulse to quicken. He wraps his right hand around his width, stroking himself slowly. Even with his vast hand clinging on, it does not hide his intimidating size. Never in my life have I seen anything so mouth-watering.

Theo's head falls back onto the headrest. This is a whole new level of sexy, and the visual he's generously giving me is now seared into my brain.

For a moment, my mind travels back to our little hot excursion in the ocean and how challenging it was to take him fully in my mouth. I've faced difficult challenges my entire life, and this one, I have to admit, is my favorite so far.

I position myself as best as I can with the little space provided in this sports car. My lips are now just inches from where I want them. I lap my needy tongue gently around his smooth tip. Theo sucks in a breath, stilling his hand movement. I take it as an opportunity to fill my mouth with as much of him as possible. I slide my lips tight around his hard length until I reach where his hand still holds firm.

"Fuck, Olive," he rumbles.

I continue my pattern, purposely slamming my lips against his hand. He finally lets go, firmly wrapping his hand around my neck.

Now, with Theo's grip, in one quick motion, I slam myself as far down as I can take. His large tip reaches the opening in my throat. Tears build in the corners of my eyes from the sudden force.

A loud growl leaves his mouth, only fueling the already

blazing fire deep inside me. I hollow out my cheeks, loving the feel of his silky skin sliding beneath my lips. Our moans, mixed with wet slurping noises, flood the car.

I quickly wrap both hands around the base of him, creating a perfect hand motion to match the sucking and sliding of my mouth movements. Tears stream down my face as I continue to consume his massive length.

"You keep sucking my dick like that, and I'm going to wreck this fucking car," Theo strains out through closed teeth. The sound of him struggling to hold his composure sends immediate pleasure down my untouched center. Desperately, I push my hips forward in my jeans, searching for friction on my sensitive spot.

Theo's fingers lace through my hair as I pick up speed. I can feel my lips becoming pleasantly numb from the brutal suction I have created around him. He pushes and pulls on my hair. Deep, uneven breaths slide from his parted mouth as he relentlessly fucks the back of my throat. Spit, mixed with tears, races down my chin.

I feel the car slow down, and I can tell we've pulled into somewhere. There's no way we're back at the apartments. I concentrate back on my good deed; I know he is close to his release. Salty remnants hit my taste buds; I can't stop the needy moan that vibrates off his dick.

Theo clutches my hair, halting my movements. I feel the car make a hard turn. Theo then slams on the brakes and puts the car in park. Before I can ask where we are, he has adjusted his seat. He pushes my head down gently, rubbing my swollen lips on the head of his length. Deep, lustful moans rush from his throat.

He breathes out, "Open wide for me, baby."

I lick my mouth one good time and follow his order. He continues his grip on my hair, pushing my head down with force, then pulling it back up to where my lips clamp onto his pulsing tip.

I join in, moving my head with the rhythm of his hand, swirling my tongue around his velvet-like skin. He slams himself down my throat; I'll be feeling that tomorrow. I don't even care; I want all of him in my mouth right now.

His grip tightens on my hair, causing a slight sting on my scalp. I already know mascara has stained my cheeks, and that's what I get when forcing something in my mouth that is not meant to fit. Theo thrusts his hips up, adding more blunt force into my abused throat. Delicious growls fill the air, filling my insides with pleasure. The sounds leaving this man's mouth are feral and hot as fuck.

He pumps his hips up at the same time he forces my mouth down onto him, causing his length to go further down my throat. "FUUUCK!" he growls.

Theo stops, keeping me still as he floods my throat with his release.

The taste of warm, salty seed fills my tastebuds, taking me back to the ocean and his pleasant taste.

He lets go of my hair, rubbing his hand down my back. I sit up and swallow down his remains. I sit back, looking up at him. He tilts his head towards me and lays against the headrest. His mouth is parted as he catches his breath. Those contagious blue eyes burn into mine, and I can almost see the dying fire pick back up. His loose, damp, dirty blond curls peek under his cap, sweat beading around them.

Theo reaches over and grabs my head, and our mouths clash together. His tongue explores mine, and within seconds, my tired tongue catches a second wind, matching his talented movement. We breathe each other in, savoring the taste of one another. I want more; no, I need him inside me to fill the creeping distance between us.

As our desperate mouths pull apart, he greedily sucks my bottom lip into his mouth, nipping at it before releasing me. His full lips curl into an intimidating grin, his sapphire eyes never leaving mine. "I love that I can still taste myself on your tongue. You took me so well, like the good girl you are."

My sensitive center sings a pleasurable tune at his sinful words.

Is it selfish that I want to take him in every way possible until my body is limp and worn from overexertion? Distracted by his presence, I didn't realize that we were sitting in what looked like an undeveloped neighborhood. Bulldozers sit along dirt lots, and there is not a person in sight.

I look back at Theo, who's now opening his door to get out. I watch as he walks around the front of his car, his dick still hard and exposed.

He reaches my door, slinging it open with force. "Get out of the car, Olive," he demands.

I suck in my lips, making eye contact with the gift he carries below his waist. I quickly get out, standing before him; I anxiously bring my eyes up to his. His long length nearly touched my stomach.

Theo chews on his bottom lip as his brows pull together in a serious manner. "Take your pants off," he murmurs.

I pause for a second, making sure I heard him correctly.

I look around us, making sure we are, in fact, the only people here. The only light available is from Theo's headlights and one streetlight at the bottom of this massive cul-de-sac. I place my hands on the center of my jeans' button.

He steps a centimeter closer, his tip grazing the bottom of my blouse. "What's wrong, Olive? Are you worried someone will hear you screaming out for me?"

I suck in all the air surrounding me, swallowing it along with Theo's effective words. My legs clench together as I slowly unbutton and slide my jeans down my legs, leaving them lying on the pavement.

Theo scans below my waist, pleased to see I am bare beneath my jeans. A smirk plays across his edible lips. "There's my little criminal," he hums.

He then hoists me up, wrapping my legs around his stomach. I can feel his hard length rubbing against my bare ass. He easily carries me to the front of his car, laying me on the hood. A shriek leaves my throat. I was expecting the hood to be cold against my lower back, but it is pleasantly warm from the engine running.

He crouches down on his knees, wrapping his arms around my thighs and sliding me down to where my ass sits right on the end of the hood. He then places my legs on his shoulders. My breathing is unhinged at this point. This man causes me to lose all control of my body.

I look down at him, seeing his eyes focused on my bare center; he slides his tongue along his lips.

Instantly, I feel my arousal run down my crease. A deep growl leaves his chest. He runs his thumb through my center. My curious eyes stay glued to his movements. Helpless moans crawl from my mouth.

Theo leans in closer, examining the wetness on his thumb. His eyes closed for a moment while he licked away any evidence of me off his thumb. He shoots his eyes back between my legs. "Mmm, let me clean up this sweet mess for you." He then positions himself, wrapping his arms back around my thighs and using his hands to expose me fully.

He first plunges his thick tongue inside of me; in return, a dramatic screech jumps from my mouth. His lips are now suctioned to my sensitive spot. I can already feel the war between coming undone and passing out. He pulls his tongue from inside me and begins lapping it slowly around my sex, caressing every fragile nerve between my wobbly legs.

My head is buzzing from the ecstasy of Theo's talented tongue and mouth. In one swift movement, he unwraps his arms from my legs and grips underneath me, lifting my ass in the air and pulling me flush up against his shoulders. His mouth connects back to my center, devouring my throbbing clit.

Within seconds, my vision blackens, and the pressure shoots through my center so harshly that my body goes limp, and all I can do is ride out the pleasure that has consumed me fully. Theo kisses my inner thigh before gently scooting me back on the hood of the car. My weak legs dangle over the front as I regain my senses.

I blink my eyes profusely, trying to bring my total vision back. And what I see before me is like nothing I've ever seen in person or a movie. Theo now towers over me; his pants are down around his ankles. His hand holds firm to his massive size between his thighs. The look in his eyes is murderous, and honestly, I'd let him end me right now. He's already brutally stabbed me with his tongue, and I'm ready for whatever he wants to stab me with next. I am hoping it's with his dick.

We observe each other for a moment. This man is unreal. How was he so beautifully crafted? The car lights beam around his tall stature, shining in all the right places.

I can see the definition in every muscle along his arms and how his sharp jawline connects to his neck. I notice his firm Adam's apples slowly bobbing when he clenches his jaw. Screw a snack; this man is a full-course meal and some.

He scoots closer, grabbing my calves and placing the bottoms of my legs on his shoulders. He holds his length and runs it between my folds. I arch my back up from how sensitive it is down there from my orgasm. Theo smiles at my reaction as he rotates his ball cap, putting it on backward. It's one thing for a man to wear a hat, but it takes it to a different level when wearing it backward.

Cold chills travel down my body, causing my nipples to harden beneath my shirt and bra. From the look that he is giving me, I may end up leaving this neighborhood in a wheelchair once he's done with me.

Theo quickly lines himself up with my opening. I bite my bottom lip, preparing for the pressure of him stretching me. He slowly slides his generous tip inside of me, pulling the breath from my throat immediately. I watch his mouth fall open, his tongue skating across his bottom lip.

I feel so helpless and vulnerable right now. Theo is in complete control of both of our bodies. And I love that he likes to be in the driver's seat. Not only is he an expert driver, but he knows how to work all the essential gadgets.

And now, in minutes, I know he is about to drive me into oblivion.

I plant my hands onto the car's hood, preparing for his blunt entrance. He stays put, placing his strong hands above my knees for support. In an instant, his eyes go feral. He plunges forward, filling me completely.

We both gasp at the same time. My head falls back onto the hood.

He rolls his hips beautifully with each lubricious thrust. I can already feel another orgasm churning inside me. This one just might kill me because of its intensity. He slides his hands down the front of my thighs, keeping my legs firm on his broad shoulders.

He presses his hands flat onto my lower stomach, pushing my back flush to the hood.

My eyes follow his movements. He then bends his knees and slowly thrusts back inside me. This time, the feeling is more intense, like he's hitting a new wall inside me. My legs shake from the heaviness building quickly between my legs. Noises I've never heard before are leaving my mouth.

He picks up his speed, ramming every thick inch of himself deep inside me. "Gods, I love how tight your pussy wraps around me," he breathes out. His yummy words melt into my flushed skin. Through gritted teeth, he then mumbles, "Tell me, Olive, How does it feel to be fucked by a man?" My loud moans answer for me.

My vision becomes blurry again while my head buzzes from my fast-beating pulse. Theo stills himself inside me at his full length. He quickly slides me down and grabs me on either side of my waist, picking me up from the car's hood.

I place my arms behind me, using my hands to hold myself up on the hood.

He grips me tightly and relentlessly slams my body onto his. With how easy Theo makes this look, I feel light as a feather right now. My head instantly falls back behind my shoulders. Another orgasm slams through me like a raging tsunami. Our breathing is both uncontrolled and unnatural.

"That's it, baby, scream my name while you cum all around me," he chokes out.

I see nothing but stars now, and I'm not referring to the ones in the night sky above us. My entire body convulses uncontrollably. "Oh my god, Theo!" I cry out.

We both let out a drawn-out moan, coming undone together, grinding out our orgasm. Theo is a high I will never come down from ever again.

My arms give out underneath me, and he grabs me before I slam into the car. He gently lays me back against his hood. I pull my legs from his shoulders, allowing them to dangle again from the vehicle. My legs feel like Jell-O while my battered vagina pounds between my thighs. Theo hovers over top of me, propping up on his hands.

His mouth hangs breathless, and beads of sweat cling to the ends of his damp locks. He leans forward, planting kisses along my steamy neck.

He then motions for me to scoot over while he pulls his pants up and zips them. He walks to the driver's side, cutting off the car and headlights. I observe him, admiring the man who just drained my soul entirely, then graciously recharged it, bringing it back to life.

When he returns, he slides off his flannel, exposing more toned muscles, even those peaking beneath his white tank. He lays back on the hood, pulling me in to lay my head on his chest and my body fixed against his. He then places his flannel over top of my bare lower half, covering me perfectly.

His arm holds me tightly, pulling me close. The warmth of his muscular body envelops me, filling me with a sense of security and something else I can't quite identify.

Maybe one day, I'll be able to articulate the undiscovered feeling swirling within me, but for now, I'll simply embrace it.

The two of us are lying underneath an endless sky filled with twinkling stars. Tonight, the crescent moon shines brighter than ever. I rest my head on his toned chest, and for a moment, I close my eyes, feeling his steady heartbeat against my ear. This moment is real; Theo is real.

Olive

CHAPTER 25

"I can't believe I let you talk me into this shit," I scoff while gawking at myself in my body mirror. Danielle stands beside me, turned to the side, running her hands down her shimmery dress.

She clicks her tongue. "Well, maybe next time you won't keep secrets from your best friend. Plus, this is your chance to redeem yourself after running away from a guy you're now banging on the hood of cars."

I bore my eyes into her reflection in the mirror. It doesn't faze her as she continues examining her outfit. If we hadn't spent an hour fixing our hair for this stupid party, I'd tackle this cunt.

Instead, I bite my tongue and respond, "Funny, because

you're ramming his best friend any chance you get."

Danielle brings her bright eyes to mine in the mirror. "Damn straight I am, and I plan on sneaking off from the party tonight to do exactly that," she admits.

A dramatic sigh leaves my lips. "If you bang in Chase's truck, please stay clear of the backseat where my ass will be sitting."

Danielle curls her lips into her mouth for a moment. "It doesn't matter, bestie; we've already banged there several times."

Of course, they have. I pinch the bridge of my nose gently, trying to avoid messing up my makeup.

Danielle gives me an innocent smile, and I can't help the grin that takes over my mouth. "On a different note, we look freaking HOT!" she brags.

I shrug at her response but bring my eyes back to the mirror, staring at our reflections in awe. For a split second, I picture Danielle and I as kids playing dress up at her house.

Now, as adults, we are still playing dress up, but instead of dancing to The Backstreet Boys or filling our bellies with endless candy in the middle of the night. We're dressing up to go to a party to get shit-faced drunk and probably twerk to the Ying-Yang Twins.

I bring my attention back to us in the mirror. We outdid ourselves tonight, and we would take the medal home if there were a costume contest. Last weekend, after Theo brought me home from the family dinner and our innocent stroll through the new construction, Danielle was waiting on the couch for me like parents would do when their kids had a curfew and returned home past the allotted time.

She told me that Taylor was having a 1920's Gatsby party to celebrate her twenty-first birthday the following Saturday. She then proceeded to guilt-trip me into the four of us going together, using my "little secrets" as leverage. She had it all planned to bombard me as soon as I walked in the door.

Chase had already gotten on board and called Theo after he dropped me off. There was no way of me getting out of it. *And she wants to talk about being sneaky.*

We had six days to choose our outfits. Thank goodness for Amazon's two-day shipping with Prime! We had no idea what the boys had ordered for themselves, but we intentionally provided them with a detailed description of our dresses, hoping they would pick matching colors. I guess we'll find out soon if they passed the test.

My dress is made of black, sleeveless mesh covered in shimmering sequins. When the light hits, the sequins glimmer with different shades of blue and white, reminiscent of the night sky. The front features a deep V-cut that reveals just enough cleavage while fitting tastefully to my figure. The hem reaches just above my knees, and shiny black tassels hang at the seams, falling below my knees. I wear black fishnet tights that hug my legs and simple black heels. My hair is styled in tight curls that frame my face, and a black headband adorned with a glistening feather wraps around my hair.

Danielle has a similar dress, but hers is a bright gold garnished with shimmering gold tassels from top to bottom. The dress reaches mid-thigh and features a rounded neckline that reveals more cleavage than mine. She wears long black gloves extending above her elbows and dainty tasseled earrings cascading down her chin. Her shiny black hair is styled in a curled updo, resting at the nape of her neck and pinned on one side with diamond-shaped clips.

We both went all out on our makeup and took it seriously, following a tutorial on YouTube. We applied black sparkly eyeshadow with a golden color on the inner eyelids, dark eyeliner with mascara, and deep red lipstick. *We are the hottest Flapper bitches.* And I won't admit it to Danielle, but I'm a little excited about this party.

Maybe it's because things have been going well with Theo this past month. Or perhaps it's because the four of us are going on an adventure together. I don't know, but I actually feel like I have something to look forward to.

My phone pings from the dresser; it's Nora. I tried calling her yesterday, but she didn't answer or reply. Relief washes over me immediately when I see her name flash across my phone screen. Tomorrow is Jake's birthday, and I want to ensure she's okay. I 've been hoping to spend some time with her. It's his first birthday not here, and I can't imagine what she and Jake's parents are feeling.

As I snatch up my phone from the dresser, Danielle motions she will prepare some shots for us to pregame with before the boys arrive. *That's my best friend.*

I quickly answered my sister's call. "Hey, big sister!" I shouted into the speaker.

"Hey, Olive Oil. Sorry I missed your call yesterday," she rasps on the other end of the line.

"It's okay; I just wanted to see you for a little tomorrow only if you feel up to it." I

anxiously tap my fingers on my dresser.

Nora lets out a sigh. "Honestly, I plan to take it easy and spend some time with Michelle and Daniel, considering what day it'll be."

I nod my head as if she can see me. "Oh, I get it. Just know I'm here, okay?"

The phone line goes silent for a moment.

"I know you are. Let's see how I'm feeling after tomorrow. I could really use a day trip to the beach with my favorite little sister."

A smile touches my mouth. "Yes! Please! You tell me when, and we'll go!"

She laughs lightly. "So when did you plan on telling me about this boy you have the hots for?"

I hold my breath for a moment. *How the hell does she know about Theo?* "I-I was planning on it. I just didn't know if it was a little fling, that's all," I admit.

She snickers lightly through the speaker. "Uh-huh, it didn't seem like a little fling from the texts he sent the night I was there." I suck my lips into my mouth. I am such a fool. I should have just told Nora about him from the start.

"I'm sorry, I should have told you. I-I know you have a lot on your mind, and I didn't think it was important enough to tell you just yet." I pinch the bridge of my nose, wanting to shove my black heel up my own ass.

"Olive, you're important to me, and so is your happiness." She pauses momentarily. "Does he make you happy?"

I can't control the grin her question gives me. "He really does, Nora," I admit.

"Good, because I'd beat his ass if not."

I let out a giggle. "Oh, I know you would!"

Nora's laugh echoes through the speaker, causing warmth to flood my skin. *Her laugh is contagious.*

I trail back to the beach conversation. "I can't wait to blast Fleetwood Mac the whole way to the beach."

Nora snorts. "And scream every word of every song?" she asks.

"You fucking know it, sister." The phone line goes quiet for a moment. "Nora, please call me tomorrow if you need me. I'm here, okay?"

I can hear her shuffling around before she responds. "I know you are, and I will, I promise."

Relief washes over me. I hope she knows I will come straight to her if she needs my company. I'll do whatever it takes to distract her from the grief that is undoubtedly to consume her tomorrow.

"Okay, good. I love you so much."

"I love you too, little sister, to the moon and back."

I smile at my moon bracelet, wondering if she's still wearing hers. *I love you to the moon and far beyond the stars, Nora Ray.*

Is it wrong that I'm already slightly buzzed from the two shots Danielle and I took back to back? Honestly, It's a blessing right now. The tequila is drowning out some nagging nerves pricking at my skin. I haven't spoken to Taylor since seeing her at the housewarming party over a month ago. Where I'm sure she witnessed me hightail it the fuck out of there. And if she didn't, someone indeed did.

My goal tonight is to be on my best behavior—drunk… *but on my best behavior.* It's almost comical to think that the very reason I left last time was because of Theo and how intimidating he was. Now, here we are, going to where I ran away from him. *The irony is uncanny.*

My sweet fluff ball runs to the door, wagging her tiny pompom tail while barking excitedly. *The boys are here.* Danielle struts over to the door, careful not to sprain an ankle in her three-inch stilettos. I throw back my third shot, telling myself this is the last one, until having a drink at Taylor's place.

Danielle flings the door open, and what I see before me stops the burning liquid from rushing down my throat. Its consistency turns to honey, coating my insides with a warm, thick residue. Suddenly, I feel scorching hot from the inside out. I went from comfortably content to feeling stranded in the middle of a safari.

Chase is leaning against the door frame, licking his lips while eye fucking Danielle's presence. He wears slate gray suspenders with a matching bow tie. Underneath is a white long-sleeved button-up tucked into black slacks. His shaggy chestnut brown hair peeks from underneath a gray Fedora. He looks astoundingly handsome. *Danielle will definitely be ramming that tonight.*

Just as Chase enters the door, my eyes stay trained on Theo coming up behind him. For a moment, time stops, just like it did when I first laid eyes on him.

My legs feel like heavy weights are pulling them down, causing me to grip the kitchen island behind me. I quickly realize it's the weight of his existence, crowding my five senses. What I see before my eyes causes my insides to evaporate.

Theo strides through the door in slow motion, evocative

of a dramatic scene from a movie. He wears a three-piece black tweed suit, which includes a long jacket, fitted black slacks, and boots. On top of his head, he wears a flat cap. Dirty blond relaxed curls twirl around the sides and front of his cap. He looks like he was made for his outfit. *Could he look bad in any outfit? Doubtful.*

I feel like I am in a scene from Peaky Blinders, and sorry, Cillian Murphy, but Theodore Rivers is the main character. And now I'm wondering if he time-traveled to the present because holy shit, this is unreal.

My vagina is screaming his name as he approaches with his eyes zoned in on me. The sweet smell of oak whooshes across my face. And his scent claims the very air I breathe.

Once he's in front of me, he slides his hands around my waist, kissing my cheek warmly. His mouth then tickles my left earlobe as he whispers. "Keep eyeing me like that, and instead of going to a costume party, we'll play dress up in your bedroom, resulting in every piece of clothing being removed from your delicate body." A squeak rushes from my throat.

Theo pulls back with a devilish grin on his face, causing my thighs to rub together, almost starting a fire between my legs. *This tasty bastard knows what he's doing to me.* And I won't give him the satisfaction of knowing that I'd much prefer him to throw me over his shoulder and lock ourselves in my bedroom for hours.

I quickly fix my face, turning my expression to stone, hiding any evidence of my silly arousal. "I'd much rather go to the party," I retort.

Theo stands mere inches from me, and even with my heels

on, I still have to crane my neck to look up at him. His blue orbs stare into my honey irises, not blinking once.

His gaze intensifies my heartrate; blood pulses through me, trying to keep up with my fast, pounding heart. He pulls his bottom lip in, gently gliding it along his top teeth. "Mmm, strange. You may have control over your pretty little face, but your eyes are screaming for me to reach between your thighs and feel just how turned on you are," he utters softly.

Fuck, I failed miserably.

My expression slackens from his words, words that ring true.

He presses his body into mine, causing my back to push into the kitchen island. I grip tightly to the counter behind me, trying to prevent my spine from taking all the weight.

Theo grabs under my ass, pushing my lower half into his. I can feel his bulge press against me. My breath quickens. He runs his hand underneath my leg to the crease of my knee, pulling my leg around his waist. I watch his head tilt down, focusing on my leg.

"These tights are doing something savage to me," he growls, his grip tightening on the back of my leg. I let go of the counter and lace my arms around his neck.

Our noses are one movement away from touching. I breathe in his scent, wanting to melt into him.

His mouth grazes mine. "You make me fucking rabid, Olive," he breathes into my mouth.

I slide my tongue along my lips, purposely touching his as well—the taste of cool mint stains the tip of my tongue. I quickly retort, "I suppose it's meant to be because I become feral the moment you touch me."

He presses into me harder. We are basically conjoined twins now, and I'm okay with it.

As our mouths part further, the sound of a door slinging open grabs our attention. Theo and I turn our heads towards the small hall. Chase first walks out. His hair is disheveled, and his hat is crooked. Danielle's short self trails behind him, peeking from beside him.

She is unbothered while applying more lipstick. *These fools somehow did a little bump and grind. How the hell? And was I that hypnotized by Theo? I didn't even catch them sneaking off.*

Chase gives me an innocent smile while adjusting his suspenders. Theo and I exchange disbelief-filled glances. I turn my attention to Danielle as she picks up our purses. She suddenly stops and stares at me.

Just as I'm about to speak, she interrupts, "Are you done drooling over your man so we can go to this party?"

We all stand in silence for a moment, looking at one another. I gaze back at Chase and see him biting his lip, trying not to laugh. Within seconds, the four of us erupt into laughter over nothing at all. The ridiculousness of the moment makes it even more hilarious.

We all pile into Chase's enormous truck. Theo lets me sit by the window, which I requested. I expected him to sit at the other window, but he sat in the middle next to me. It's a tighter fit for his long legs, but he doesn't seem to mind. Having him close is comforting.

Danielle turns her head in her seat and gives me her brightest smile. Then she leans over, turns up the radio, and kisses Chase on the cheek. *Lovebirds.*

Within minutes, we have introduced the boys to our car karaoke, which features a mix of Lil Wayne, Lady Gaga, and various random throwbacks. I glance at Theo several times; he doesn't seem bothered, sporting a lopsided grin.

However, I still wondered if they might want nothing to do with us afterward.

The sun is setting now, casting bright oranges and pinks across the sky. I gaze out my window at the endless fields we pass by. I think of Nora for a moment, and guilt washes over me. I am on my way to a party while she is going through a tough time alone. How can I enjoy myself knowing my big sister is in pain?

I grab my phone from my purse and quickly text her, reminding her how much I love her and that I'm always here for her. I gently lay my head against the cool window, watching darkness take over the landscape. A warm hand slides along my knee, sending tingles up my leg.

I lift my head and tilt it toward Theo. He silently studies me, his face relaxed. We stare at each other for a moment. The creeping night highlights his sharp jawline and pronounced brow. I'll never get over how damningly beautiful he is. I run small circles around his hard knuckles where his hand rests on my knee.

He leans into me, slightly pressing me into the door. He tenderly places one of my curls behind my ear before bringing his lips a hair's breadth away from me. "What's on your mind?" he mumbles into my ear. His rich, gentle tone sends chills down my spine.

I bring my eyes to him before laying my head on his shoulder. I let out a long, breathy sigh. "I'm just worried about Nora," I admit.

He lifts my chin, resting his fingers beneath my jaw, tilting my eyes to meet his. He gives me an understanding nod. "She wouldn't want you to stress or worry. If she needs you, she will reach out. And if you need to go to her at any point, I will get you there as quickly as possible. You say let's go, and we'll go, baby." His tender words melt away some of the strain in my chest, but the feelings evading my mind still linger.

I return his lazy smile and follow it with a sensual kiss on his soft lips. My fingers lift to his face, gently tracing the light stubble along his chin and jaw. I think back to when I first met him with a clean-shaven face. And I find myself enjoying the stubble; it suits him and reflects the man he is and continues to become.

Olive
CHAPTER 26

"Damn, there are a lot of people here!" Chase yells over the music blaring from the radio. And he's not exaggerating; cars line the street on both sides, with many parked in the front yard and driveway.

After almost an hour of riding, my buzz has mostly faded, and seeing all these cars sends my anxiety into overdrive. More people means a higher chance of running into someone I'd rather avoid. Taylor mentioned to Danielle that there would be alcoholic beverages at the party, and I plan to take full advantage of that.

We pull into a parking spot across the driveway, three cars back from Taylor's house. The boys, ever the gentlemen, quickly hop out of the truck, swing open our doors, and extend their hands to help us step out. *Chivalry is very much alive.*

As we stroll across the street, the enticing aroma of grilled food envelops us. The familiar music from the backyard creates a lively atmosphere, while the sound of laughter and animated conversations weaves through the air, elevating the vibrant energy of the scene.

Danielle and I share arms, smiling as we ascend the steps to the front door. "Deep breaths, Olive," I murmur under my breath.

Glancing over my shoulder, I spot the boys trailing right behind us. Theo gives me a devilish wink, quickly waking the butterflies in my stomach. I blow him an innocent kiss and pull my focus back on the front door decorations: the entrance features black and gold balloons dancing lightly in the breeze.

A small letter sign hangs over the top of the door frame: *Happy 21st birthday, Taylor!*

Stepping up to the mat, I reach to knock, but Danielle steps forward and opens the door before I can, giving me a lopsided grin as she enters. *This bitch.*

The music and chattering are much louder than before. Every room resonates with laughter and beer bottles clanging together. A table sits to the right. Long black and gold tassels hang from the wall above it. Each side of the table holds gold vases with black and white feathers sprouting from the top. Long beads of pearls scattered around the surface.

A fancy menu sits in the middle of the table, featuring five different cocktails and their ingredients. Surrounding the menu are rows of clear cocktail glasses filled with enticing beverages. I start with the Bee's Knees, a delightful mix of honey, lemon, and gin. I take a generous sip; the sweet notes of lemon caress my taste buds while the gin provides a pleasant warmth at the back of my throat.

Woo, I pucker my lips at the amount of alcohol I taste. If every drink is as potent as this, I might want to limit myself to just two glasses.

Danielle selects the Aviation cocktail, a stunning dark purple hue that catches the eye. I'm definitely going to try that next. As I turn to ask the guys what they'll be drinking, I see them pulling beers from a large cooler by the front door. Looking around, I realize every guy has a beer in hand—except for one.

He's sitting on the couch with a girl nestled on his lap. I observe him, taking quick sips of his hidden cocktail, cleverly concealing it behind her, clearly trying to hide his beverage. *What a douchebag.*

"Hey, girls!! " a familiar voice shouts from behind me. I turn to see Taylor approaching us; Ryan is over to the side, talking with Chase and Theo.

I forgot they went to school together, just as Danielle and I did with Taylor. She is wearing a gorgeous plum-colored thigh-length dress. Her short silver-blonde hair hangs right below her chin. She's wearing a headband wrapped in pearls with gold feathers on one side.

Danielle and I wish her a happy birthday and thank her for inviting us to her birthday festivities. I watch as Taylor looks back and forth between us and the boys. She tries stifling a grin by placing her gloved hand near her mouth. "I see you ladies lucked up and got a packaged deal," she murmurs playfully, cutting her eyes to Chase and Theo.

The three of us turn our attention to the boys.

She continues. "I've only been around them a few times since Ryan and I started dating, but he has rambled on about their loyalty." She looks at me specifically.

My cheeks flush immediately. I know she is referring to Noah. Everyone who knows me from school has whispered around about the time my close friend screwed my boyfriend and then got her ass whooped in a parking lot. I refrain from responding, giving her a quick nod before guzzling some of my drink.

Relief washes over me, knowing that I won't run into them here. I don't know if Taylor still talks to Chloe, but I never expected her not to after what happened. It was just known for us to never be in the same place at the same time.

My icky thoughts evaporate when I feel strong arms wrap around my waist from behind. The delicious smell of oak cocoons around me. A delightful scent that will stick with me forever. Theo presses his hard body into my backside, pulling me flush to him. I feel his stubble tickle my earlobe.

"I couldn't resist being away from you any longer." His words melt into my hot skin. I lay my head back onto his chest. "I look around at these other girls, and all I see is you, and somehow you're all mine," he mutters into my ear.

My eyes slam shut from the intensity of his rich, deep voice.

"Good gosh, love birds, save it for later!" Danielle's voice fills my ears.

My eyes fly open; Taylor and Ryan are headed for the backdoor while Danielle and Chase stare at Theo and me.

Danielle rolls her eyes. "Let's check out the backyard festivities!" She then turns on her heel, smacking Chase on the ass in mid-walk. I muffle a laugh as Theo clasps our hands together to walk outside.

Taylor and Ryan went all out for the backyard. The patio has multiple tables where people are playing poker. Some men take it as far as puffing on cigars while shuffling cards. Starting at the backdoor, there is a red carpet running out to the middle of the yard. There are posts set up in a square shape with lights stringing from them. In the center, groups of people dance and sip on their beverages.

Behind the small dance area, I see the fire pit where I first spotted the man standing next to me. I glance over at him, still captivated by his presence. Life has a funny way of bringing people into our lives. If I had never attended that party here on my birthday, I would have never met Theo. The thought makes my stomach churn. Yet, something tells me we would have found each other somehow, regardless.

"Let's dance, bitch!" Danielle chants, grabbing my wrist and leading me toward where others are dancing. I look back at Theo, who is showcasing his best-crooked smile.

Chase shakes his head playfully, leaning in to say something to Theo.

I give them both a shrug before bringing my attention back to Danielle. We really got the package deal with those two.

Whoever controls the music must have read our minds because throwbacks are now playing on the speakers. Danielle and I shriek in excitement. We both chug the rest of our drinks, tossing the empty cups into a nearby garbage can.

My body relaxes now that I've had a strong cocktail, and I can feel myself moving to the music. Every beat pulses through me like a warm liquid, and each song evokes a memory from our early high school days. We remember every dance to each song, literally dancing our asses off and laughing so hard that my stomach hurts.

Danielle twirls me around several times, and when I regain my balance, I look towards the fire pit, catching a glimpse of something out of the corner of my eye. I sway back and forth to the music, keeping my eyes fixed on the fire and the people gathered around it.

A light breeze stirs my hair, giving me a feeling of déjà vu. I watch as the smoke from the fire wafts away, and there he stands—tall and beautiful.

I stop moving, never taking my eyes off him. His brows furrow as he gazes at me intensely. He strides toward me, his hands comfortably resting in the pockets of his slacks. Memories flood my mind from the first time we met; I remember feeling frozen as he approached, stealing the air from my lungs.

He still has that intoxicating effect on me, but this time, I surrender completely to it. Instead of the internal struggle I often face, I allow my longing soul to take control.

As his body slams into mine with a graceful force, I am acutely aware of the electric connection between us, as if our very souls are woven together in an intricate dance. His hands explore the delicate curve where my arched back meets my hips, his fingers tracing along my skin and igniting sparks of desire. With each movement, he pulls me closer, our bodies swaying rhythmically to the pulsating music around us, lost in the intoxicating moment that feels both exhilarating and utterly consuming.

I finally look around and realize that Danielle and Chase are gone. "Where did they go?" I ask.

Theo presses his lips together before answering, "Chase said they needed to get something from the truck. They scurried off pretty quickly."

I shake my head, both of us aware of what they're really up to. A part of me wishes it was Theo and me sneaking off instead. He looks at me with a smirk, almost like he can read my thoughts.

He then spins me around, grabbing my hips and pulling my backside into him. The memory of us under the pier flashes through my mind. I remember I had finally lost control at that moment. And damn, it felt so good. I focus back on Theo's grasp on my hips, placing my hands over his. I slowly roll my hips to the beat of the music.

He brings his mouth to my left ear, brushing his lips on my lobe, causing goosebumps all over my body. "I've already thought of different places we could sneak off to," he purrs.

Excitement runs through my veins, so much so that I show him just how turned on I am. I buck my ass back, grinding into him. I create a perfect motion with my hips, rubbing my ass in the right places. I feel a groan vibrate through his body.

Theo grips onto my hips harder, moving his body with mine.

His warm breath tickles my ear again. "Mmm. I could take you right here. But one thing about me, Olive, is that I don't share what's mine."

My breathing has changed its pace. He plants a kiss right behind my ear, then another further down on my neck. My head falls back, resting on his chest. I close my eyes, letting music and pleasure roll through me.

"O-Olive?" a familiar, deep voice shakes my core. There's no fucking way.

My eyes fly open, and so does my mouth. I feel Theo stiffen behind me. I stand frozen, catching gnats in my gaping mouth as I watch Noah and Chloe approach me. My hands fly to my sides, forming tight fists.

Adrenaline vibrates through me as my heartbeat picks up speed.

He has changed so much in a year. His onyx-colored hair is trimmed much shorter now than when I last saw it, and he has stubble along his jaw and chin. His face is more structured. I can tell his body has changed; he looks more like a man now.

I never once thought about how opposite he and Theo are besides their similar height.

My eyes move to Chloe, and instant heat builds inside me. I stare at her while she nervously hides behind Noah. She looks the same. Her long dark brown hair reaches to her stomach, and her brown eyes flick back and forth between Noah and me.

Noah's eyes stay on me the entire time, and something changes when I look back up at him. I almost see guilt behind his hazel gaze. I feel pity for him for a split second, but then it's quickly burned away and replaced by anger. Fuck both of them.

Noah steps towards me, and when he does, Theo removes

his hands from my hips, quickly steps in front of me, and puts one hand on my thigh. I watch as Noah cuts his eyes at Theo. My stomach turns to lava. One thing about Noah is that he has a mouth on him. I can see the look he's giving Theo, like, "Who the fuck is this guy?"

I peek around Theo's arm, looking up at him. His expression is stone cold, fixed on Noah.

Noah brings his attention back to me. He reaches up, rubbing the back of his neck in a nervous manner. "I just wanted to say that I'm s—" his words are cut short when Theo sucker punches him in the nose.

Noah falls back, almost knocking Chloe down. A shriek leaves her dainty throat. My hands fly to my mouth, unable to comprehend what just happened.

Theo calmly walks over, towering above Noah, looking down at him as he wipes gushing blood from his nose. He then kneels down, grabbing the collar of Noah's jacket.

"You've had a whole fucking year to apologize for not being able to keep your puny dick in your pants," Theo growls. He twists his fist into Noah's jacket, pulling him closer. "She doesn't need your apology. She forgot your name the moment she started screaming mine."

Holy shit... that was hot. My thighs rub together like an overworking cricket. Theo stands back up, nonchalantly swiping his slacks off and adjusting his long jacket.

Chloe hurriedly crouches down to check on Noah. She pauses for a moment, her eyes wide; I watch her mouth open to say something. But I step forward, cutting her off before she can speak. "Chloe, just keep your fucking mouth shut before I drag your ass like I did in the parking lot."

Her mouth seals shut immediately, and her attention goes back to Noah.

Theo turns and steps in front of me, gently placing his hands on my arms. "Are you okay?"

I look around us, not realizing that the music had stopped and a crowd of people has begun to circle us. Whispers and quiet chuckles surround us. Taylor and Ryan push through the crowd, stepping into the center. Her eyes go to Noah and then to me.

She looks remorseful. "Girl, I'm so sorry. I didn't think they were coming. I would have told you otherwise."

I wave my hand in the air with a sigh, dismissing her concerns. I clutch my small purse on my shoulder and head for the back door of the house. Theo trails behind me, placing his hand on my lower back. Once I'm inside, I beeline it to the drink table. I snatch up a cocktail, not caring which it is, and chug it in two big gulps. I slam the glass back down on the table and head for the front door.

Once we reach outside, I pause at the driveway. I don't know what has come over me, but I can't help the laughs that churn in my lower stomach and belt out of my mouth. I laugh so hard that tears fall from my eyes. Theo stands watching me intensively, holding back a smirk of his own. Once I get all the adrenaline and giggles out, I wipe my eyes, looking up at Theo.

"Come on," I say, turning on my heel and heading up the driveway. Theo follows me.

"Where are we going?" he asks.

I peer over my shoulder. "We're sneaking off for a moment."

He stays quiet, letting me lead the way. Once we reach the street, I head towards Chase's truck, ready to kick Danielle and Chase out, but my eyes catch on something.

Noah's precious Mustang sits to the right of me. I grab my purse, digging in the bottom. Once my fingers find what I'm looking for, a sinister smile plays across my face. I pull the spare key to Noah's Mustang out of my purse. I've had his spare key since we first started dating, just for emergencies. And when I found him in Chloe in the parking lot, I was thankful to have the key with me.

I guess they felt protected behind a locked car door, but I changed that feeling of security for them quickly. The key was in the purse I carried tonight the entire time. At one point, I planned to throw it away. Noah never tried reaching out to get it back. And now I'm glad that I kept it.

I hit the unlock button, slamming the driver's side door open. Theo walks up beside me, his face confused. "What are you doing, Olive?"

I scoot back from the door. "Get in the car," I demand.

Theo looks at me for a moment as one side of his mouth quirks up. He says nothing as he moves forward, sitting down in the driver's seat.

I climb into the tight space, straddling his legs and shutting the car door. Theo observes me as I recline the sit back some and scoot it back as far as it'll go to give us more room. It's snug in here, but it'll do. I throw my purse and the key in the passenger seat, bringing my eyes back to the beautiful man sitting in front of me.

I scoot my ass back into the steering wheel and begin twirling my fingers around the zipper of his slacks; his pupils dilate from the interaction. He grips my thighs, sliding his hands up them, pushing my dress up to my stomach, now showcasing my bare center. His eyes light up in anticipation.

We stare at each other, both hungry for lust. I bite down on my lip, already feeling pressure build in my lower stomach. "Unzip your pants," I breathe out.

Theo listens, slowly unzipping his slacks, waiting for my next command. He's letting me be in control, knowing that I need this moment for myself. I fix my breathing.

"Now, touch yourself," I order.

I pin my eyes on his hand, fixated on him, easily lifting his hips with my weight on top of him. His massive dick springs from his slacks, and his hand wraps around it, slowly stroking the base as I ordered. I gasp. I feel a tingling sensation build at my center.

Theo's hooded eyes never leave mine. I spread my legs a little further, exposing my throbbing pussy. I run small circles around my sensitive spot, showcasing my pleasure for him. Tiny moans leave my lips as I rock my hips into my working fingers.

"Holy fuck, Olive," Theo grits out behind closed teeth. We watch each other as we touch ourselves, our moans melting into one another.

I remove my fingers, bringing them to Theo's mouth. I slide my fingertips slowly across his lips, watching his eyes close as he licks off my arousal. His lips part, and I slide my middle finger in his mouth. He sucks and swirls his soft tongue around my finger, removing any evidence I once had. *So damn hot.*

I need him inside me now. I place my hands on his

shoulders, adjusting my weight. I pull myself up, aligning my opening with Theo's thick tip. He keeps his hand at the base of him as I slowly slide down on him. My head falls back at his thick length, stretching me.

Theo growls at our connection. He removes his hand, placing both on my ass.

I move my hips up and down slowly, wrapping my hands around his neck for support. Theo's head falls back on the headrest, and my eyes roll back from the ecstasy building in my core. And my mind wanders off. The thought of Chloe and Noah fucking in this exact seat is quickly replaced with Theo and I. And the thought of them completely washes away.

I roll my hips slightly forward with each pump, hitting every wall inside of me. The feel of his silky cock caressing my inner walls sends pleasure to my center. The windows are now fogging up from our heavy breathing and heated bodies. I quickly reach back, grabbing one of Theo's hands.

"Touch me, please." Theo pulls his bottom lip into his mouth, biting down on it.

He takes his thumb and presses it into my clit, making small circles as I continue to ride him. My body is buzzing with pleasure; I'm so close to my release. My legs shake from the constant up and down movements. He senses my tired legs, giving my clit a few more sensual rubs. He then wraps his hands around my sides and creates a push-and-pull motion with my hips.

My breaths are choppy now. I quickly bring my mouth to Theo's, sucking his bottom lip into my mouth. A deep growl escapes his throat. He parts his mouth, allowing my needy tongue access to his. Once they connect, they swirl and lap around each other. We explore each other's mouths, feeling every bit of passion passed between us.

Theo pulls away, and his expression hardens. He stills our movements, and I watch his parted mouth and the way his tongue slides across his bottom lip. He removes his hands from my waist and places them on my neck. His thumbs rest along my jawline. He studies me with a look of admiration on his handsome face.

A lopsided grin pulls across his mouth while his eyes look murderous. For a moment, I swear they become glossy. His thumb slides across my wet lips as he speaks. "You know, from the moment my eyes found yours that first night, I knew you'd be mine. And I felt it right then."

My eyes search his, waiting for him to finish. "You felt what, Theo?" I pressed.

His face hardens as he gazes into my eyes. "That I loved you." His words are like smooth velvet.

My stomach drops while my heart flutters in my chest. Right now, here with him, I feel whole. I grab his face, slamming my mouth into his. We kiss each other like it's our very last.

I stop, our parted mouths still touching as we breathe each other's air. "I love you, too," I breathe.

Theo moans loudly, kissing me again.

He wraps his arms behind my back, grabbing onto my shoulders. I prepare myself for what's next. With no remorse, Theo thrusts his hips up while slamming me down onto him. I gasp at how much his length consumes me, filling me whole.

I grab onto his jacket, and my head falls back, letting my rapture build to its highest point. "Oh, Theo!" I gasp.

"Mhm. I'll never tire of you screaming out for me, baby," he murmurs hoarsely. His raspy voice wraps around me entirely. He continues deliciously assaulting my inner walls. My orgasm slams into me, exploding throughout my body, so forceful that I fall forward, collapsing into Theo's chest. My hand bangs onto the fogged window, leaving a handprint. My body jerks over and over from the pleasurable impact.

Theo's undoing comes seconds after mine, stilling our movements as he releases inside of me. We both climb down from our intimate high. He wraps his arms around my back, keeping me flush to his heaving chest. Heavy panting and the faint sound of our pounding hearts fill the car.

I lift my head, taking in the man I gave my broken heart to. And I realize this entire time, Theo has slowly filled the broken parts with pieces of him.

Theo's kind eyes scan my face as he gently pulls sweaty strands of hair from my forehead. "As much as I'd love to reenact everything we just did, it would probably be smart for us to get the fuck out of this car before I have to break homeboy's nose again." He laughs under his breath.

My eyes go big. *Oh shit*. The realization of what we just did hits me. I broke into my ex-boyfriend's car and made love to my new boyfriend.

I snatch my purse and the key from the passenger seat. Glancing out the window, I make sure the coast is clear. Theo gives me the go to get out once his dick is back in his pants. I climb out, looking around. I take the spare key and leave it sitting in the driver's seat.

My eyes stop on the window, where my handprint is still visible. I can't help but grin. I've never been one for revenge, but damn was it exhilarating. *I got my redemption.*

"Olive, what the fuck?!" Danielle's voice echoes down the street.

I spin around, catching Chase and Danielle just a few cars down from us, heading in our direction. Danielle is hopping on one foot while trying to put her other heel on. Theo and I glance at each other, stifling a smile.

The first thing she does is look at Noah's Mustang, instantly spotting the handprint on the window. Her mouth falls open, almost reaching the pavement. She whips her head in my direction, cutting her eyes between Theo and me. "You'd better fucking explain yourself," she demands.

Poor Chase looks so lost and confused. "Can y'all fill me in, please?" he asks.

Theo chimes in. "Well, a lot of shit went down while y'all were getting something from the truck for, uh, an hour." We all cut our eyes at each other.

I made the mistake, yet again, of bringing my attention to Chase. His bottom lip is twitching from trying to hold back a laugh. On cue, we all bust out laughing for no good reason. I finally catch my breath after laughing so hard. "Bestie, we will tell y'all everything, but first, let's get the hell out of here." Danielle rolls her eyes but nods her head.

Walking back to the truck, I looked at the three people with whom I've spent most of my time recently. Theo reached over, clasping our hands together as we walked side by side, giving me the cutest wink. Somehow, in the most comforting, unexpected way, the four of us have become a little family.

And I am so thankful it's with my best friend.

As if she sensed my thoughts, Danielle looks back at me, giving her best smile.

Olive

CHAPTER 27

Buzz buzz... buzz buzz. I slowly pry open my sleep-crusted eyes, focusing on the repetitive vibrating noise. *Buzz... buzz.* It's so dark in here that I reach my arm over, patting the bed, searching for Theo's body. My hand grazes across his arm. I finally turned over and slapped my hand along my nightstand, searching for my buzzing phone. *What time is it?*

I squint my gritty eyes at the bright screen, struggling to open them fully. It's 2:01 a.m. Michelle's number flashes across my phone screen. *What the hell?* My confused brain still tries to process that I'm awake, but instant panic hits my stomach. I quickly press the answer button.

"Hello, Michelle?" I whisper, trying not to wake Theo. I

hear her shuffling on the other end. "Olive, honey, I'm sorry to call you this late. Is Nora with you?" I can hear the urgency in her tired tone.

I pause for a second, dread heating my entire body.

I pop up, scooting to the edge of my bed. "Uh, no, she's not here. I thought she was at home with you guys?" I press.

Michelle lets out a long, shaky sigh. "She was. She had gone up to her room around 8 p.m. Daniel and I had cut a movie on and ended up falling asleep, and we just woke up and realized Nora wasn't home. And she's not answering my phone calls." Her voice cracks.

I close my eyes, laying my head in my hand. This is not like Nora; where the hell would she be at this time of night? I calm my breathing and brainstorm. "Maybe she couldn't sleep and went to Jake's gravestone, considering what day it is?" I theorize.

Daniel mutters something in the background.

I take a deep breath. "Let me figure this out. Please try not to worry. I'll find her."

Michelle sniffles quietly. "She has been hurting for a while now, and I just hope she knows we love her and want her back home." Her voice breaks.

My throat tightens as I reassure her that Nora is okay before hanging up. I use my phone light to locate my sweats on the floor, accidentally slamming my phone back down on the nightstand, forgetting that Theo is still asleep just feet away.

I hear him shuffle around in the bed. Once my sweats are on, I snatch my phone, dialing Nora's number. The phone rings over and over. I try a couple more times with no answer. I swiped through, going to my text, realizing she had never answered my "I love you" text from yesterday evening. My heart quickens with every minute that passes.

"Olive, what's going on?" Theo groans out from the bed.

I cut on the small lamp on the nightstand, trying to calm the storm inside me.

I sigh heavily. "It's Nora. She's not at home, and she's not answering phone calls. I may know where she is, and I need to get there now."

Theo rubs his eyes before running his hand through his sleepy hair. He reaches over and taps the screen on my phone. "Olive, it's 2:20 in the morning. I don't think you need to drive, considering you drank a decent amount last night," he admits calmly.

I know he's right, but I have no choice. She's my sister, and it's my turn to be there for her.

"Either you take me, or I'm driving, Theo. I need to go NOW!" I bark louder than I expected.

Theo's expression stays neutral as he gives me a quick, understanding nod. He then jumps out of the bed and dresses within seconds. "Let's go, baby."

Lottie whimpers at the end of the bed, wagging her little pompom tail. I give her a quick kiss on the head before exiting my bedroom. "We'll be back soon. Go back to sleep, sweet girl," I say under my breath.

As much as I know Danielle would have wanted to help, there was no time for us to spend waking her and Chase up to fill them in. Honestly, I should already be at the gravesite. Theo gases his car, feeling my urgency to get there. My chest is heavy, staring into the endless night. The uncertainty eating at my flesh as we drive in dead silence. Nothing but the car engine and my toxic thoughts ring in my ears.

I replay last night in my head. Not once did I check to see if Nora reached out, which she didn't. But I should have checked in periodically, even if I never received a response from her.

Once we arrived at Taylor's party, so much had transpired that it slipped my mind. By the time we left, I was still buzzed, and adrenaline coursed through me from the events that took place. Once we got home, the boys stayed, and we all crashed around 12:30 a.m. *I'm the worst little sister.*

"Olive, I don't know where to go," Theo says softly, squeezing my trembling hand. Focus, Olive. I glance at the time again—it's 2:42 a.m. Why does it feel like we've been in this damn car for an hour? I look back up at the road.

"Oh, shit. Turn left here!" I shout.

Theo quickly veers into the graveyard, and I motion him to continue straight. Please be here, please be here. I keep repeating those words while frantically searching for Nora's car.

"Stop right here, please." Theo hits the brakes and puts the car in park. I jump out and search for Jake's gravestone using my phone's flashlight. "Here it is," I mumble under my breath.

But there's no sign of Nora or her car parked anywhere. It's just Theo and me surrounded by loved ones who have passed. My chest aches. I was so sure she would be here. Or maybe I just made myself believe that to protect myself from the worst.

I glance back, shining my phone's light onto Jake's

gravestone. I notice flowers and a photo leaning against the right side of the stone—fresh daisies, to be exact. I gently rub the petals between my fingers before picking up the photo propped beside them.

It shows Nora and Jake in their first picture together when they were still in high school. Jake stands behind her, giving her a bear hug and kissing her cheek. Nora is laughing, her eyes nearly closed from joy. She looked so happy and in love.

I flip over the picture, and to my surprise, I find Nora's gorgeous handwriting.

Sunday, 12:00 a.m.

Happy Birthday, Jake. I miss you so damn much that you haunt my mind and dreams, breaking my heart all over again. It's all I have left of you, so I accept it.

I will love you forever. I can't wait to be with you again.

XOXO your Nora

I stare blankly at her words, feeling guilt build in the corners of my eyes. Nora was here, but where is she now? She doesn't seem to hang out with anyone that I know of. My mind wanders momentarily, searching for answers I don't have.

A warm hand gently rests on my shoulder, and I turn my head slightly to look up at Theo. He gives me a half-smile that doesn't fully reach his eyes. I'm sure he can read the defeat written in bold letters all over my face. Theo clears his throat. "Is there anywhere else she might be?"

I shrug my shoulders, feeling helpless. What if she's somewhere crying alone? Or worse, what if she's hurt? Every worst-case scenario races through my mind.

I blow out a shaky breath. "I don't know—" I freeze

momentarily as an imaginary lightbulb flickers violently above my head. "Our mom's," I whisper, the words barely escaping my lips.

Somehow, Theo hears me, releases my shoulder, and quickly approaches his car. He then calls over his shoulder, "Tell me where to go, babe."

Mom isn't answering her phone, and it's no surprise—it's almost three in the morning. But that doesn't matter; I need to see that Nora isn't there. I motion for Theo to turn left into the neighborhood. Embarrassment washes over me, making my already flushed skin feel even warmer. I never intended for him to come here or potentially meet my mother.

What if she's high or drunk? My thoughts drift back to when I stopped by her place a month ago; the yard and house were messy. I can only be thankful that it's nighttime, and most things aren't visible right now.

Instant relief floods through me when I spot Nora's car parked in the driveway. It's weird that she would come here instead of calling me. She knows she's always welcome to stay with Danielle and me. But I don't even care right now. I am just relieved that I found her. She probably just fell asleep after going to visit Jake.

But something in my gut tells me I need to make sure. We didn't drive all the way here for nothing. I need to see her physically to ease this nagging gut feeling. I tell Theo to wait in the car while I knock on the door. I want to avoid him meeting my mom, especially since it is an unexpected visit in the middle of the night. Mainly because there is no telling what state Jewels is in right now.

It is pitch black, except for the headlights from Theo's car.

And there are no lights on in the house, which tells me that whoever is in there is asleep. I stop by Nora's car, checking through the dark window—no Nora.

Once I reach the front door, I give a couple of light knocks, listening for footsteps on the other side of the door—nothing but silence. I knock again, but it's more of an aggressive pound this time. I hear shuffling from inside the house, and the living room light flicks on shortly after. I see the blinds bend, someone peeking through. My patience is running thin.

Mom swings the door open. She's wearing the rose-colored robe she's had since Nora and I were kids. Her curly hair is pulled back into a messy bun, with sprigs sticking out in all directions. Confusion fills her tired eyes. "Olive, what in the hell are you doing here at this time of night?" she mutters. I swivel my head, glancing past her to see if I can spot Nora in the living room, but Mom quickly pulls the door shut behind her, blocking my view.

She must have a guy in there, probably some low-life piece of shit. I can't believe I brought Theo here. Honestly, it doesn't even matter at this point. I just need to know where the fuck my sister is! A wave of dread and panic washes over me again. My words come out strained. "Mom, is Nora in there?" I already know the answer, but I ask anyway.

Mom's brows furrow together. "Why on earth would she be here? I can't even get her on the phone when I try calling her—" Her voice trails off, becoming nothing more than a muffled noise in the distance.

The treehouse! Why didn't I think of it before all of this? Ignoring Mom's continued rambling, I turn on my heel and run as fast as possible to the backyard. My thoughts scream in my head while different voices yell at me. I can't understand what they're saying; some are cries, and many are outraged.

I swore I heard Theo's voice yelling my name for a moment, but my legs wouldn't stop if I wanted them to. Like a robot, I've been programmed to complete a task: get to the treehouse as quickly as possible.

I reach the grown-up trail leading to my destination. Darkness swallows it whole, leaving nothing but a faint gleam from the moon in the distance. I scramble for my phone in my sweats, unable to locate it in either pocket. Fuck, it must have fallen out while running back here. I take a deep breath, putting my arms out before me as I slowly move forward.

As I push through the blackened trail, twigs, vines, and briars slash at my arms and hands. I battle through it and even stumble a few times on stones and roots along the trail.

After being abused by nature, I finally see light at the trail's end. The treehouse comes into sight. The moon shining all around it is strange at this time; usually, it has already moved. I sprint over to the wooden stairs leading up to the crooked door. I notice that it's not latched but cracked open slightly.

As I climb up, I call out Nora's name, praying to hear her voice. But I receive nothing but the repetitive sounds of the woods. Crickets chirp loudly while the light breeze rattles tree limbs throughout the dreary forest.

Once I reach the top of the ladder, a heaviness consumes my body, and an eerie feeling pricks at my battered skin. I slow my breathing, closing my eyes just for a second. Once I open them, I slowly push on the small door to the treehouse. "Nora, are you…" My words are cut short.

As the door creaks open, I see feet lying just a few steps away. Once it's fully open, I find Nora lying on her side by the exposed window. The moon flickers its ghostly glow around her limp body.

No, no, *no*. I dive through the small door, crawling on my hands and knees to her. This can't be happening. Once I reach her side, I catch a glance at her phone lying near her, and the screen lights up. Mom's number flashes across the screen, and there is a long list of missed calls and texts from Michelle and me. The time shows 3:03 a.m.

My breathing becomes deranged as I take in what's in front of me. Nora lies on her side, one arm pinned underneath her. Her left arm rests beside her, and I notice a foil-like object in her lax hand. Flashbacks of our mother unconscious in the bathtub flood my mind. *No, Olive, focus; we have to be quick!* Nora's voice and urgent words hit me like a bag of bricks.

I begin greedily taking deep breaths while searching my surroundings. Nora's bag sits underneath the window of the treehouse. I quickly retrieve it, dumping out the items inside.

Not caring about what I touch, I sift through the items, scattering them on the wooden floor of the treehouse, all while focusing on what I'm looking for. *Damn it.* It's not here…where the hell is the Narcan?! My heart pounds against my chest.

I glance back at Nora nervously. She looks so peaceful. Her head lies flat, her lips slightly parted, and her curly hair spreads around her head like blossoming wildflowers taking over a forbidden garden.

Seeing her like this fills my eyes with tears. I quickly reached for her phone to call 911 but realize it is locked with a password. My hands tremble as I attempt to guess it, but nothing works. Then it hits me—her password is probably Jake's birthday! Why didn't I think of that sooner? Just as I'm about to enter it, the screen locks again, leaving me with a one-minute timeout. Fuck!

Frustration floods over me, and in a moment of panic, I toss her phone against the wall, the sound of shattering glass echoing around us. I lean closer to her still form, grasping her shoulders and shaking gently. "Nora! Please, wake up!" I plead, my voice a mix of desperation and hope.

I do chest compressions, pushing down with all my strength, refusing to let despair creep in. I can't give up! I take a deep breath as my vision dims, and the world spins around me. I have to keep going for her. I won't let her *die*. That three-letter word burns through my mind and into my throat like acid.

I glimpse up at her, taking in her beautiful features. I don't know if the moonlight adds to it, but her tan skin begins to pale. Realizing what has happened stabs its way through my heart and soul. But I can't accept this; it can't be real. I grab her arms, pulling her up from the floor. Her head quickly falls behind her shoulders, dangling lifelessly. The sight of it makes me lose my grip, causing her head to slam onto the wooden floor.

My hands instinctively cover my mouth as a distressed cry escapes me, muffled by the weight of agony. I gently place two fingers on her neck, searching desperately for a pulse, but the chilling absence of life is a punch to my gut. The realization that I couldn't save her wraps around my heart like a heavy stone, suffocating me with its unyielding grip. "THEO! HELP! Please, help me…" I barely croak out, my throat tightening as anguish swells within me.

My balance falters, and the room spins around me, the world blurring into a dizzying black void as if caught on a wild merry-go-round that has suddenly lost control. I lean against Nora's chest, yearning for the comforting rhythm of her heartbeat that once reassured me.

Tears stream down my trembling lips, mingling with the salty taste of fear and sorrow as I whisper against her, "Oh, Nora, don't leave me. I need you, I love you… please." Each word feels like a plea cast into the void, swallowed by the merciless silence surrounding us.

As everything around me fades to black, the only sound I can hear is the frantic beating of my own heart, echoing in the stillness like a desperate drum, wrapping me in a swirling haze of grief. In this profound darkness, I feel as though I'm gently drifting away, suspended in an endless void that threatens to engulf me.

My eyes, the only part of me I can control in this strange dream, dart around, taking in the swirling chaos of colors and shadows surrounding me. In the distance, a luminescent light begins to manifest, growing steadily more prominent as I float toward it. I soon realize it is the moon, hanging in the vast expanse of the night sky like a radiant beacon. Its brilliance is so intense that my eyes strain against the overwhelming glow, feeling like they might burn from its exposure.

I squeeze my eyelids shut to shield myself, but despite my efforts, the moon's power draws me in, relentless and mesmerizing. Every moment, I find myself being pulled closer, unable to resist its enchanting allure. Panic rises within me as I attempt to pull away, hoping to escape its grasp, but it is futile.

The moon's pull becomes stronger, and in an instant, it envelops me completely, swallowing me whole. I am consumed by its ethereal light, becoming one with its dazzling entirety.

There's a slight ringing in my ear as I continuously blink, my vision becoming less blurry with each shutter of my heavy lids. As my senses recharge and my mind is aware, I check my surroundings. I realize it is nighttime, but the moon's ethereal light is much brighter than ever before. I am standing in front of the trail to the treehouse. But what was before is no longer. The trail is clear, with no briars or branches. Something pulls me closer, almost telling me to walk through its path.

I don't fight it; my mind and heart feel calm and at home. As I travel through, I am enveloped with a sense of nostalgia. Throughout the clear path, colorful wildflowers sprout and bloom around me as I walk by. And the sweet smell of honeysuckles tickles my nostrils. I breathe in my surroundings as the moon pulls me to where I belong. Once I step from the trail, a delightful gasp leaves my throat.

Before me sits our treehouse, its outer walls wrapped in beautiful, large wildflowers and greenery gifted by nature. I watch in awe as vines wrap and twirl along the wooden ladder leading up to the small door. The moon is double its size, its haunting glow cascading everywhere. A sense of warmth feels me from the inside out, so intense that I close my eyes, drinking in every ounce. When my eyes fly open, I stand before the ladder, one hand resting on the step above me. My hand is much smaller than before, like a child's hand.

A sense of familiarity consumes me, causing a genuine smile to form along my lips. Cheerful giggles fill the air; my head shoots up to the treehouse. The small door slowly swings open. And again, my body feels the pull of something telling me to continue forward. As I climb the ladder's steps, I hear familiar laughter ring through my ears, urging me to climb quicker. Once I reach the top, I peek through the open door. My eyes sparkle with excitement.

I'm frozen, watching a young Nora Ray twirl in circles in the moonlight, its blue aura dancing around her like a protective shield. Her beautiful, long brown hair floats around her with each spin. "Olive Oil! Dance with me!" she chimes. Her child's voice is a voice I haven't heard in a long time but cherish wholeheartedly.

I quickly climb through, rubbing my small hands along my clothes. I look down, seeing I am in a dark blue nightgown with sparkles splashed all over, reminding me of the starry sky.

Nora grabs my hand, and when I look up, I realize she too wears the same nightgown. We say nothing more, grasp hands, and spin in circles, feeling the night sky with our nostalgic laughter. "I'm so happy you're with me, Olive Oil, one last time."

Her words hit my chest, but before I could ask her what she means, she pulls me in for a tight hug. My arms wrap around her, and my eyes seal shut.

Our memories together as sisters flood my mind so crucially that I collapse onto the ground, but Nora kneels, holding me close, never letting go. Memories shoot through like a projector, memories I've held onto for so long, and ones I've never seen, visions of Nora younger than I remember holding a baby, kicking her feet with excitement, the feeling of genuine love wraps around me. I'm the baby that she's holding in her arms. She was the big sister that was ready to protect her little sister.

Warm tears flow down my cheeks as every moment stamps in my mind and tugs on my heart. Nora then picks me up, spinning me gently. I hold tight around her neck, wanting to stay in this moment forever. She puts me down; I keep my eyes squeezed shut.

"Open your eyes, Olive." Her childlike voice is now gone. I open my eyes to find Nora and I standing at the treehouse window. My hands are no longer small. My moon bracelet dangles from my wrist.

I look up at Nora; she's no longer herself as a child. Her bracelet rests along her wrist as she holds onto the wood of the cutout window. Her contagious smile blooms around her, that smile I've missed for so long. I observe her as she turns and stares at the moon, a sense of peace glowing around her body.

When I look at the large moon, I realize it is slowly approaching, growing in size. I look back to Nora; her eyes grow big, not with worry but longing.

"Thank you for being the best little sister," she breathes. With those words came the realization that she was leaving me. And this was our goodbye.

My lips tremble as I place my hand over hers. "Please, don't go. I can't do this without you."

Nora looks at our touching hands, and a star-like tear rolls down her cheek when her brown eyes meet mine. "That's not true, Olive; you don't need me anymore, not in that way. You are the strongest person I know. And I'm so proud you're my

little sister. Since I first held you, I loved you with all of me."
Her voice cracks.

I shake my head profusely. "No, no... please." I cry out.

"Shhh... It's okay, Olive Oil. He's waiting for me." Nora
looks to the moon. And in that second, I knew she was talking
about Jake.

Jake is waiting for her. My body pulls away like a magnetic
field. I grab Nora's hand tightly, the only thing keeping me
from sliding further away from her.

Nora smiles at me. "You have to let go, Olive."

Desperate cries leave my throat. "I can't, please..." I strain
out.

The pull on my body became stronger, causing my grip on
her hand to slip slightly.

Nora retorts. "When you feel far from me, look to the moon.
I'll be right there, always." A humming noise surrounds us.
"Look at me, Olive. Remember, sisters forever."

I give a slow nod, accepting I have to let go. I can't be selfish
anymore.

"Sisters forever," I whisper. As my hand slides from her, I
keep my eyes on my beautiful big sister, soaking her in for the
last time. I choke out, "I love you, Nora Ray, to the moon and
far beyond the stars."

A single tear falls from her eye. She gives me a slight nod
and turns to the window. As I'm pulled further away, her eyes
slam shut, and I watch as her body becomes nothing but a
bright light so intense that I have no choice but to close my
eyes. A hum so loud that I cover my ears.

For a moment, I hear Nora's comforting tone in my mind.
"I will love you forever, little sister."

In one quick breath, everything goes silent, and blackness swallows me whole again.

Theo

CHAPTER 28

I sit patiently, tapping my thumb along my steering wheel while watching Olive knock on the front door of her mom's house. I wish she wouldn't have asked me to stay in this fucking car. I selfishly want to be beside her every step of the way, but I understand her reasoning.

I'm genuinely concerned about her well-being. She consistently puts up a façade to hide her pain, but tonight, I caught a glimpse of her true emotions as her mask slipped away. It was painful to see how vulnerable she truly was beneath that exterior. She puts so much effort into appearing strong and resilient, yet she doesn't seem to recognize that her strength already shines through, even in her moments of fragility. It kills me to think that she faces her struggles in solitude, battling her demons without the support she deserves. *We're going to work on that, though.*

I sigh and lean my head back against the headrest, keeping my eyes fixed on Olive. Finally, the front door opens, and a woman steps out, slamming the door behind her. I assume that's her mother, Jewels. I've only ever seen pictures of her sister, Nora.

Olive's posture suggests that her sister isn't in the house. So where could she be? Olive had already checked her car earlier, so perhaps someone picked her up. I hope she's okay, for Olive's sake. I can't hear the conversation, but it seems like her mom is rambling about something. Olive doesn't even appear to be paying attention.

I glance at the time, seeing it's almost 3 a.m. When I look up, I see Olive is no longer by the door. Suddenly, her mom is sprinting down the stairs, yelling something. Where the hell did she go? I quickly turn off the ignition and step out of the car. "Olive!" I call out, but she doesn't respond.

Her mom is heading my way, and she doesn't look happy. "Who the hell are you?" she shouts. I shut my car door and calmly respond, "My name is Theo. I brought Olive here to look for her sister."

She stops about six feet before me, looking me up and down. I see a lot of her in Olive. Even with her current state, she is a beautiful woman. I don't know what Olive's father looks like, but I see where she received many of her features.

"Could you please tell me where Olive went?" I request.

Jewels places her hands on her hips and looks towards the backyard, letting out a heavy sigh. "She didn't say, but I will assume her and Nora's treehouse. A trail at the end of the yard leads to it."

I remember sitting on the beach with Olive, and she told me about their treehouse and how special it was to her and Nora. I give a quick nod and thank Jewels.

I sprint towards the backyard, dialing Olive's number. The line continues to ring as I navigate my surroundings. I hear a faint buzzing ahead of me; I move closer and spot a small light beaming from the grass. Olive's phone lies facedown on the ground. I retrieve it and place it in my pocket. She must have dropped it running back here.

I turn my phone light on and search all around me. I am close to the end of the yard, and there is nothing but woods beyond this point. To the left, I see what looks like a small opening into the woods. I shine my light in its direction. Once I approach it, I realize it's a grown-up trail; this has to lead to the treehouse. I move forward, holding my phone in one hand and using my other to push briars and twigs out of the way.

My movements stop when I hear a loud cry, followed by Olive screaming my name. *What the fuck?* I pick up my speed, disregarding the cuts and scratches forming along my arms. Finally reaching the end, I look up at the treehouse. I spot the small open door leading to the inside. I slide my phone into my other pocket and climb the ladder quickly. My heart is minutes from pounding out of my chest.

As I reach the top, I push the door open, slamming it into the wall. What I see is unlike anything I've ever witnessed. Olive is on the floor, lying peacefully across Nora's chest. Her slender hand gently intertwines with Nora's. Items are scattered around them and near their joined hands, and neither of them is moving. The remaining rays of the moon reflect off their weightless bodies. I quickly climb through the small opening of the door, knocking my shoulders against either side.

I quickly examine both of them. First, I check Nora for a pulse. Her skin feels oddly cool to the touch, causing me to pull my hand back instantly. Aside from a faint gleam from the moon, there is barely any light in the room.

I pull out my phone and shine the light on Nora's face. My eyes are immediately drawn to her lips; they are blue, and her face is pale, almost like the moonlight.

I cover my mouth with my closed hand in shock. She's gone; it's too late. I look at her one more time. She is so beautiful, like her sister, and I notice that her hair is curlier, unlike Olive's wavy locks. Her curly hair reminds me of their mother.

I shake my head and focus on Olive; she hasn't moved at all. I take a moment to calm my heavy breathing and clear my mind. First, I crouch down and place my ear near her mouth to listen for her breathing. I anxiously wait for ten seconds, but there's nothing. Gently, I grab her and attempt to roll her onto her back, ensuring that her head is flat against the floor.

The most difficult moment came when I had to separate their hands. It felt deeply wrong to pull them apart as if I were tearing something precious. My gaze was drawn to the matching moon bracelets Olive had lovingly chosen from the beach—a symbol of their bond now bittersweet. As I stare at their lifeless hands intertwined with such determination, a wave of emotion washes over me, and my heart aches at the sight. It was as if their connection was still alive, even in stillness, making the act of separation even more painful.

I listen once more for any signs of breathing, but there is still nothing. I've always managed to stay calm and not overthink situations, but I won't lie—I'm absolutely terrified right now. If I lose her, I can't even begin to imagine what that would mean. I position myself beside her, placing my hands on her chest, ready to begin compressions.

I realized there wasn't enough time to call the cops; paramedics would never get back here in time. And I don't know what the address is. I tried replaying the roads we traveled, but I can't remember. I have to save her.

At this moment, I am grateful that I paid attention in school when I learned CPR —it's the one useful skill that I gained. I start the chest compressions, mentally reviewing the steps. I glance down at Olive, taking in her angelic features. "Come on, baby, I can't lose you," I plead. I've never been one to pray, but I pray anyway. "God, please save her," I choke out.

I lean down, cradling her small head in my hands, tilting it back to ensure her airways are completely open. I close her tiny nose with a gentle yet firm pinch, sealing it shut. Taking a deep breath, I blow air into her mouth twice, each puff feeling both urgent and delicate. As I sit back on my heels, my eyes are fixed on her chest, but it remains still, unresponsive.

With growing concern, I repeat the steps, feeling a pang of guilt as I press my weight onto her fragile chest; it feels like I might crush her small frame, and my heart is heavy with worry.

I breathe my air into her mouth once more, willing to

sacrifice the air in my lungs for her. The feeling of desperation takes over me. I pause, listening and watching her chest for movements. Still nothing. The night is silent. My breath becomes shaky as I run my hands through my hair. I bring my eyes to her face, realizing I've failed her. Tears brim the corners of my eyes. I should have been with her.

Feeling helpless, I grab my phone from the floor and dial 911. Just as I go to click the call button, I hear a weak sound come from Olive's mouth. I freeze, focusing on her; a few seconds pass, and I see her chest slowly rise and fall. A sound leaves my mouth that I've never heard before, and relief surges through my entire body.

I lean down softly, brushing strands of hair from her delicate face. Her mouth is now parted, and the beautiful sounds of breaths rush through her lips. Her eyes remain closed as life slowly comes back to her. I so badly want to kiss her but refrain from doing so. My head falls back as I close my eyes, focusing on my breathing and thanking God for answering my selfless prayer.

I bring my watery gaze back to the young, beautiful woman who captured my heart from our very first hello. I gently wrap my arms under her neck and legs, lifting her into my lap. Cradling her tightly, I lay her against my chest and rest my cheek on her head.

I close my eyes, listening closely to Olive's steady breathing—a sacred sound that I will cherish for the rest of my life.

"You are okay," I whisper into her silky hair.

I promise myself that I will never leave her side again, no matter what happens. I know she will resist, and that's perfectly fine. I love her feisty spirit; it's one of the qualities that drew me to her in the first place.

She can challenge me day and night. I don't care. Olive Sage Landers, you are mine, forever.

Olive

CHAPTER 29

The familiar smell of oak clouds all my waking senses as my eyes slowly open. The loud ringing sound gradually dissipates from my ears. I blink profusely, trying to clear my blurred vision. My head feels foggy from the deep sleep I was in. Confusion doesn't take long to wash over me as I regain consciousness.

Strong arms are wrapped tightly around my body, cradling me close. A deep, rich voice whispers above me, "You are okay." I take a moment to realize that it's Theo's voice.

I squeeze my eyes shut and then open them again, remaining still as I scan my surroundings. It's dark here, except for a small light shining nearby. Tilting my head up, I see Theo looking down at me. Although it's hard to see clearly,

I notice his brows relax, and a small smile spreads across his face. He looks relieved.

I search my brain for answers to what happened and where we are. I try replaying what I can remember, but I draw a blank. And when I try to speak, words won't form.

"Shhh, it's okay, Olive," Theo whispers softly, squeezing me gently.

My eyes shift back and forth, searching for answers. I yank his arms off of me, acid burning through my esophagus. I lift myself too quickly, my legs almost giving out. I spread my arms, trying to balance like a baby learning to walk. My legs feel like Jell-O beneath me.

Theo tries to reach for me, but I swat his arms away aggressively. My equilibrium feels out of whack, causing me to sway back and forth. I wait a few more seconds, trying to give my body time to regain its strength. I take a few wobbly steps.

From my peripheral, I catch Theo quickly standing behind me. "Olive, please don't," he pleads with remorse. Just as I slightly turn, attempting to form words to ask him what he's talking about, my eyes catch on her…

Disbelief rattles through me as I stare at Nora Ray's lifeless body. It's within seconds that the events of the night erupt in my mind, replaying everything that happened, each moment like a bullet wound to my feeble heart. My hands fly over my mouth just as my legs give out.

Theo wraps his arms from behind me, saving me from collapsing to the floor. I slowly crumble onto my knees, with Theo crouched behind me, arms still wrapped tight around my waist.

My eyes stay fixed on my sister's cold, pale body. The

realization hits me hard: Nora is dead because I couldn't save her. She is gone forever. I try to scream, but my throat feels constricted as if a python is wrapped around my neck, slowly tightening its grip on my airways. A numbing emptiness replaces the ache in my chest.

I no longer struggle as Theo pulls me into his embrace, cradling me like a fragile child. My eyes remain locked on my sister, and the warmth within me evaporates, replaced by a numbing cold that grips my heart. Tears that long to escape break free, cascading to the floor like delicate icicles in a silent winter.

The moment Nora died, a part of me left with her, leaving me hollow and adrift in my newest friend: grief.

I lay restless in my bed, replaying the night that changed everything for me. When it's not consuming my thoughts, it haunts my dreams. Three miserable weeks have passed since my sister's death, and things have not improved. If anything, they've only gotten worse.

The days blend together; I often find myself unsure of what day it is.

Sometimes, I forget she's gone and reach for my phone to call or text her. Then the reality hits me all over again—a painful jab to my chest that knocks the breath out of me. First comes the shock, followed by disbelief, dread, and finally, a wave of weariness.

My mind seems to be working against me, or perhaps it's the lack of sleep and proper nutrition. I can't remember the last time I had a full meal.

Once, I loved eating, but now I have to force a granola bar down my throat just to keep my body from shutting down. It's strange how the body and mind interact. During traumatic events, one craves nourishment while the other insists on starvation. I don't know; maybe it's different for others.

But how can I eat or focus on my health when I am constantly reminded that my sister is no longer here? I feel guilty for eating, hell, even breathing, for that matter. Life can be so unfair and cruel. She had so much life to live and spent most of it protecting me as best as possible. I am not worthy of living on, am I?

I'm not suicidal by any means. I would never leave my sweet Lottie behind; she needs me. Plus, Danielle would hold it against me and attempt to whoop my ass once we were reunited in the afterlife. But I won't deny that it's crossed my mind, not doing it, but what it would feel like. In a sense, it sounds peaceful, with no pain or suffering.

I don't think people understand that mental pain is just as detrimental as physical. It's a nagging ache that takes over.

Honestly, I feel very much dead internally. Nothing but a vessel. Danielle keeps telling me this is part of the first stages of grief. I couldn't help but laugh at her statement when she told me. How the fuck are their stages to this?

And what the hell happens in the next stage?

I learned quickly that grief is my enemy.

No one will change my mind about it. I've tried to fight it off, but it's clever in how it works. It beats you down first, then swallows you whole. And I've had no choice but to drown in it.

Imagine being stranded in the middle of the ocean, with no land or people in sight. You focus on staying afloat and screaming for help, but heavy waves continue to form and crash around you, pulling you under repeatedly. You fight for air until your body loses every ounce of strength.

Eventually, you stop fighting and let the ocean current pull you under. You watch as your body sinks further away from the surface. Panic sets in as you breathe in water, filling your battered lungs. Darkness creeps in, and just as death taps you on the shoulder, you blink and find yourself back, floating once again in a deserted ocean, drowning all over again. Grief feels like living in your own hell.

Nora Ray was pronounced dead at 3:44 a.m.—Jake's birthday. The paramedics estimated she had been gone for about two hours, judging by her decreased body temperature and the discoloration of her skin.

It was heartbreaking for the police to determine that it was an overdose, especially since fentanyl was found scattered around the scene. I can't help but feel responsible for that; I had dumped her purse in a moment of panic. In her hand, there was also the piece of foil with a burned substance on it, a stark reminder of the struggles she faced.

Why didn't I notice the signs that were so painfully obvious? I knew she was struggling with Jake's death and the weight of our past, but I never imagined it would drive her to purchase the same lethal drug that took Jake from us. She had promised me she would get better and heal, and I believed every word she said.

In my mind, I've replayed countless scenarios, trying to piece together the moments leading up to this tragedy. I remember her laughter that sometimes felt hollow and her eyes that would occasionally betray a deep sadness. But the cruel truth remains that I may never fully understand why she felt this was her only escape.

The uncertainty gnaws at me, leaving a void filled with regret and sorrow that I can't shake. It feels as though I'm trapped in a nightmare, wishing desperately to turn back time and somehow save her from this fate.

Watching them try to get Nora's body down from the treehouse was the hardest part. Theo tried to pull me away, but I resisted; I felt I had to witness it. I deserved every ounce of pain and trauma that came my way. They had to cut part of the door to make the space larger. Once they succeeded in widening the entrance, they realized they needed more hands to safely lower her down the ladder with no accidents. Theo offered to help, but they refused, stating that it would interfere with the scene.

Mom was hysterical when she realized what was happening. At one point, as they placed Nora's body into the ambulance, I watched her, my expression stone-faced, as she ran around yelling at the police for answers. At that moment, I felt nothing but anger towards her for the upbringing she had given us. Did I blame her for Nora's death? No. But a part of me believed she, along with our absent sperm donor, had played a role in it.

Theo urged me to get checked out by the paramedics to understand what had happened to me. I explained to the EMTs how things unfolded, and Theo shared his perspective on finding us. They encouraged me to take a drug test, which I did in the second ambulance that arrived. To my surprise, I tested positive for a small amount of fentanyl, likely from digging through her purse and then touching my face. I must have wiped some residue on my nose or mouth, resulting in an overdose, especially since I had no tolerance for it. Theo found me just in time and saved my life.

That's just another reason I've been avoiding him. I can't face him right now. How could he want anything to do with me after witnessing what he did? I feel like I've selfishly burdened him with my problems and trauma, dragging him down from the peaceful life he once had. I'll never forgive myself for that.

I last saw him the afternoon after everything happened. When we returned that morning, we were exhausted and went straight to bed. In that difficult moment, I needed him close to me. We slept through lunch and probably would have slept longer if Danielle hadn't burst into the room. That was the last time I truly slept; I think my body was in shock from everything at that point.

Once we were all awake, I asked Theo and Chase to leave so I could talk to Danielle about everything that had happened. She was unprepared for the heavy news I had to share with her. It was the first time I had broken down since finding Nora. The weight of my grief was overwhelming, and I couldn't hold it back any longer—I needed my best friend.

Danielle broke down with me, and we cried together for hours. Since then, no one has seen me cry. Why should they? It's not like crying will bring my sister back.

I feel so grateful for my best friend during this difficult time. She has done her best to support me while also respecting my need for space. It was so hard for me to share the news, so she took it upon herself to call Michelle and Daniel.

I was dreading this moment, and hearing Michelle's cries on the phone was absolutely heartbreaking; it made me feel physically ill. I kept replaying the words I had promised her, assuring her I would find Nora and that everything would be alright. It breaks my heart to think about what she's going through, losing both her son and daughter-in-law in the same year, especially on her son's birthday, is an unimaginable pain.

These last few weeks, I've spent a lot of my time researching death and how the brain works when someone passes. It's a temporary distraction that has become my addiction. No one knows about the dream I had while death almost claimed me.

Research shows that when someone dies, their brain can replay memories or moments for up to nine minutes. Many survivors who were brought back to life have spoken about out-of-body experiences.

The challenge I face is that I haven't yet discovered a story that echoes my experience. It was an encounter so vivid, so intensely real, that it lingers in my mind. I often find myself lost in thought, pondering whether Nora was indeed waiting for me as if our souls were interconnected in that fleeting moment. It felt as though I shared a dream with her before she transitioned fully to the other side—a goodbye that was meant to happen.

I can't shake the feeling of absence from when our hands parted, witnessing her soul gracefully depart to fulfill its destiny, floating gently towards the moon, where I believe she now resides. I know that if I tried to share this experience with others, they would find it hard to believe, dismissing it entirely. But in my broken heart, I know the truth of our connection and our last moments together—by the moon.

I've done my best to follow her words from our shared dream: "When you feel far from me, look to the moon. I'll be right there, always." Her voice lingers in my heart.

Each night, I gaze at the moon, feeling a profound sense of longing, and I cry until every tear is gone. I call out to her, yearning for a sign that she's with me. Despite that, I find no response. It's a heavy feeling, knowing that I'm reaching out in the darkness and not finding her. Some nights, I feel tempted to give up, but the moon's pull demands I keep reaching for the light it offers.

Today marks a significant step for me. I've been staring at the two boxes sitting on my bedroom floor for an entire week. Last week, Danielle and Chase went to Michelle and Daniel's to collect some of Nora's belongings that Michelle thought I would want.

This was the first time I spoke to Michelle on the phone since the time I found Nora.

I appreciated her effort in boxing up Nora's items. I told her to keep anything she wished to hold on to from Nora, and I hope she did.

I've often hovered my fingers over the boxes, almost ready to open them, but I've held back. I can't postpone this any longer. Danielle insisted on being here when I opened the boxes, but I declined. I need to do this alone.

I've been alone for the past few days; Danielle has been staying at Chase's most nights to give me the space I need. At least when I'm by myself, I don't have to hide my emotions.

I kick the covers off and stare at the ceiling of my

bedroom, trying to run my fingers through my matted hair. Dread begins to take hold in my mind. Taking a deep breath, I reach for my phone on the nightstand. It's 2 p.m. Four notifications flash on my screen: one from Danielle, one from Theo, another from my mom, and a final one from my work friend Vanessa.

I slam my phone down and rub my eyes, deciding I'll get back to those later.

Lottie nudges my arm, squeezing her way onto my lap. She has been extra clingy lately, sensing my distress. On the nights when I toss and turn, wishing I had Theo's strong arms wrapped around me, Lottie nestles close, helping to soothe the constant ache in my chest. She's the best companion.

A hot bath sounds inviting right now, and it would probably be good for my body to soak for a while. I finally force myself out of bed and retrieve a hairbrush from my makeup tote. I brush gently through the tangled mess, wincing each time I encounter a pesky knot.

Looking in the mirror, I see my red and puffy eyelids, a result of crying on and off. Dark circles form under my eyes, revealing my lack of sleep.

I take a moment to examine my figure, noticing that my sweatpants no longer fit snugly at my waist.

I've truly let myself go. For all these years, I hid my struggles so well, but now they are visible both on the inside and outside. I can no longer conceal them. I've come face to face with my demons—the same demons that Nora used to protect me from. I let out a loud sigh of defeat as I head to the bathroom.

As I sink into the tub, the scalding water burns my skin in

a strangely pleasurable way. If my tired body could express pleasure, it would moan contentedly. I lower myself until my chin barely stays above the water's surface. I watch the steam rise from the water.

Closing my eyes, I try to savor the surrounding silence. Just as I feel heavy and relaxed, a nagging reminder hits me again, screaming in my mind.

I close my eyes and sink completely under the water, trying to drown out the noise. I hold my breath, feeling my lungs begging for oxygen. The voices remain, but they are muffled beneath the water. This must be what it felt like for Nora, who had to fight her mind daily, drowning in constant pain.

I squeeze my eyes shut, struggling against my body's instinct to search for air. "You have to let go, Olive," Nora's soothing voice fills my mind, pushing away the stifled voices.

I shoot out of the water, gasping for air. My hands grip the sides of the tub tightly as I take in deep, long breaths. As my breathing calms, a heavy sensation fills my chest, and a familiar ache rises in my throat. I pull my knees up to my chest and wrap my arms around them. Warm tears flow down my cheeks as I cradle myself.

I cry for my child self and all that she has lost. I cry for Theo and the pain I caused him. Mostly, I cry for Nora—the life she deserved but never had—and for her absence.

I sit on the floor in front of the boxes, mentally preparing myself for what I might find inside. I shake my head slightly as I open the first box. Inside, I see some of Nora's neatly folded clothes. I run my hands along the fabric of a plaid sweater before sifting through the clothing. My eyes land on a black t-shirt, and I unfold it, realizing it's the Stevie Nicks shirt I got her during one of our day trips to the beach for her twenty-second birthday.

I bring the shirt to my face and close my eyes, inhaling the scent of the fabric, which carries a mix of Nora's favorite perfume and the familiar smell of Michelle's house.

Next, I glance into the second box and discover a pile of pictures. I grab the box and bring it to my bed, eager to look through the photos. Some are snapshots of Nora and Jake throughout the years, starting from their high school days. I also find a couple of pictures of Nora with her old friends from middle school.

As I dig deeper, I spot a picture of our mom—one I've never seen before. She appears to be almost full-term, her hand resting under her swollen belly. Young Nora stands beside her in a sundress, playfully kissing her belly.

Another picture catches my attention. It's of Nora and me; she looks to be about nine or ten, which means I was five or six. We are sitting on her bedroom floor, surrounded by various stuffed animals. Each of us is holding three in our hands, smiling widely for the camera. For a moment, a bittersweet smile tugs at my lips. I remember that day. It feels so long ago, but I cherish the memory.

As I dig through the piles of photos, I spot something brown underneath. I pull it from the bottom of the box; it's a leather journal of some sort. An engraved palm tree with a moon above it sits in the center. I trace my finger along the moon and scan the pages inside to find Nora's beautiful handwriting. The journal is filled with her words. I slam it shut, not wanting to invade her privacy. Maybe one day I will read them, I tell myself.

After going through some of Nora's belongings, I finally respond to Danielle's text, leaving Theo's message unread. I had promised myself I'd get back to him before the day was over, just not right now. I opened Mom's text; she has been checking in on me almost every day. She mentioned she has been sober since Nora's death. While I'm relieved, it feels a lot like false hope.

We've been through this so many times, but I'm trying to stay positive and give her another chance because, in one week, she will be checking into a substance abuse facility that also addresses mental health. This is a significant step for her—one she has never been willing to take before. It breaks my heart that it took losing a daughter to substance abuse for her to finally realize she needed to turn her life around, not for me, but for herself.

What scares me the most is the thought that if Nora's death wasn't enough to motivate her to get better, what if it's the very thing that drags her down even further? Nora struggled immensely, but Jake's death was the final straw for her; it pulled her into the depths of addiction.

How could Mom possibly make it through if Nora didn't? The thought of losing the last piece of my family fills me with dread. I have to cling to the hope that Nora's memory is enough to inspire change.

Theo

CHAPTER 30

I thrum my fingers along my steering wheel as I stare at Olive's apartment building. It's been three damn weeks since I last saw her—the night everything went down, to be exact. She has been avoiding me like the plague. I've given her the space she's wanted, no questions asked. But I won't lie and say it hasn't rocked me to my core. I've missed her so much.

Three fucking weeks of worrying and wondering. The only peace I've gotten is getting updates from Danielle. It seems she has been out of the "Olive loop" as well, but she has at least spent time with Olive and seen her weekly. I can at least be grateful for that.

My parents have been worried sick about her. Little Emma

has asked multiple times when she'd see Olive again, and I've just had to tell her that Olive needs time. Mom begged me to let her call her, but I declined. I know right now isn't the right time. I need to get to her first.

These last few weeks haven't been easy. I've had many restless nights, wishing I was holding her close to me. The dreams are ruthless, constantly reminding me of that night. I can't deny that the events of that night fucked me up. And the one person I've wanted to confide in and be close to has kept her distance. I don't blame her, though. I understand. Knowing Olive, she blames herself for everything. And that kills me.

I should be with her, comforting her, keeping her safe. I made a promise that night that I would never leave her side again. And I've already bent the rules, giving her the time she wished for. And as much as I like bending the rules, this ends today. She's going to fight me like hell on it, and that's fine; I love that about her. But I won't take no for an answer, no matter how hard she fights.

I've almost left twice, sitting in this damn car for about an hour, anticipating how I'm going to bombard her out of nowhere, but I've stuck to my guns. Danielle gave me permission to stop by. She warned me of how Olive may react, but she gave me the go to come here, and that's enough for me.

The sun is setting as overcast hovers in the sky. It rained intermittently for the last few days, so our jobs for the week were postponed, and I was stuck at home in my thoughts. Leo didn't seem to mind me being home, though.

My phone pings.

Danielle: She just texted me back, so she's up. If she asks why you came, you tell her you came of your own free will. I'm not in the mood to get chewed out by a distressed Olive.

Me: Noted. I appreciate your help. Give Chase a smack on the ass for me.

Danielle: Noted and done. He screamed like a little girl.

I take a deep breath through my nose, sliding my phone into my front pocket. There is a light drizzle, so I throw my black hoodie on and head for the stairs to her apartment.

Once I reach the door, I hesitate to knock. What if this is a bad idea? I despise people who show up unannounced, and here I am doing just that. It had to be this way, though. I don't know how long she would have gone without me, but I can't go any longer. I can admit that I fucking need her near me.

I knocked three times on the door to the apartment. Tiny footsteps tap across the floor on the other side of the door, followed by whimpers. The little rodent knows I'm here. A few seconds go by, and I hear the door unlocking. I take a step back as the door opens.

Olive peeks from the door's crack, surprise written all over her face. Her gorgeous mouth opens, but she pauses for a second, almost like she's thinking of what to say. I wait patiently, giving her the opportunity to speak first.

She finally opens the door a little more. She chews on the inside of her mouth, looking up at me. "What are you doing here?" she murmurs.

My eyes scroll down her body, examining every inch of her I can see. Her hair is pulled back into a low-side ponytail hanging over her shoulder. Long strands pull to the front, framing her face. She's wearing burgundy sweats with a black Stevie Nicks t-shirt.

I lock my eyes back with hers. I can tell she hasn't slept well; the underneath of her eyes has darkened. Her eyelids are puffy and red, exposing that she has been crying more than usual. That fucking kills me.

I reach over to rub her cheek but refrain quickly, sticking my hand into my pocket. My lips press together. "I came to see you, Olive," I retort.

Her eyes flicker at the sound of my voice. She sucks her bottom lip in as she looks back into the apartment, letting out a soft sigh. Her eyes meet mine again as she opens the door all the way for me to come in. Relief washes over me as I step into her apartment.

She doesn't say a word as she heads for the couch. I follow behind her, giving some distance between us. I scan her body, noticing she has lost a little weight since the last time I saw her. Regret pings at my chest. I should have come here sooner. I would have made sure she was eating properly.

Olive plops down on the couch across from the loveseat. I eye the spot right beside her but choose to sit on the loveseat. *She needs space, Theo. Give her space.* I pull my hood off, running my hands through my hair. Olive silently watches as she chews on her bottom lip.

Her expression falters as I search her tired eyes for answers. All I see is defeat. Normally, she hides her thoughts so well, her eyes being the only thing giving answers. Today, it's written all over her face.

"Why didn't you call or text before coming?" she presses.

I clasp my hands between my legs. "Would it have made

a difference?"

She pulls her eyes to the floor, rubbing her hands together. It takes all of me not to rush over and place my hands on hers. I clench my hands together tight.

She lets out a shaky breath. "I've just needed time."

I shake my head at her response. "And how much longer did you need to avoid me?" Her eyes shoot to mine, shock written on her face. She opens her mouth but then closes it, rubbing at her temples. I slowly stroke the stubble on my tense jaw. "I should have been here with you, Olive," I admit.

Her eyes flick to mine for just a moment. I can see the battle in her eyes.

"I've already put you through enough, and I can't handle ruining you more than I already have." Her words come out almost a whisper.

My hands shoot to my hair, pulling at the roots as I try to ease the frustration coursing through my blood. "Stop blaming yourself for things you cannot control. You never forced me to do anything; I was beside you because I fucking wanted to be," I breathe.

I watch her hands form into fists at her sides. "The longer you stick around, the further I'll pull you down with me. I'm nothing but a disease contaminating everything in my path." Her mouth wobbles as she fights the tears sure to fall.

I can't hold back anymore. I shoot from my seat and stride to her, kneeling in front of her. She looks at me, one tear rolling down her flushed cheek.

I place my hands on her knees, focusing my gaze on hers as I reply, "Then pull me down with you, baby. Infect me. You are a disease worth spreading in this world." I reach up and connect my thumb with the fresh tear on her cheek.

Her eyes close as she takes my hand and presses it against her face. "I don't deserve you, Theo. I deserve nothing. I've let you down; I've let Nora down..." Her voice cracks. "You'll eventually grow tired of me."

Anger slams through me, not towards her but towards how hard she is on herself. "I'm not going any fucking where, Olive! At least, not on purpose. We can't control everything in this life. Things happen; people die for no reason. You can't sit here and dwell on it; you'll be miserable for the rest of your life if you do. Good people die, along with the bad.

"And there will never be an answer as to why, not here on earth, at least. I will gladly let this world take me out however it pleases as long as the time I have here revolves around you. Don't you fucking get it? Please look at me, baby," I demand.

Her lip quivers as tears stream silently down her cheek. She brings her watery eyes to mine.

I take a deep breath, keeping our eyes connected. "You were made for me; I know it. We just had to find each other. Our souls can't survive this fucked up world without each other. And I know this to be true, and when I die, my soul will wait for you on the other side, and no matter how fucking long it takes, our souls will meet again." My voice breaks. "Death isn't the end of us; there is no end to us. This is only our beginning. Do you understand me, Olive?"

Tears prick at my eyes as I confess my love to her.

"I love you so goddamn much. Never hold that shit against me. If you're going down, I'm going down with you, baby. You're the match, and I'm the flame. We'll burn to the ground together until there's nothing left but our ashes." My throat tightens at the realization of my own words.

A cry leaves her mouth as her face falls into her hands. "I'm so sorry, " she cries.

I quickly stand and move beside her on the couch. I grab her and pull her into my arms as I lay back on the couch. "Shh, it's okay. You've done nothing wrong. I'm here," I whisper into her hair.

She nestles into my neck as sobs vibrate through her tiny body. *This fucking hurts me.*

I hold her tight to my chest, rubbing her back.

"She's dead, Theo. Nora's dead. Oh, my god!" I barely understand her words behind her sobs. Remorseful tears slowly fall from my cheeks into her hair.

"Baby, I know. I'm so sorry," I rasp out.

I know at this moment, all I can do is be here and comfort her because no words will ease the pain of her losing her sister.

"Nora wouldn't want you to beat yourself up. She'd want you to heal and be happy. Let her memory live through you." I continue rubbing her back, trying to soothe the pain of her tragic loss. She sniffles against my neck as her crying calms.

We lay in silence for a good while, just embracing each other's warmth.

Olive props up on her arms, using my chest as leverage. Her eyes find mine as she runs her hands along my jaw. She moves her eyes to my lips.

She then leans forward, connecting our mouths. Warmth shoots through my entire body, feeding the hunger I've felt since not seeing her. Our tongues reunite, swirling around one another as we drink in our tears. She pulls her mouth away and speaks, "I love you, Theo."

A shit-eating grin tugs at my lips. "I love you too, Olive. So damn much."

I watch her as she gives me a lazy smile, almost reaching her eyes. "Happy birthday. I'm sorry I didn't get you anything," she whispers. She remembered my birthday.

I gently grab her face, resting my thumbs under her chin. "All I ever wanted was you, and I couldn't have asked for a better way to end my birthday," I admit.

She gives me a genuine smile, laying her head on my chest. And we say nothing more. Everything is silent. We lay holding each other, filling up the emptiness we felt while being away from each other. Our souls once again danced as our hearts beat against one another.

I missed being this close to her, and right now, I never want to let go.

Olive
CHAPTER 31

It has been three months since Nora left this world and today would have marked her twenty-fifth birthday. I have been dreading and anticipating this day in equal measure, knowing how much it meant to her. I decided to come to the beach, our special place filled with memories of laughter, where we spent countless summers together.

As we arrive at the familiar access point, I feel a wave of nostalgia wash over me. I tightly grip the urn resting on my lap, feeling its cool surface. Being reminded that it contains the ashes of my sweet Nora. I hope that somehow, I can honor her memory today. This is what she would have wanted.

I gaze out of the car window, my eyes drawn to the shimmering reflection of the full moon dancing on the water at the pier. The sky, a deep indigo canvas, is peppered with twinkling stars that seem to whisper secrets of the night. Theo, sitting beside me, tenderly places his hand on my leg, his fingers warm and reassuring as they give a gentle squeeze.

"Are you sure you want to do this alone?" he asks, concern etched in his features, his voice soft yet firm.

Turning my gaze to him, I lean in and plant a quick, lingering kiss on his cheek, feeling the warmth of his skin beneath my lips. "I'll be okay, I promise," I assure him, trying to convey my confidence amid the flutter of nerves in my stomach.

He responds to my gesture by gently grabbing my chin and pulling me in for an intimate kiss. After pulling away, he caresses my cheek and says, "Take all the time you need. I'll be right here waiting for you."

I return his words with a soft smile, take a deep breath before exiting the car.

The night is eerily calm, blanketed by a sky adorned with shimmering stars, and there isn't a single soul in sight along the deserted beach. The late October air is crisp and invigorating, prompting me to pull my arms tightly around myself for warmth.

As I dig my toes into the cool, slightly damp sand, I find a strange comfort in its softness, grounding me in the moment.

In this tranquil setting, my mind drifts back to a vivid memory of Nora beside me. I can almost see her infectious grin lighting up her face. With boundless energy, she dashes toward the ocean's edge, her laughter ringing out like music as she kicks up clouds of sand behind her. She twirls with such joy, her long, curly hair flowing freely, catching the wind as if it has a life of its own.

The recollection brings a smile to my lips, but a deep ache in my chest, a reminder of what once was, and the warmth of her presence that I long to feel again quickly accompanied it.

I find a spot to sit in the soft sand, gently placing my small bag beside me while still holding the urn close to my heart. I take a deep breath, inhaling the salty night air as I absorb the ocean's deep hues, the moonlight casting a gentle glow on the waves.

Nora always loved the ocean, just as I do. This place was our sanctuary, offering a sense of peace that often eluded us back home. When we were together, even for a fleeting moment, all our wounds seemed to fade away. I glance beside me, imagining my beautiful sister sitting there, her feet buried in the sand, arms wrapped around her tan legs, lost in thought as she gazes out at the horizon. The memory of her presence brings both warmth and heartache, reminding me of the bond we shared.

I level out a place in the sand beside me and gently place the urn on the ground. Reaching for my bag, I pull out my phone and Nora's leather journal.

I place it on my lap, running my fingertips along the brown leather. I haven't opened it since the day I went through her box of things. I thought about it long and hard, deciding that a part of remembering her on her birthday would be to reminisce about the raw memories that she felt and expressed on paper.

I take a deep breath while turning on my phone. Then, I open Nora's journal and scan through the pages. It was filled with memories that meant something to her. I read through one dated back to when she was in high school; she had just met Jake a few days prior. And she was rambling on about how nervous and giddy he made her feel. I found pages talking about our nights in the treehouse as kids and the times we played hide-and-seek for hours.

So many happy memories fill the pages of this journal.

As I approach the end of her journal, a page catches my eye. I flip back to it. There's no date, but at the top, it reads, "My sweet Olive Oil."

My throat tightens at the sight of my nickname in her writing.

Taking a deep breath, I start reading.

My sweet little Olive Oil,

Where do I begin to express how thankful I am to have you as my little sister? I still remember when Mom found out she was pregnant with you. I was so excited to have a baby brother or sister. I prayed every night that you would be a girl so I could play with your hair and dress you up like my own personal doll.

We didn't find out your gender until you were born. I remember the nurse bringing me into the room, and I was jumping with excitement. Mom was cradling you in a yellow quilted blanket. I stood on my tiptoes to get a better look at you. As soon as I saw your little chunky face, I knew you were a girl.

I will never forget the first time I held you at the hospital, right after you were born. I looked down at you and realized that I was your big sister and that I would always protect you as best as I could. I can't express how proud I am of you. I always knew you would grow into a strong, beautiful woman.

Even in my darkest days, you were the light I always needed.

From the very moment I held you as a child, you saved me in so many ways. I hope you always know that no matter what, I will always be there for you. I love you to the moon and back.

Love your big sister,

Nora Ray

Tears flood my eyes as I read the words Nora has written to me. I search the page for answers, hoping she just wanted to express herself in that moment.

Her words of admiration envelop me completely. I glance back at the ocean, trying to focus on the sound of the crashing waves. I close the journal and put it, along with my phone, back into my bag. Wiping my eyes, I stand. It's time.

I lean down, carefully gather Nora's ashes, and begin my slow trek to the shore.

Cold chills run up my legs as the salty water washes over my feet and ankles. I cradle her remains in my arms and look up at the moon. It stares back at me, bright and ethereal. I let Nora's voice resonate within me, remembering every little detail about her: her laugh, her smile, her annoyed expressions, her scent—every feature flows through me as the moon casts its comforting glow around me.

After all this time, I finally understand. Nora is at peace and has returned to where she was always meant to be. The night the moon called her home was the night her soul was set free from all the pain she endured.

Every happy moment and memory cradled her as she journeyed to her rightful place. In my heart, I now know that one day I will see her again. For now, she is with me every time the moon shines.

Tears stream down my cheeks as I descend further into the ocean, stopping where the water reaches just above my knees, soaking my jeans. I twist the lid off her urn and gaze out at the vast sea. As I softly whisper words to my beloved Nora, reminding her of how much I love her, I slowly pour her ashes into the ocean. I watch as they dance along the salty water. A light breeze blows through my wavy hair, and for a moment, I feel Nora close to me.

As I gently pour the last bits of her ashes, a soft breeze picks up, swirling them gracefully in the air. I take a moment to watch as they dance around me, and for just an instant, I can smell Nora's favorite perfume. In that fleeting moment, as the final remnants of her ashes rise toward the moon, it feels as though Nora is reminding me that she is still here with me and always will be.

I grab my bag and head back toward the pier. My phone vibrates, so I stop to check it. "A Bridge to Recovery" flashes on the screen, so I quickly answer.

"Hey, Mom," I say.

"Hey, baby. How did it go?" she asks.

I look back at the ocean. "It went as well as it could. She's free now."

I hear her sniffling through the phone. "That's great, baby. I know it's what she would have wanted."

I sigh lightly. "I think so too. How is rehab going?"

She clears her throat. "It's going really well, Olive. In just a week, I'll have completed three months here so far."

A smile crosses my face. "I'm really proud of you, you know? And I know Nora is, too."

Her voice cracks as she responds, "Thank you, baby. I've always been proud of you and Nora. I love you."

I nod my head and reply, "I love you too, Mom."

As I reach the parking lot, I spot Theo leaning against the passenger door, arms and legs crossed. His eyes shift from the moon to me, and a lopsided grin spreads across his gorgeous face. He stands up as I approach and pulls me into his warm embrace.

"Are you ready?" he asks.

I take a deep breath and reply, "Yes, I'm ready."

He opens my car door and gently shuts it behind me. I place my bag and the urn in the backseat, feeling a wave of relief and contentment wash over me.

Once Theo is settled in the car beside me, his hand slides across my thigh, holding me gently as he gazes at me with admiration sparkling in his ocean-blue eyes. I return his stare, savoring everything that has unfolded since I met Theo.

When I met him, I was deeply broken and feeling profoundly lost, consumed by a heavy heart filled with heartbreak and insecurities that seemed insurmountable. That fateful night, when our eyes locked for the first time, I felt an undeniable spark that signaled a change within me—a shift so powerful that no amount of denial could hold it back.

I had long believed that I was beyond repair, a shattered mess with pieces scattered all around me. But then Theo entered my life like a breath of fresh air, graciously capturing my soul with his kindness and understanding. He slowly began to heal the deep wounds that had long been left open, mending the parts of me that had been in disarray and lying broken on the floor, feeling abandoned.

People often say that time heals all wounds, and while there is some truth in that statement, I have come to realize that love truly has the power to mend even the deepest scars. And that's exactly what Theo brought into my life: a pure, genuine, and transformative love.

As we move forward together, I can't predict where life will take us. However, I am certain that, no matter the challenges we face, we will stand firm by one another's side.

Together we can navigate the turbulent waters because, ultimately, bumpy roads lead to smoother paths. I feel ready to live not just for myself but also in honor of Nora. She made so many sacrifices for me throughout her life, and I refuse to let her memory fade into oblivion.

Her spirit will always be cherished and remembered for everything she was and everything she did for me.

My commitment now is to share our story with the world, driven by the hope that it will touch someone else who is struggling as I once did. I know that this is exactly what Nora would have wanted—to inspire others to find strength within their own struggles.

I want to emphasize that healing from trauma is not only possible but also achievable. Recovery from dark times is within reach if you are willing to fight your way through. You must hold on and keep pushing until the light eventually overtakes the darkness. The daylight always returns, bringing with it new hope and possibilities.

Theo squeezes my leg. "Let's go home, baby," he says.

I place my hand on his and nod in agreement. Leaning over, I switch on the ignition, and the radio comes to life.

My breath catches in my throat as a familiar song begins

playing. "Dreams" by Fleetwood Mac blasts through the car speakers. I jerk my head toward Theo and catch a genuine smile on his face. I let the music wash over me and turn to look at the moon.

A big smile spreads across my face. As we drive away from the beach access, I whisper to myself, "I love you, Nora Ray, to the moon and far beyond the stars."

ACKNOWLEDGEMENTS

Oh, my gosh! Where do I even begin? I want to thank many amazing people for believing in me and this book.

First, I want to thank my sweet husband, Shane, and our two beautiful children for always believing in me and loving me daily. You three keep me grounded, and I love you so dearly. I want to thank my family and close friends for being a big part of this amazing journey. You all mean the absolute world to me. To my close friends who were excited and took the time to read my raw work, I love you to the moon and back.

To my cheerleaders in heaven, my Nana and my big sisters Megan and Stacy, sometimes I receive sweet little signs that I like to think you sent as a reminder that you're always with me. I hope I continue to make you proud. I can't wait to hug you again one day.

To a few of my author friends, Allie Cole, Sierra Marie, and Kyle Snow, thank you so much for answering my questions. I couldn't have done it without your knowledge and support, which means so much to me. I am beyond thankful for the genuine friendships we built. I have loved watching you all grow into the successful authors you are. I will always cheer you on and support you as best as possible.

I will forever scream how grateful I am for my book community. Reading has been my escape from reality for many years, and I always knew that when the time was right, I would pursue my dream of becoming an author. I still remember the day when I announced my writing and healing journey. I felt extremely nervous about the outcome. I never expected to have so many loving readers in my corner, cheering me on, supporting me, and being genuine friends. You have helped me grow, watched me from day one, and virtually held my hand the whole way. I can't thank you enough for the love you've continuously shown me. No matter where my author career takes me, please know that you will always have a friend in me.

Lastly, a huge thank you to my amazing TROTS Street team for rooting me on and for being a genuine friend. I adore each of you so much and will forever be grateful for the lasting friendships we formed along the way. I love you all.

AUTHOR'S NOTE

This book holds a deeply cherished place in my heart. It reflects real-life experiences that have shaped my journey. Healing has become an integral part of my daily life, and this novel has played a significant role in that process.

On April 3, 2023, and July 21, 2023, I faced the profound loss of two beloved sisters who fought their battles with addiction, mental illness, and trauma. My sisters were beautiful both inside and out. They were not just sisters but also daughters and mothers. Losing them less than four months apart was a heart-wrenching experience, and saying goodbye to them far too soon has left a lasting impact on me. Not a day goes by that they're not on my mind.

My hope for this book is to provide healing for those who struggle and to help others understand the profound significance of trauma, mental illness, and addiction—three realities that can deeply impact anyone's health and overall well-being. Many individuals face these challenges in solitude, grappling with their pain in silence. Having witnessed how these struggles can devastate families and close friendships, I recognize the fragility of life and the vital importance of seeking help when needed. Remember, you are not alone in this fight; there is hope for healing and recovery.